SHOLOM ALEICHEM

The Nightingale
Or, The Saga of
Yosele Solovey the Cantor

Translated by Aliza Shevrin

A PLUME BOOK

NEW AMERICAN LIBRARY

NEW YORK AND SCARBOROUGH, ONTARIO

NAL BOOKS ARE AVAILABLE AT QUANTITY DISCOUNTS WHEN USED TO PROMOTE PRODUCTS OR SERVICES. FOR INFORMATION PLEASE WRITE TO PREMIUM MARKETING DIVISION, NEW AMERICAN LIBRARY, 1633 BROADWAY, NEW YORK, NEW YORK 10019.

English translation copyright © 1985 by Aliza Shevrin

Original Yiddish version copyright © 1917 by Olga Rabinowitz

This is an authorized reprint of a hardcover edition published by G. P. Putnam's Sons and simultaneously in Canada by General Publishing Co. Limited, Toronto.

 PLUME TRADEMARK REG. U.S. PAT. OFF. AND FOREIGN COUNTRIES REGISTERED TRADEMARK—MARCA REGISTRADA HECHO EN FORGE VILLAGE, MASS., U.S.A.

SIGNET, SIGNET CLASSIC, MENTOR, ONYX, PLUME, MERIDIAN and NAL BOOKS are published *in the United States* by NAL PENGUIN INC., 1633 Broadway, New York, New York 10019, *in Canada* by The New American Library of Canada Limited, 81 Mack Avenue, Scarborough, Ontario M1L 1M8

Library of Congress Cataloging-in-Publication Data:

Sholom Aleichem, 1859–1916.
    The nightingale, or, The saga of Yosele Solovey the cantor.

    Translation of: Yosele Solovey.
    I. Title. II. Title: Nightingale. III. Title: Saga of Yosele Solovey the cantor.
PJ5129.R2Y613   1987   839'.0933   87-11214
ISBN: 0-452-25933-9

First Plume Printing, December, 1987

1 2 3 4 5 6 7 8 9

PRINTED IN THE UNITED STATES OF AMERICA

SHOLOM ALEICHEM, one of the greatest Yiddish writers, was born in 1859 and died in New York in 1916. He is perhaps best known for the "Tevye" stories, which were the basis for the Broadway musical *Fiddler on the Roof*. His works include *In the Storm* (available in a Plume Fiction edition), *Marienbad*, and several collections of short stories: *Holiday Tales, Some Laughter, Some Tears, Old Country Tales,* and *Stories for Jewish Children*.

ALIZA SHEVRIN is one of America's premier translators. Her numerous translations from the Yiddish include some of the novels and stories of Isaac Bashevis Singer and I. L. Peretz. She translated the award-winning *Holiday Tales, Marienbad,* and *In the Storm*, all by Sholom Aleichem.

For Marsha,
    My sister, my friend

Translator's Introduction

Sholom Aleichem is certainly known to have been an imaginative and gifted young artist—indeed, he was also self-taught—so it is no surprise that, early on in his writing career, he wrote three novels (as well as several short stories) whose heroes were creative artists. *The Nightingale, Or, The Saga of Yosele Solovey the Cantor* was written in 1886, when Sholom Aleichem was just twenty-seven, and published in 1889 in the author's then newly established literary journal *Yidishe Folksbibliotek.*

Yosele Solovey, the original title of the book—literally, *Yosele the Nightingale*—was the second of the trilogy. The first of the three was *Stempenyu*, a novel about a violinist, which was published the year before *Yosele Solovey* in the same journal, and the third was *Blondzhende Shtern (Wandering Star)*, about an actor. *Yosele Solovey* provides particular insight into Sholom Aleichem's early struggles as a novelist intent on giving fictional form to his own experiences as an artist, and it is the only one of the three that has never before been translated into English.

The Yiddish scholar Dr. Anita Norich has made a study of the trilogy called "Portraits of Artists: Three Novels by Sholom Aleichem" (see the journal *Prooftexts*, September 1984). She makes clear that Sholom Aleichem was attempting to write about the artist's fate in a Jewish world dominated by the strictures of religious orthodoxy while at the same time seeking to depict love relationships in the manner of nineteenth-century writers. And he made this attempt despite the discouragement of his mentor, Mendele Mocher Sforim. Although Sholom Aleichem felt that conventional romance was meaningless within the Jewish world, he was also convinced that a novel without romantic interest would be equally meaningless, and he sought to reconcile this apparent contradiction in each of the three novels.

"The narrative perspective in these novels," Norich states, "wavers between the romantic heroes who pursue their way in a romanticized plot on the one hand and, on the other, a much broader social interest in which the perceived realities of the Jewish world dominate. The tension between these perspectives is never resolved." The artist, capable of being set free by his imagination, is confined within the narrow shtetl walls and its strictly defined expectations. A gifted singer might be allowed to chant the synagogue services and could one day become a respected, impoverished cantor, but only if he had the requisite character and training. If he was lucky as well as talented and was prepared to uproot himself from his shtetl, he might become a renowned star in the cantorial world. But even on this larger stage he had to adhere unreservedly to the stringent requirements of piety and religious observances, however tempted he might be by success and public acclaim to abandon his fundamental values. Without the protection and constant reminders of family, community, and religious obligations, the artist was in danger of losing his bearings, his sustaining beliefs, and his integrity—the loss of which must inevitably lead to excess and to artistic and spiritual downfall in the eyes of God and of the community. The power of imagination that strengthened his artistry would also delude him into overidealizing reality, into making bad decisions based on exaggerated perceptions of people to whom he foolishly turned over control of his life. Yosele the Nightingale, cantor *extraordinaire*, personified this conflict between the demands and requirements of the religious world in which his art was embedded and the temptations of the secular world opened to him by success.

The cantor, or *hazzan*, has been particularly vulnerable to the opposing tugs of secular adulation and religious commitment. The *Shulchan Aruch*, the collection of ancient laws and prescriptions governing the life of an orthodox Jew, tells us he was required to have a pleasant voice and appearance, be married, have a beard, be fully familiar with the liturgy, be blameless of character, and in all other respects be acceptable to the members of the community. The three letters in Hebrew of the word HaZaN have been interpreted as the initials of *Hakham* (a man well versed in the Torah), *Zakayn* (at least thirty years of age and possessing a flowing beard), and *Nasuiy* (married). The cantor is referred to as the *shaliach tzibbur*, a messenger or emissary of the congregation. Like J. S. Bach, whose title was Kantor, he fulfilled many roles, including that of composer, leader of the service, conductor, and musical director. In Temple and Talmudic days he was a general communal functionary; around the sixth and seventh centuries he became the reader who recited aloud the prayers before the congregation, because as late as the Middle Ages he was the only one who possessed a *siddur*, or prayer book. With the advent of printing (c.

9

1456), each worshiper was able to read for himself, and the cantor could then stress the musical and vocal aspects of the prayers.

Ironically, the growing popularity of the cantor made him the most controversial communal official. His dual role of religious representative and artistic performer inevitably gave rise to tensions that persist even in modern times. As priority was given to a beautiful voice and musical skill over the traditional requirements of learning and piety, many cantors indulged in needless repetition of words and extended the chanting of prayers with the sole purpose of displaying the richness of their voices. The potential for theatricality and exhibitionism was always present, and with the rise to popularity of the traveling "star" cantor, many were seduced into becoming celebrities, with the concomitant monetary rewards and self-aggrandizement.

With the emancipation of European Jewry in the early nineteenth century, traditional melodies, heretofore passed along orally, were set down in musical notation, with harmonies to be sung by cantor and choir. New melodies were composed under the influence of modern European musical trends and techniques, and a new improvisational style, *hazzanut,* was invented in which the cantor with true artistry gave musical expression to the meaning of the prayers. Cantors performed in a coloratura style, employing unusual melodic contours and modulations that were influenced by Oriental Jewish music, European opera and oratorio, and traditional church music. But it was a two-way street: in the nineteenth-century period of emancipation and enlightenment Christians showed more congeniality toward Jews and greater interest in their music and were attracted to the synagogues by the cantorial music. Innovations, influenced both musically and ceremonially by the Protestant

Church, were instituted by such leaders as Solomon Sulzer (1825–90), chief *Hazzan* of Vienna, followed by others.

The cantor had a choir, which generally consisted of young boys, *meshoyrerim* (singular, *meshoyrer*), who were apprenticed to him and who could follow his improvisations with instinctively felt harmonies, often in four parts. A *meshoyrer* had to have a good voice and a retentive memory, for he was often required to cue the cantor. A chorister who excelled could eventually become a cantor himself. Throughout the eighteenth century and well into the nineteenth, even an itinerant cantor on tour might be accompanied by a group of choirboys.

That a cantor might stray from the straight path is not merely a hypothetical fear; tales abound of just such cantors in recent history. In *The Nightingale*, Sholom Aleichem frequently refers to Yoal Dovid, the Vilner Balabeysl (Little Master), whose real name was Joel David Loewenstain-Straschunsky (1816–50) and whose story foreshadows Yosele's spectacular rise and fall. As a boy of eleven the Balabeysl was already famous as a great singer possessed of a magnificent lyric tenor. Married and independently wealthy while still very young (hence the nickname) and living—in the words of A. Z. Idelsohn, the acknowledged authority on *hazzanut*—in a "fantastic realm of self-glorification," he was beloved and venerated by the people to the point of idolatry. Legend has it that on one of his extended tours the Balabeysl was attracted to a Gentile Polish woman singer, fled to Vienna with her, and there was soon plunged into a melancholy from which he never recovered. He lost his voice, became mentally deranged, and assumed the life of a penitent, walking from community to community with-

11

out speaking to anyone, studying the Talmud in seclusion until his death in an insane asylum.

It was no accident that Sholom Aleichem so often wrote about music; next to writing, music was the great passion of his life. He loved to improvise on the piano. Music runs through many of the stories drawn from his childhood and youth. His own ambition to play the violin is marvelously depicted in a popular children's story, "The Fiddle." In her fine biography of Sholom Aleichem, her father, Marie Waife-Goldberg relates that one day a poor man called upon him to plead for his musically gifted son of only nine. The father was convinced the boy was another Paganini, who lacked only the ear of the musical world to succeed. Sholom Aleichem responded by arranging a recital for the supposed prodigy, personally raising funds for the occasion. The boy, threadbare and barefoot, performed masterfully, stunning the audience with his virtuosity. The listeners showed their appreciation by taking up a collection to provide the money for the youngster and his father to travel to Western Europe in order to find the right teachers. A few years later, in 1904, the now thirteen-year-old lad launched a brilliant career. His name was Mischa Elman.

During the time Sholom Aleichem was writing *The Nightingale* he was living on his father-in-law's estate in Kiev, where he happily devoted himself to his literary pursuits. At one point he inherited 220,000 rubles and began trading on the Kiev stock exchange. For a time he did fairly well, increasing the family fortune, but in the autumn of 1890 he lost it all. Some blame his losses on his lack of attention to money management, as his prodigious literary output during those years would suggest, whereas others attribute it to the market crash of 1890. Waife-Goldberg writes that Sholom Aleichem once told his son-in-law, I. D. Berkowitz, that *Yosele Solovey* had cost him 30,000 rubles, so absorbed had he been in its writing that he completely neglected the stock exchange.

Several of the main characters in the novel are described as being in the thrall of a popular romantic literature of the time. Sholom Aleichem appears to condemn these characters and to blame them in some measure for Yosele's fate. Depicting realistic love within the novel can be understood as a reaction to the trashy novels he deplored. In 1886 Sholom Aleichem published a diatribe, written in the form of a dramatized trial, against the most popular Yiddish romance writer of the time, N. M. Shaykevich, whose pen name was Shomer. This writer Germanized his Yiddish to make it "high class" and wrote romantic, heartrending stories filled with facile daydreams and sentimental happy endings instead of dealing with the realities of Jewish life. The Jewish intelligentsia, including Sholom Aleichem, considered this fiction to be little more than trash, or *shund* literature. Sholom Aleichem's pamphlet *Shomer's Mishpet (Shomer's Trial)* succeeded in swaying the Yiddish reading public against Shomer's writing. Professor Dan Miron, in his splendid book *A Traveler Disguised*, describes how the "disparagement of Shaykevich went hand in hand with the establishment of 'the great tradition' in Yiddish fiction." Sholom Aleichem nourished this tradition by using his own funds to commission Jewish writers to submit Yiddish fiction and poetry for publication in his *Folksbibliotek*.

Sholom Aleichem's intent to render in realistic fiction the nature of Jewish life results in a number of surprises to modern sensibility. Perhaps the greatest surprise in *The Nightingale* is the treatment of women. The author describes with fidelity the arranged marriages, the desperate need for a large dowry in order to ensure a good match, the absolute authority of parents, the limitations of a woman's education. It is therefore interesting to read of women who were considered superior to men in business, who made the major decisions financially, and who were respected by the community at large for their shrewdness and capability, often at the expense of their husbands.

Perhaps because there is a span of almost a hundred years between the time of writing and the translation of this novel, I have found the task to be more formidable and challenging than other Sholom Aleichem works. The language of the shtetl, particularly the way the women speak, is quite archaic, almost a local and vanished dialect marked by many incomplete sentences and phrases, as if the speaker assumes the listener is familiar enough with the idiom and speech patterns to complete the thought. Some terms uttered by a few of the women neither I nor anybody I know had ever heard before. In addition, many of the characters are given to using—often even inventing—aphorisms to make a point, combining not only Yiddish and Hebrew but Ukrainian and Russian as well, usually incorrectly. For the translator the task is one of constant problem solving: finding native speakers—who are, virtually by definition, elderly—checking every possible spelling of transliterations in various dictionaries, and then coming up with an equivalent translation in modern (but not too modern) English that will sound natural as spoken by a person of a particular status and age living in the 1880s. When this is achieved, euphoria results, equal to the exhilaration produced by finding a treasure with the aid of a very old map.

Especially difficult were the sections in which cantorial singing and its effect on the audience is described, for there were no musical terms in Yiddish comparable to "falsetto," "embellishment," "coloratura," and other such expressions.

14

At one point Sholom Aleichem describes Yosele's trill as sounding like little *arbes* (garbanzo beans) rolling over one another. Garbanzo beans??!! But that's what it says, and what other image could one use? I chose chick-peas, but I still think it sounds odd. Also, I would like to offer a prize (a small prize) to anyone who can tell me what *chata pokrishke* means. I have lists of foods, clothing, and animals in the original Yiddish which have sadly died along with their speakers. Yet I did find out that the Cold Shul, the synagogue where Yosele and his father sang, was given that name simply because the building was too large to be heated. Other synagogues, like the Butchers' Shul, were small enough to be heated by a small wood stove. My father said he prayed in a Cold Shul in his small town in Hungary.

The Yiddish language can tolerate more repetition than English. When it was not necessary to maintain the rhythm of the original, I took a very few liberties in deleting unnecessary connective words and redundant phrases. Aside from these modifications, I have insisted on retaining the nuances and idioms as written and intended.

To achieve this goal I was assisted by many friends, patient relatives, and scholars, often finding all three roles in one person. Special honor goes to my parents, Rabbi Eliezer and Rivka Goldberger. In spite of my father's recent loss of much of his eyesight, his remarkably lucid and almost total recall of Talmudic and biblical references was of enormous help. Rabbi Allan Kensky kindly read for accuracy and spelling the sections of the book in which the hero sings the Musaf service. Also to be thanked are Dr. Tikva Frymer-Kensky, my friend Anita Norich; Joan Blos; Dr. Shoni Guiora; Serge Shishkoff; Basya Genkina and Anya Finkel, my Russian speakers; Dr. Marilyn Krimm; Faith Sale, my

15

splendid editor; Louise Lindemann, the superb copy editor; Dorothy Foster, my typist; the Sholom Aleichem family as represented by the lovely Bel Kaufman; and above all, my husband, Howie. He was especially indispensable in the translation of this work because of the inherent problems already mentioned. He read aloud and acted out all the parts for me, thus helping me establish the correct speech patterns and rhythms. He has an unerring sense of language and the way it is used to convey personality, *and* he is also fluent in Yiddish. I am very fortunate in having his collaboration and support. Should this novel ever be dramatized, I can recommend him for every role.

Aliza Shevrin
Ann Arbor, Michigan
Pesach 1985

Since this introduction was written, my beloved father, who placed his extensive knowledge of Judaism at my disposal, has passed away. He will be sorely missed in many ways.

Dearest Friend!

My second Yiddish novel, *Yosele Solovey*, I bring to you today on the occasion of your birthday. I hope this gift will be pleasing to you, but not because I've convinced myself that it has no faults. I know very well that I haven't fully obeyed the *Zayde's*, Reb Mendele's, rule that "a work needs to be polished and repolished," and this I haven't done for two reasons. First, there is no time. One is, alas, no more than a frail human being, and only half a writer at that; or more accurately, half a businessman and half a writer, as is usually the case among Jews. One has also to keep in mind *this* world, not only the world to come. Second, we are, after all, young people who rarely have time enough; we are couriers, always rushing, always busy, always afraid we will be too late. So what do I want to say? I am counting on you to realize that, as much as possible, I toiled very hard on my *Yosele*, until God helped me and I finally lived to see him at least resembling a living person.

Accept this gift of mine, then, dear friend, as it is, and may it serve as a token of how you are loved and valued by

Your true friend,

The Author

Kiev, December 1889

Contents

Part Two

Part Three

Part One

I

Yosele Is Burning to Sing

Such spendthrifts as the elders of the Cold Shul in Mazepevka are not to be found anywhere in the world. The townspeople can often be heard saying, "May each of us have for himself what they spend a year on cantors." The reason for this largesse is that the Mazepevka Jews are, as is well known far and wide, connoisseurs without equal of vocal music. Search the world over, you will not find such devotees of singing as the elders of the Cold Shul. Where does the renowned Pitzi sing when he comes to Mazepevka? In the Cold Shul. Where can you hear Yerucham? Or Nissi? Or Mitzi? In the Cold Shul. That's the way it's always been, and that's the way it has to be, no one questions it. It's no easy task for them to select the right prayer leader who will bring them pleasure and who won't embarrass them before the congregation. They are willing to go through no end of trouble until they find a cantor who will please each and every one of them, suiting each one's taste. But once he has been selected, he is theirs for good, for all time, and for him there can be no better place anywhere in the world. That's the kind of people the elders of the Cold Shul are, and that's the kind of cantor Shmulik was. Shmulik's voice could sound as deep as a lion's roar or scale the heights of a sweet falsetto trilled with the greatest virtuosity. They said that his *mim'kom'cha*, adapted from the Krutier's version, was a sheer delight. His tone was rich and his Hebrew impeccable, his recitations were "pure gold." "If, let us suppose, our Shmulik"—that's the way the elders of the Cold Shul spoke of him—"If, let us suppose, our Shmulik knew how to read music, he would undoubtedly be superior to Pitzi and Mitzi and Yerucham and all the international cantors currently the rage. Our Shmulik, if he had a mind to, could this very day outdo with one of his little Musaf prayers or his rendering of a Rumanian *Vulechl* all of today's virtuosos along with their big choirs!"

During the High Holy Days, Shmulik used to conduct the services assisted by a small choir made up of his son, Yosele, with his young voice, and two other singers—a bass and a high tenor—and that sufficed. Most of the service Shmulik performed himself with his own "golden voice." The variations that Shmulik would improvise for each holiday were thenceforth sung by the townspeople the rest of the year. Not that they ever gathered someplace in order to sing, for that there is no time, and furthermore, people are rarely in such high spirits that they suddenly burst into song. But each person in his own way, perhaps at his table or while walking down the street, would softly hum Shmulik's original variations. Shmulik knew nothing about notes. He knew there were cantors who could read music, but he had heard that only once, when Pitzi came through

Mazepevka with his eighteen-member choir. Shmulik had heard many cantors in his life, but they had all sung in the old style, following the established oral tradition or composing the melodies extemporaneously. Shmulik had only to hear the great Paretzer cantor chant the Musaf once without benefit of notes and he would remember the flavor of it for the rest of his life. But when Pitzi came through Mazepevka with his choir of eighteen, Shmulik heard for the first time how it was to chant with notes. He was so overwhelmed by Pitzi's chanting that he was riveted to the spot.

"So that's what notes can do! Notes!"

All that Sabbath he paced restlessly about in a state of consternation.

"So that's what notes can do!"

After having impatiently awaited the end of the Sabbath and the performance of the concluding Havdalah service, he announced to his wife, Zelda, that there was no way out—he simply had to go to Reb Shavtai's inn and have a talk with this Pitzi face-to-face. After the Eliyahus prayers Shmulik tied his cord belt around his waist and, accompanied by his son, Yosele, set off for Reb Shavtai's inn. After discussing cantorial matters for a while, Shmulik asked Pitzi if he might take the trouble to go into greater detail about notes and clarify how they were useful. At first Pitzi ridiculed him and joked about it at Shmulik's expense, but as he gazed into Shmulik's naïve yet earnest face and after testing his voice, Pitzi was impressed by the cantor. He performed several compositions from Sultzer's *Siddur* for him, accompanied by all of his eighteen choir members. Shmulik was in seventh heaven, his eyes filled with tears.

"What is there to say? Now for the first time I realize, Reb Pitzi, what an incompetent, the devil-knows-what I am,"

Shmulik said humbly. He then pointed to his Yosele. "Do you see this youngster, Reb Pitzi? He's mine, my son. You ought to listen to him."

Pitzi listened to Yosele and liked his voice very much. Shmulik heard Pitzi pronounce: "The child has talent, he has a very fine soprano, and with time, if he works at it, something might come of him."

Those words went straight to Shmulik's head, and from that time on he never stopped thinking, What can be done for Yosele? As for me, I'm past help—what is there to say? I'll die an incompetent, but my Yosele? Just let him grow up a little, start to put on *tefillin* and, with God's help, I'll apprentice him to a big cantor, to Pitzi or to Mitzi or even to Yerucham."

From that day on Shmulik always imagined that Yosele would one day become a renowned cantor like Pitzi or perhaps even like Nissi. And why not? Haven't we all witnessed how a mere stripling of a boy can become a man?

"Yosele," Shmulik called to his son as the youngster ran in from *cheder*, his face flushed, his cap atilt, "Yosele, you little devil, would you like to become a great cantor some day?"

Yosele stood still, deep in thought, his eyes sparkling. His father needn't have asked. Of course he would like to become a great cantor. Ever since childhood his ambition had been to become a cantor. Yosele could not imagine anything greater or better. And since hearing Pitzi's chanting, the zeal to become a cantor had intensified. As with Shmulik, Pitzi's chanting in Mazepevka with his eighteen-member choir had shaken Yosele to the foundation of his being. While Shmulik had been occupied with Pitzi, Yosele had joined some of Pitzi's young choirboys, from whom he had learned many things. They told him how they toured all over the world and how wherever they went they were met with great pomp and fanfare. They were carried on people's shoulders, they were regaled with the best and finest. In short, it was the kind of life anyone would envy! Observing these choirboys with their fine caftans and their round velvet caps, Yosele was truly envious of them, he envied not only their caftans and caps but the fact that they sang on the same pulpit with Pitzi. He would consider himself lucky to be like them, to be one of Pitzi's choirboys. How I wish I were already old enough to be bar mitzvah, Yosele thought, and those fortunate singers never left his thoughts for so much as a minute. At school his mind would often wander from the Pentateuch until the rabbi reprimanded him. "Look at that boy with his head in the clouds instead of in his *Chumash!*"

Cheder was for Yosele a heavy burden, and no sooner did he have a free moment than he would practice his singing, imitating Pitzi's tenor, trying to rumble in the low registers like Pitzi's basso, or attempting Pitzi's impossible vocal feats in the highest registers, which were like climbing straight up bare walls. He had the feeling that if he could only let loose and sing at the top of his lungs, he would be greatly relieved.

II

Shmulik the Cantor Tells Stories About Cantors and Yosele Listens Intently

The world in which Yosele grew up was alive with singing and talk about cantors. From childhood on he had heard Shmulik recounting tales about world-famous cantors who had achieved renown and were remembered wherever there were Jews. Tales about Hershele the Yingele, the Vilner Balabeysl, Arke Fiedele, and others gave him no rest. He would dwell on them day and night. Yosele would imagine that he himself was Hershele the Yingele, who at eleven years of age put on a small prayer shawl and conducted the service at the pulpit, causing a sensation. When Yosele would find himself alone at home, he would don his father's prayer shawl, stand facing the wall, and, pretending to pray, would mimic cantorial gestures while straining to reach the highest notes and trilling in a cracked falsetto. Once when Shmulik caught him at it, he scolded him and sent him back to *cheder* where he belonged. But Yosele had little enthusiasm for *cheder*, and the rabbi had his hands full. He could not understand how a young boy could always be so lost in thought, his mind in the clouds.

From his earliest remembrance, Yosele's greatest pleasure came when the High Holidays were celebrated. Shmulik would need to prepare the holiday service. Six weeks before Rosh Hashanah he would start rehearsing all the parts with his choir. At those times Yosele felt his soul ascend the heights. He could barely wait until that happy moment when the rabbi would send the children home to eat. He would come running home, gulp down his supper quickly, and slip into a corner unobtrusively, where he would listen to his father, whose sweet voice poured out melodiously, his hands in an attitude of supplication, singing, "Oy vey, oy vey, oy vey, oy vey!" And the choir echoed, "Oy vey, oy vey, oy vey, oy vey!" Yosele was content if no one noticed him and he could sit in his corner listening to the entire service until the Avodah. Best of all, Yosele loved to hear the stories his father would tell his choir members about famous cantors and how they had made names for themselves. He especially liked the story of how Pitzi became a cantor.

"Bardichev is where he was from," Shmulik said, relating the story about the great cantor, "Bardichev, from beyond the Greblye. His father was a *shamesh*, a synagogue sexton. From childhood on, Pitzi showed he was a prodigy. At first he was a choirboy, but when his voice changed he was apprenticed to a goldsmith. But since he loved to sing, he always made it his business to be in the company of cantors and musicians. He was a jack-of-all-trades. He was a drummer, played the cymbals, even the pipes, until he met up with the great Reb Tzalel. Reb Tzalel told him, 'Foolish boy, how do you come to play the pipes? You have a better instrument—your voice!' In short, he made his way to Lemberig, and when he returned from there he had a glorious name, may half of it fall to my Yosele, God in heaven!"

Hearing those words spoken by his father, Yosele's heart leaped for joy. He imagined that he also was being sent to Lemberig and would also return with a glorious name, like Pitzi. Shmulik had a sackful of stories about cantors, one better than the next. He had learned these stories from their original sources.

"How does a Bachman happen?" Shmulik said to his choir. "Tell me—how? What is there to say? The great Bachman! What was he before that? Go to Kishenev and they'll tell you. Do you think you wake up one morning and you're a Bachman, a Pitzi, a Nissi? And then there was Sender Mider who was a rich man, very wealthy, and he sang only for pleasure; it's his *Yer'u ayneynu* that I sing. You can find good cantors these days too: there's a Nissi Belzer, a Chazkele, a Pitzi, an Eli David Chernigover, a Shkuder cantor—What is there to say?—and plenty more cantors. But the cantors of old are not to be found nowadays.

Where, for example, can you find today a cantor like Arke Fiedele, the Vitebsker? The whole world flocked to hear his voice, which was more like a violin than a voice. Or where today would you find someone like the Canarik, on whom the Kaiser Franz Josef himself bestowed a gift? Or, for instance, where can you find today someone like Reb David Chmelniker and his three sons? He truly was the cantor of cantors, worthy of singing before the Emperor himself! He used to stand up before the congregation, warbling plaintively, wearing the long fringed ritual undergarment, with an incongruous top hat on his head. Oh, it was a delight to see! Or, I ask you, is there nowadays a cantor like the Krutier cantor who was actually Nissi's grandfather? Or, for example, Reb Abraham Chassid from Lemberig, who was one in a million? Or Kashtan, whose confession of faith on his deathbed is a legend? Or, for instance, someone like the Vilner Balabeysl, as he was called? Where can you find his equal today? What is there to say?

"Have you ever heard the story of the Vilner Balabeysl? It's a good story, worth listening to. His name was Yoal Dovid. He had a personality seldom found in this world. As for his talent—nothing need be said. If you can imagine it, by the age of eleven he was already conducting the High Holiday services on the pulpit. His reputation had spread so far and wide that soon the count himself had heard of him. The count wanted to hear what the crowds were buzzing about, and so he sent for him.

"Yarmulke on his head, Yoal Dovid came before the count, who was surrounded by great lords and ladies. At first the Balabeysl was intimidated by such an illustrious audience, but he stood with his face to the wall and began to demonstrate his feats, performing with great virtuosity as only he could. He was accompanied on the violin, and the stunned audience was left speechless because they couldn't tell which was the voice and which the violin—that's how pure Yoal Dovid's voice was and that's how high his voice could reach. Toward the end one of the violin strings snapped and the musician had to improvise an octave higher. What do you think happened? The Balabeysl hesitated a moment, and—What is there to say?—accomplished with his voice what only a violin can achieve. And to top even that, he threw in several nightingalelike ornamentations. When he had finished, the count could no longer contain himself. He rushed up to Yoal Dovid and planted a kiss on his forehead.

"The count was a very good person, but she, the countess, may her name be obliterated, was a wicked woman who hated Jews. When the Balabeysl arrived wearing the yarmulke, she was ready to chop his head off. But once he began to sing she became enchanted, and afterward she went up to him, took him by the hand, thanked him many times over for his singing, and asked him his name and how old he was. Yoal Dovid answered all her questions, keeping his eyes averted because she was a person of high rank. But *she* certainly looked at *him*, devoting a long time to gazing at his face, not letting go of his hand and not taking her eyes off him continuously while squeezing his hand and thanking him.

"The following day a message arrived, again from the count, commanding that he appear at the palace without fail. What could one do? There was no choice. If the count commanded, one could not be an ingrate and refuse. It turned out to be a ruse—the count wasn't even at home, but the countess was, cursed be her name. Festooned with gold and diamonds from head to toe, she came out to greet Yoal Dovid and his choir. She offered him her hand in the most friendly manner, as if they had known each other for years. She politely bade the choir members wait in the Great Hall while she led Yoal Dovid into her private chambers. She seated him on an expensive velvet divan, offered him sweets and, naturally, wine, but he would not drink under any circumstances. No matter how she pleaded, it was in vain. When the evil countess realized her wiles were not having their effect, she seized his caftan, as Potiphar had once tempted Joseph the Righteous, and Yoal Dovid barely escaped with his life. From that time on, they say, she became even more wicked, and when she saw a Jew she would become enraged. She finally convinced the count himself to become an enemy of Jews. As for the Balabeysl, she wreaked revenge on him in her own way, by other means. There are to be found, even among Jews, people who for money will do away with a person. Such people were hired by the countess. They gave the Balabeysl a poisoned drink that robbed him of his voice. As soon as the poor Balabeysl realized he had lost his voice, he fell into a deep melancholy and went completely mad. He wandered about the world, tattered and torn, not speaking a word to anyone. That was the end of the Vilner Balabeysl—and all because of her, may her name be cursed."

To Yosele these stories were profoundly exciting. "Balabeysl," "Fiedele," "Canarik," "countess," "Potiphar"—those images were never far from his thoughts. His imagination constantly drew him back to Pitzi, to Nissi, to Yerucham. At last his eleventh year was behind him. Another year and then another year and he would become bar mitzvah and his father would send him off to study. His every day was filled with a chorus of great voices and sweet melodies. Cantors and choirs never left his thoughts, and when the rabbi labored with him and the other students

34

over the Gemorah—that was when Yosele's mind would wander far afield. Occasionally there would escape from his throat a little whistle, a screech, or some strange sound like the crowing of a rooster. At those times the rabbi would usually give him a sharp slap. "On the pulpit with your father you can crow, not here!"

In shul Yosele assisted his father only during the High Holidays, and that was his favorite time—first, because he was allowed out of *cheder* a month early, and second, because of the singing. The singing was very precious to him. Once on the dais he was no longer afraid of being slapped. His voice was liberated and he could lift it in song to his heart's content. During the High Holidays both voices could be heard together—Shmulik's voice joined with Yosele's reedy young voice, and the congregation was delighted with both. The musical experts said that Yosele would one day surpass his father. But Shmulik derived little pleasure from that praise. Of what use was praise when he saw Yosele growing up in poverty and there was nothing he could do about it?

Although Shmulik the cantor was esteemed by the community, it was not beneath him to acknowledge that he was a poor man like all the Mazepevker religious functionaries, who had to depend on locally provided stipends. In Mazepevka, as is well known, the salaries of cantors, synagogue officials, ritual slaughterers, and rabbis were not overly generous. If local clergy had had to rely on their meager salaries alone, they would have died of starvation. The largest share of their income came from what they could make on the side—the donations and gratuities that came their way from the plate that was passed in the shul on Yom Kippur eve, from Chanukah money, Purim gifts, and donations for reciting prayers on special occasions. Shmulik the cantor may have had a rare voice and may have performed like a Nissi, like a Pitzi, or even like a Yerucham Hakaton, but when Chanukah time came, it did him no harm to take his staff and lantern in hand and go through the town wishing each congregant, "May we all live till next year" and accepting in return—charity. At Purim time it would not be beneath his dignity to fill a plate with lekach and strudel and have it sent around from household to household and accept in return—charity.

III

How Shmulik Meets His Neighbor, Zlate the Shopkeeper, and How Their Children Meet

In Mazepevka it was no small matter to own your own place—the smallest piece of property, a hole in the wall, a clod of earth—so long as it was your own and you didn't have to put up with neighbors. Zlate the shopkeeper owned no grand palace with spacious rooms but lived in her own little house with three small low-ceilinged cubbyholes whose walls slanted inward, making for sharp-angled corners. Although there was a kitchen of sorts, the house could not boast of a hallway, a yard, or so much as a shed—only a garret above and no more.

Yet that would have been tolerable if the roof had really been a roof. But the poor pitiful thing was made up of two rafters covered with black straw and overgrown here and there with green weeds, so that from a distance it appeared as if the house were a sukkah covered with thatch. Yet that too would have been tolerable if the count, the landowner of the district, had not been harassing the residents with his caprices. One fine day he was suddenly taken with the idea that the entire town should improve its appearance by using roof tiles, wrought-iron trim, or, at the very least, wooden slats, and he further specified that no straw be visible at all. Zlate the widow had to work her fingers to the bone in order to put a groschen by a groschen so that she could comply with this edict. But a new misfortune replaced the old: no sooner had she begun to pull down the old roof than Shmulik the cantor burst into Zlate's house, shouting, "Madwoman! In God's name, what are you doing? Do you want to ruin me? What have you got against me? I slave and slave till I finally live to have a bit of property and now you come along and try to wreck it!"

"This is just what I needed! What wreck?" Zlate was astounded. "Who's bothering you and your property?"

"*You're* asking who's bothering *me?*" Shmulik said, changing his tone of voice. "A woman remains a woman—long on hair, short on brains."

"Let me tell you something," Zlate answered him, working herself up, "even if you are the cantor of the Cold Shul, and please don't take offense if I tell you straight out, since God created fools, He never created as big a fool as you."

"Oho! A big mouth too!" Shmulik flared up. "It's not enough that you're destroying my house, utterly ruining me, but you have the gall to insult an honest Jew? I've had all kinds of neighbors in my lifetime, both men and women—Ach! To the devil with it!"

"*You* go to the devil, along with everything you hold dear, Lord Almighty. May you and all my enemies suffer, wherever they are, dear God! I too have had neighbors, and as I stand here on my own two feet, I have never in my whole life met anyone like you. How does a man allow himself out of the clear blue sky to burst into someone else's house, fly off the handle at a poor widow, and spit in her face?"

"Sha, quiet down, what's going on here?" broke in the cantor's wife, Zelda, who had come running in, frightened. She was a short, dark-skinned woman with lovely, kind eyes. "What's all this shouting about?"

Shmulik and Zlate both blurted out their grievances to the cantor's wife, telling her all that had taken place, shouting and interrupting each other so that Zelda couldn't figure out who was in the right and who was in the wrong.

"Do you know what, Shmulik? You go home. I've prepared a cup of chicory for you. And you, Zlatenyu, please sit down right here next to me on the bench and we'll talk together calmly. What's the good of shouting? The neighbors will come running and will think, God forbid, that people are being slaughtered in broad daylight."

Once Shmulik left, Zlate and Zelda had a chance to talk it over and made some sense of things. The trouble was this: Zlate the widow's house and the adjacent house, which Shmulik the cantor had recently bought from Reb Sholom Shachne the shochet on installments, were separated by nothing more than a wall, the two were, in fact, one house sharing several beams and covered by the same roof. Understandably, when one beam was moved, the whole roof threatened to cave in, including the part over Shmulik's house. And that is why Shmulik had flown into such a rage. Zlate and Zelda, who had until then only nodded at each other from a distance (because Zlate thought of herself as upper-class—after all, she was Reb Avrahaml's daughter-in-law—but more about this later), grew so close after this chat that they soon became as one soul. It was decided that if they covered the roof together, it would cost less and the garret could become shared space. At least, blessed be His name, they trusted each other not to cheat or take advantage, heaven forbid.

"Your husband," Zlate said to Zelda, "is an honest man. Who doesn't know that? And you, Zelda, are not, God forbid, one of those wives who casts eyes on another's belongings."

"And you," Zelda replied to Zlate, "don't need my little sack of potatoes. Do you think people don't know about you? I've heard tell that my mother, may she dwell in Paradise, used to spend a great deal of time with your Bubbe Estherl, doing all kinds of shopping for her. And your grandmother had a house, may its like be granted to all Jewish housekeepers! Your daughter is named after her, I suppose?"

Zlate almost wept with tender feelings after Zelda spoke those sympathetic words, and from that time on, a powerful kinship sprang up between them. Their children also grew close; Shmulik's son, Yosele, and Zlate's daughter, Esther, were often together, almost as if they had been sister and brother. Later, when Zelda died and Yosele became an orphan, the children grew even more devoted to each other. "Tragedy," they say, "binds; sorrow creates friendship."

As long as Zelda lived, Shmulik the cantor was content. He struggled and survived as so many others did. But tragedy struck him down. His wife died. Zelda the cantor's wife was a pious, honorable Jewish woman. Her sudden death was a great catastrophe for her friends, and for Shmulik it was a shock he swore he could not survive. He was convinced he would soon follow Zelda into the grave. He could not be persuaded otherwise. There was no question of re-marrying. When hair grew on the palm of his hand, Shmulik declared as he sat *shiva,* only then would he marry anyone after Zelda. Many in the town visited him daily and pleaded with him, "Reb Shmulik, you think you are smarter than anybody else and believe you can go against human nature? Human nature is human nature for all time. A man should not live alone. And you think you are clever enough to change that?" People worked on Shmulik so long that a few weeks after the thirty-day mourning period, he drove to Bardichev with Reb Kalman the matchmaker and soon re-turned home with a woman in a Turkish shawl.

Bardichev, thank God, was well known as a place where one could, for ready cash, obtain that sort of merchandise: for a widower, a divorced man, a bachelor—whichever you were. Bardichev was a bounteous land that supplied the other cities in the district with all kinds of women: widows, divorcées, or spinsters, according to one's liking. Should a widower pay a visit there, he would be escorted from home to home and shown the selection of available wares. You can be certain he would find something to his liking, would strike a bargain, and return home with a partner. That is where our Shmulik made a quick visit. It didn't take him long. After a few words—a wedding. And considering he had to hurry back for Shabbos, the beauty he had selected wasn't so bad, praise be God. "A woman—What is there to say?—she looks like a respectable person, doesn't seem bad-natured, speaks honestly, smiles . . ." But a few weeks after returning home poor Shmulik first realized what a calamity, what an affliction God had visited upon him; his new wife made him old and gray before his time! Shmulik suffered a miserable old age at her hands. And poor Yosele also suf-fered. He always seemed to be in her way. "That boy," she kept complaining, "will drive me into my grave! From morning till night all this creature wants to do is eat! That mouth of his never closes for so much as a minute, and he's always talking back too. If you tell him something, he cries and acts like a spoiled brat!" God only knows what would have become of Yosele if not for Shmulik's neighbor, Zlate the shopkeeper, and her household, who came to the rescue of that poor innocent orphan.

IV

Zlate the Shopkeeper and Her Daughter Esther

Even before she was married Zlate was considered to be one of the most respected shopkeepers, not only in Mazepevka but in the entire district. Her name was well known in the large fairs and markets. In those days when people everywhere were still debating whether women should be allowed to work or should be restricted to home, kitchen, and children, when great minds had been pondering the matter for years, wasting vast amounts of paper and ink, the Mazepevka Jews went their own way, heaping scorn on all such theories, because in Mazepevka, as long as people could remember, women had played exactly the same role as men, and the wife was considered no less important than the husband. On the contrary, one could say that almost all the business of Mazepevka was in women's hands. It was not uncommon in Mazepevka for the woman's reputation to completely eclipse her husband's. One could even find men who were totally unknown; people knew only who "she" was, and that was all. Zlate the shopkeeper was one of those women who were known as *eyshes-chayiles*, "women of valor." Even while her husband lived, Zlate was known in town as Zlate the shopkeeper, not Zlate Levi's. It was Levi who was known as Levi Zlate's.

So it had been with Zlate's mother, Basya the wholesaler, as she was called. She too was an *eyshes-chayil* and raised her daughters to be *eyshes-chayiles* so that they could support their husbands. The sons-in-law Basya the wholesaler obtained for her daughters were those rare, pampered, delicate young scholars of aristocratic lineage intent on keeping their satin gabardines clean. For the right pedigree Basya paid dearly. For her son-in-law Levi, Zlate's husband, Basya paid a double dowry in order to procure him, because Levi was the son of Reb Abraham Slaviter, and Reb Abraham Slaviter was dripping with pedigree and related to all the important Jews. In truth, Levi was a fine young man but not in the best of health, a consumptive who was forever coughing. He died young, leaving Zlate a widow with three small children: Esther, an eight-year-old girl, and two infant boys, Ephraim and Menashe.

Although Esther was her mother's only daughter, she was not spoiled, because her parents never had the means with which to pamper her. As long as Esther could remember, there had been only sorrow and grief. She could remember her father only as ill, distressed, and despairing. Her mother was always busy with the shop, always pressed for time, always irritated, always cursing her plight and the day she was born. By the time Esther was thirteen years old she was helping out in her mother's shop, at first simply watching for shoplifters and later bringing out merchandise, dealing with customers, and eventually handling money—in short, doing business. Esther had the reputation in town of being a capable girl with a talent for trade and a good head on her shoulders. Where did Esther learn how to write and do figures? From Mottel Shprayz, who tutored all the Mazepevka girls, as a sideline, in reading, writing, and arithmetic. In Mazepevka it was possible for girls to grow up to be capable and decently educated.

Levi Zlate's was a devoted father and a refined person, a man of learning who earnestly hoped that his daughter would achieve great things. And since Esther had shown promise from early childhood, Levi had always assumed that Esther would, God willing, become a woman of many accomplishments, not like so many Mazepevka girls. Of course, this goal wasn't so easily achieved. Zlate, his wife, who always had her way, was not too eager to consent to the father's ambitions for his daughter. "What kind of nonsense is this," she would protest, "a female scholar? A hen crowing cock-a-doodle-doo? On my life, it's unnatural!" In all matters Levi gave in to Zlate his wife, but in this case he stood his ground, firm as iron: once and for all, Esther had to have a proper education! But man proposes and God disposes. It was not poor Levi's fate to see his wish fulfilled. After a few years of struggling with his illness, he was, heaven help us, carried off by tuberculosis while still in his twenties, and he left behind his dear, beloved Esther in Zlate's hands.

Esther could no longer give any thought to serious study; the little she had learned she retained and the rest she picked up in the course of her dealings with business people. And Esther proved to be an exceptional Mazepevka businesswoman. Reb Kalman the matchmaker was not shy about making this observation directly to Zlate when he came into her shop one time.

"Listen to me," Reb Kalman said, turning to Zlate, snorting loudly to clear his nose and glancing off to the side as he did so. "Look here, Zlate, you have quite a daughter there, you know, and a clever one too, a real person, be thankful for it, and quite competent, they say. How old is she, ha? It's high time to start thinking about making something of a match. How do they say it? A pretty girl is half the dowry, ha?"

"Who knows?" Zlate answered him with a pleased little smile. "What's the hurry? There's still time. Let her enjoy herself."

And Esther "enjoyed" herself. . . .

Day and night she was tied to her work, not knowing a moment's pleasure. One could say without any question that Esther was never really a child. The foolish childhood years flew by as in a dream. Early in her life she was made aware of want, worry, and poverty. She could not remember ever having been happy like other Mazepevka girls. If Esther so much as laughed, her mother would say, "What's the big celebration about? Is it because your father died and left me a miserable widow with three children so I should know what it is to struggle on this earth?" Such reproaches were worse than a beating for Esther. Whenever she was reminded of her father, her heart would break and she would lower her eyes. She remembered her father as if in a dream, because she had been so young when he died. She always pictured him as ailing, with a jaundiced, drained face but with large, kindly blue eyes that always gazed at her with pity, as if Levi knew that his poor only daughter would soon become an orphan. Esther remembered how her father would continue stroking her hair even while having a coughing fit. She would never forget that day when he was lying on his cot, unable to speak, and he fixed his gaze on

44

her with his kindly blue eyes and motioned with his hand for her to bring her head closer, all the while stroking her hair. That look she was unable to forget, and if ever, for so much as a moment, she did feel any happiness, any liveliness, she had only to remind herself of that look and in an instant the good feeling vanished, even though she was still a mere child.

But Zlate did not allow her to remain a child for long; she was soon put to work in the business. And Esther was so competent that Zlate would boast of her, "A one-and-only, thank God at least for that! What would a poor widow like me do if I had children, as *some* people do, may God not punish me for these words? With one hand the Eternal One afflicts, with the other He heals. That's the way, my child, learn all you can. At least I'll have a little help with my tiny orphans, and you yourself will also benefit from it." Esther plunged into learning all there was to know about the business, and she soon mastered it.

As skillful as Esther was in conducting trade in the shop, so was she skilled in disguising poverty at home. One has to explain "disguising poverty" in Mazepevka—not everyone comprehends its meaning. Even during the hardest times Esther was able to run the household so cleverly that one would not be able to guess when entering Zlate's house whether she was rich or poor. It was cleaner and neater than any rich person's house in town: the food—what there was of it—the tablecloth, the dishes, and the way things were served—to perfection! To succeed in preparing a supper with scraps of food, without meat, without fish, without shmaltz, with nothing more than one's five fingers, was no easy task, and that was where Esther excelled. The old-fashioned furniture in Zlate's house was worn out. Nevertheless it was always draped with white covers, and the windows were hung with clean curtains, so that the rooms sparkled and shimmered before one's eyes as in a wealthy home. The clothing, it was true, was quite out of style but was nonetheless always mended, washed, and ironed—a pleasure to look at. No child in Mazepevka was as clean or as neat as Ephraim and Menashe, Zlate's boys. And of Esther herself, what could be said? When the townspeople would see her they would say, "It looks like Zlate is not doing so badly." Esther was a genius at disguising poverty—washing it and sprucing it up and making it look so good that no one could recognize it. But the reputation Esther had earned in her own town was as nothing compared to the reputation she had in the entire district. Her name was known far and wide because of the large popular fairs that took place in Mazepevka three times a year.

These three large fairs gave Mazepevka a chance to show off before the world. It is doubtful that Mazepevka could have survived without these fairs, which were called Yuria, Spaas, and Pokrova. Every Mazepevka Jew looked forward to them the entire year, all his hopes riding on their success. For weeks beforehand people began to prepare for the fair, running around in circles like dogs chasing their tails, sniffing out any kind of spot and trying to grab the best possible locations for themselves. "No time to waste—we have to get ready for the fair!" was heard all over, even from those who didn't have a stall, a shop, a tavern, a grain cellar, or even any apple cider to hawk. Everyone was getting ready for the fair. One must wonder why a teacher or a cantor would be interested in a fair. Yet the teachers would send their pupils home early from *cheder* and the cantor would dismiss his choir in the middle of a *melech elyon*, and all would run off quickly to the fair, only to return home as empty-handed as they had gone, with deep frustration in their hearts, because it was apparently easier for others to bargain and take advantage of the good things to be had. Their wives would be ready for them when they arrived home, complaining that everyone else grabbed up bargains and why not they? "May a terrible fate descend on my enemies' heads!" the wives would curse afterward. "Look how happy he is! A big fair is not for the likes of him! Oh, no! But couldn't he at least have brought home a scrap, a little remnant of material to make shirts for the children, or even a nice string of onions for winter or—oh, the devil knows what!" The teacher or the cantor would try to defend himself: "You call that a fair? It was nothing special!" But they stood there feeling disheartened, their hands hanging down while they were forced to listen to an entire litany of curses. That's how important the fair was in Mazepevka.

So is it any surprise that open warfare would break out among the shopkeepers when Yuria, Spaas, and Pokrova time came? Is it any surprise that they would come to blows over favored locations, that they would fight over a customer, pulling at him from all sides? If you want to truly understand a Mazepevka Jew with all his virtues and faults, it would be best to observe him at a distance through binoculars during a fair as he stands beside his wife in his stall, talking to six customers at once, displaying wares to this one, bargaining with another, and measuring or weighing the merchandise for a third. There in the booth they ate and slept, be it summer or winter. The Mazepevka Jew was a genius when it came to fairs: with one tongue he could talk to ten people, with two hands he did three jobs, with two eyes he looked in four directions, spying out wherever the customer had just gone so that he could call him back, shouting in Ukrainian, "*Ab chodye syudi, tcholovitche!*—Come over here, man!" and, above all, keeping an eye out for shoplifters. "Making money is hard enough," he would say, "but the stealing that is done right under your very nose—ach! That's the hardest to put up with!"

As you observed this Jew you would conclude that he and his wife and his children were created solely for the fair. Their faces burned with excitement, their eyes glowed, their nostrils flared, their tongues wagged, their hands worked, all their limbs were in motion. "Hooray, Jews, it's fair time!" Zlate and Esther worked hard all day along with the others. From constant shouting their voices became hoarse and dull. Finally, exhausted, hungry, and faint as after a fast, with God's help, they welcomed the close of day. When night fell, the stalls were covered from top to bottom with flaxen cloths, and all the shopkeepers sat down at their tables, each counting up his profits, then sighing, "So this is all we made from the fair? A big nothing! That at such a fair we can't make any money—well, what's the world coming to!"

"I can't believe it," the old dry-goods storekeeper Reb Feivel was exclaiming. "They were able to swipe eighteen lengths of fabric from me. I've been a shopkeeper for more than thirty years and no one has ever stolen so much as a piece of thread from me—till today. Unbelievable! I don't understand it. It was lying right there, it seems, in front of my very eyes, and in a split second it was gone! Eighteen lengths of my finest linen cleaned out! What an outrage!"

People were talking among themselves, recounting stories about the fair. Among the babble of voices Esther's voice could be heard, and people paid attention, reserving friendly smiles for her while scratching their heads in amazement. "A real grown-up, Zlate's girl!" the shopkeepers said, admiring her. "Only a child, but does she know how to do business!"

Because conditions were crowded and rental space was at a premium, most Mazepevka women, those *eyshes-chayiles,* hardly had room or time for their husbands, those overly refined Jews who had no real interest in business. Although they weren't trusted to help take in the cash, they were enlisted to stand nearby to guard against thieves and, by their presence, to frighten them off. Were you to look at them, you would see fine, full-bearded men, but in fact they were useless old women in trousers, ladies with beards and earlocks. Levi Zlate's also used to be a stall-watcher, and when Zlate reminded herself of it she would become sad. "No more Levi, no one to stand guard over the booth," Zlate said, bemoaning her fate to her neighbor, Shmulik the cantor, and she suggested that since his Yosele was at that time idle, perhaps he wouldn't mind taking on some responsibility by watching over the booth, standing guard to prevent theft. Shmulik consented, and Yosele, alongside Zlate and Esther, stood guard while they took in the money. Actually, Yosele enjoyed being able to help Esther, being useful to her in any way. For Esther's sake Yosele would not hesitate to do anything. He would go to the ends of the earth, through fire and water, in gratitude for her devotion, for her good heart, and for the kind way she had treated him, a poor, lonely orphan.

V

Yosele Wanders Around with Time on His Hands and Is Drawn Ever Elsewhere

There is an old saying: As long as there is a mother, a father remains a father; without her he becomes a distant uncle. While Zelda lived, Yosele was for Shmulik the cantor, the apple of his eye; he was always basking in Yosele's promise. "My Yosele? You'll see what he'll become one day!" But after Zelda died and he brought home from Bardichev that woman with the Turkish shawl, Shmulik began to cool toward Yosele because of "her," although perhaps in his heart he loved him as much as before. It infuriated Zlate the shopkeeper to see the way they were mistreating Yosele. "Do you think, Reb Shmulik," Zlate would ask him pointedly, "that if Zelda, may she rest in peace, had remained a widow, Yosele would be wandering around with nothing to do? Do you think *she* would have taken him out of *cheder*, as you did, so he would grow up to be a who-knows-what, a wastrel?" To that Shmulik would respond with a deep sigh and a groan, trying to avoid Zlate's barbed tongue—anything to avoid hearing her words, which always struck home.

As you read earlier, Yosele spent so much time at Zlate's place that he had become like one of her own. And when he became an orphan Zlate drew even closer to him, taking great pity on him and standing up for him so that his stepmother would not do whatever she wished with him. As a result a feud raged between Zlate and Shmulik's wife. For his wife's sake Shmulik also had to quarrel with Zlate. They didn't actually quarrel, Zlate simply let him know more than once that he was letting himself be stepped on and was allowing his son to be humiliated.

"Please forgive me for coming right out with it, Reb Shmulik, but you're a sheep, not a man. Why do you listen to her, that Bardichev witch? If Zelda, may she rest in peace, were to rise up from her grave right now and see what's happening to her Yosele, she'd jump right back in again. You're some father, I tell you! I would be ashamed of myself if I were you. Is that the way a decent Jew behaves, eh?"

Shmulik would hear her out, bite his tongue, then go off with his choirboys to prepare a new *Od yizkor lanu* for Rosh Hashanah. Shmulik was more afraid of Zlate than of his wife, the Bardichever witch. It became more and more awkward for him to encounter Zlate, who was always reminding him of Zelda, and so he avoided her like the plague. He was always on the lookout for Zlate; when she came home from the market he would make sure to be occupied with his choir, working on a *m'chalelel* or a *v'yosev* for the High Holidays or practicing his scales. Still and all, Yosele spent his every waking hour at Zlate's house. Since he had been removed from *cheder*, Yosele had nothing to occupy him. He would sit in Zlate's shop looking after things or would help out with some task in the house, singing to himself in his sweet voice that Esther so loved to hear. Yosele got along with Esther as if he were her brother. They were both about the same age, had grown up together, were both orphans, and both had become acquainted with misfortune. When Esther felt downhearted, she would ask Yosele to sing "The Vilna Street" for her, and Yosele would stand in the center of the room and, striking a dramatic pose, would sing slowly in his soft, sweet voice:

When I go out
On the Vilna street
I hear a voice loudly lamenting
Alas, I hear their cries . . .

Yosele would become animated, turning his eyes upward and holding his hand over his heart, transported, while assuming the mannerisms of a real performer.

"Where did you learn those gestures?" Esther once asked him.

"I watched Pitzi's tenor when I visited Pitzi with my father. Pitzi's tenor used to say that that was the way they sang in the *theeter*. If you sing in the *theeter*, you have to stretch it out and make with your hands and with your whole body 'Ay, ay'—that's how that tenor sang. He listened to my voice and told me that Pitzi would take me on in a minute. I even thought of mentioning it to my father at the time, but I didn't want to—I was afraid. If Pitzi were to come here now, I would be a lot smarter."

Saying those words, Yosele would sink deep into thought. In his young heart there burned a small flame, and he was always drawn toward the wider, freer world. Nissi, Pitzi, Yerucham, music—these dominated Yosele's dreams, his strongest desires, in his boyhood years. To achieve those cantorial ambitions was the highest goal in his young life. Magical dreams ceaselessly floated through his brain. His favorite dream was to steal away to Odessa, where Pitzi lived, or to Mitzi in Tetrevetz in order to study music. That was also Shmulik's wish for his son, but he was never able to raise the fare for the journey. First he would have to talk it over with his wife, and that would be as difficult as the parting of the Red Sea. As Yosele's troubles mounted, he would often think that it might not be such a bad idea to go off on his own to Pitzi's: simply set one foot in front of the other and be gone! Of whom should he be afraid? Yosele had even conceived a plan, exactly when and how to do it, but he had second thoughts about leaving his father to sing alone. It was already clear that Shmulik could not get along without Yosele, who was his main support. When Yosele would sing out in his high-pitched voice, trilling up and down the scale, Shmulik could at least take a little rest and renew his strength to go on.

Yosele, as unhappy as he was, loved his father and felt sorry for him. He asked himself: "What will he do without me? Who will deliver his sweet platters for Purim, distribute the *matzo-shmura*, the first matzo, for *erev* Pesach, the *esrogim*, the citrons, for Succos?" In the good years, when Zelda, may her memory be blessed, was alive and was earning the household expenses by her own labors—by raising geese, by rendering shmaltz, by plucking feathers and such extra jobs—Shmulik didn't have to worry about every penny so desperately. But now that Zelda was dead and he had brought home that woman from Bardichev, she had increased his family by several tiny, guiltless souls who needed to eat, and Shmulik had to force himself to send Yosele for the first time out in the town to deliver sweet platters for Purim. For Shmulik it was a great comedown to see his poor son going from house to house barefoot.

Yosele wasn't at all bothered by this. For his father's sake he was willing to do anything in the world, if only he knew what. "If I were as great as Pitzi," Yosele reasoned, "I would give everything to my father in order not to see him suffer." More and more, Yosele felt himself drawn away. He would wander about, deep in thought, troubled. His thoughts were off somewhere else. In his heart dwelt a spirit that he himself hardly understood. It seemed to lift him in the air, didn't allow him to sleep, and drew him elsewhere. "Somewhere else! Once and for all—to go somewhere else!"

VI

He Finds His Garden of Eden
But Is Cruelly Driven Out

With time on his hands, Yosele would stroll aimlessly through the town, measuring the streets with his footsteps. His wanderings would sometimes take him far beyond the town, where, all alone, he would stretch out on the ground near the forest and pour out his heart in song. In his father's style, he would sing snatches from the High Holiday services. There, in the open fields, he could sing out loud, even chant to his heart's content, and the echo from the trees would respond resonantly, as if the woods were a choir accompanying him. There, in the open fields, Yosele felt more at ease than in his own home; no one prevented him from singing or shouting and he didn't have to be embarrassed before anyone. No one was there to lord it over him, no stepmother to nag him, no father bemoaning his sad fate. There, in the open fields, Yosele lived in a world of fantasy all of his own making: the woods were entirely his and had been created for his sake alone so he could sing there; the fields were entirely his, his own estate, his property, his Garden of Eden. There, in that Garden of Eden, where no one could see him or hear him, he could, if he wished, clothe himself in luxury and sing and shout and leap, make believe to his heart's content. But, unfortunately, nothing lasts forever on this earth! Though he was entirely innocent, Yosele was soon driven out of his Garden of Eden, chased out by dogs, assailed with sticks and stones.

It was a hot, clear summer day. In town, as usual, a blistering sun shone without mercy, driving the Mazepevka market folk under the carts, where they lay prostrated in the shade, fanning themselves furiously. The housewives, those stout women who could not tolerate any heat at all, were forced to go down into the cellars. The teachers in the *cheders* threw off their caftans and remained seated in their wide shirt-sleeves and yellowed *tallis-kotns*, four-fringed undergarments, their hearts pounding, lifting their yarmulkes off their sweating heads, perspiring as in a steam bath. The students were dismissed to bathe in the pond, where they splashed in the mud. It was as hot as in Gehenna, with nowhere to escape to. Old Jews, clutching their canes, barely made their way about the marketplace, their sleeves rolled up, hats pushed back, struggling for breath, saying to one another, "Whew!" "Did you ever see such a heat?" "Oy, what a day!" "Who can stand it?" Even the goats on the Shul Street, which had until then been mischievously scampering over the low roofs, nibbling straw from the eaves, licking the shul walls, leaping onto the pushcarts at the market and being constantly shooed off by the apprentices—even those mischievous goats were now exhausted by the heat and had lain down, their legs tucked under them, their heads outstretched, their little tongues stuck out, producing a silly expression.

In short, the town was sweltering, burning in the heat, and everyone was looking forward to the relief evening would bring.

But this was not the case beyond the town, in the fields near the great green woods where Yosele had secluded himself. There he could sing, shout, and raise a din, walking in the shade of trees at the edge of the woods while gulping cool fresh air with his open mouth. Yosele didn't realize how far he had strayed from town. Spread out before his eyes was a vast green expanse, so smooth, so delightful that it invited a person to throw himself upon it, to stretch out and lie there forever. Ahead the grass appeared even thicker and lusher, drawing him on even farther. He felt light-hearted and high-spirited. Something in his throat started to bubble and tickle so that he had to sing. He was struck by a new idea, a new version of the *v'al ham'dinos boh yomer*. Yosele began singing higher and louder. His voice flowed freely and effortlessly. He had the feeling that no matter how high he sang, he could sing even higher. Warbling the highest notes and trilling such intricate passages that he himself marveled at how he had come by them, he sang on, letting out all the stops. His voice created a fantasy out of sheer sound. He did not know where his improvisations would take him or how he would end them. The words and music simply came to him. *"Ashrei ish . . .* Happy is the man . . ."* Yosele sang out louder and stronger, skipping along and gesticulating with his hands, loudly intoning, *"Chol hachoshim boch! Chol hachoshim boch!"*

Suddenly Yosele heard a loud outcry, *"Ksi-ksi-ksi! Atu yevo!* Get out of here! Ksi-ksi-ksi!" He turned around, and what he saw made his blood run cold: chasing after him was a band of young herdsmen, waving their shepherd's crooks, sacks bouncing on their backs, their big hats flopping. Racing ahead of them all was a huge, black, fierce, shaggy dog. Yosele felt a sharp blow and after that he felt as if something was dragging him, tearing at him, biting him. And after that—after that he remembered nothing.

When he came to he was once again alone. Confused, humiliated, and terrified, his short caftan torn and shredded to bits, Yosele stood up and made his way back home, his poor heart sad and heavy. He burst into tears; he could not understand why God in heaven was picking on him more than on all the other boys his age. Why was He punishing him so? Didn't he pray daily, observe all the Commandments as was expected, and honor his father? He even honored his stepmother—more than she deserved.

"What have I done to deserve this, God in heaven? How have I sinned that You are punishing me so?"

And looking back for the last time, Yosele, with a sigh, bade farewell to his Garden of Eden, to the open fields, to the green shadowy woods, forever, forever. . . .

VII

Yosele Repents, But a New Misfortune Befalls Him

After being so cruelly expelled from his Garden of Eden, Yosele arrived home battered and bruised, his clothes in tatters. He expected a scorching welcome as usual from his stepmother, but even his father joined in this time. Shmulik never hit his son, but he would punish him with words.

"I ask you, is that a way for a young boy to behave? Rips his clothes to shreds? Do you think I can just go out and buy you new ones? With my income as it is these days? If your mother would rise from her grave right now . . . I hate to think of it, what is there to say . . ."

Yosele would have given the world not to hear his father's scoldings. He vowed on the spot that as long as he lived he would never again set foot in the woods and he would never again step outside the town, as surely as that day was Thursday. On the following day, Friday, Yosele ran off bright and early to synagogue, where he prayed with fervor and devotion as never before. After services he took it upon himself to help his stepmother in every way. He polished the brass and copper for her, sped to the market to buy pepper, bay leaves, cinnamon, pickling spices, and three groschens' worth of honey for the kugel and for the Shabbos kiddush. When he returned home Yosele threw himself into the task of grating horseradish, and then he set about preparing the calves' feet for dinner, splitting them on a board with a knife and pestle so skillfully that the cantor's wife could no longer contain her feelings and said, half to herself, as she peered into the oven and blew at the fire, "How else? That's the way a boy should behave—not wait till he's told what to do—keep busy, show some initiative, enthusiasm."

These words fired Yosele's spirit. He felt he had the strength to turn the world upside down, like mighty Samson. When he noticed that his stepmother needed water, without a moment's hesitation he rolled up the hem of his patched caftan, grabbed the bucket, and in a few minutes brought it back brimful. Later he sat down to read the week's Torah portion and recited the Song of Songs with such sweetness that the cantor's wife rewarded him with a plate of noodles smothered in chicken fat and onions. On the following day, Shabbos, Yosele's heart was charged with filial devotion and repentance toward God. Shabbos afternoon, after lunch, while all the other boys were strolling down Bardichev Street, Yosele sat himself down and with great zeal pored over a chapter from the *Mishneh*. Immediately after that accomplishment he eagerly immersed himself in the Book of Psalms, but he soon realized that home was not the proper place for such a sacred endeavor. All virtuous Jews chanted the Psalms in synagogue, and here he was sitting near the slop pails. Feh—he should be off to shul!

Yosele quickly donned his Shabbos caftan, tied a white scarf around his neck, and set out for the synagogue. He felt lighthearted as never before, like a person who had quarreled and had just made up. He imagined that between himself and the great living God something of a partnership existed, a kinship between himself and the entire universe which he could now see with a fresh eye! The sun, sinking rapidly, setting the horizon aglow and painting it in bright red strokes, the birds, sailing up above in formation, rising and falling like ships at sea—all things seemed close, familiar, addressing him directly. Lost in such transcendent thoughts, Yosele walked farther and farther, not noticing that he had long since passed the Cold Shul, the Shul Street as well as Bardichev Street, the stables, the forges, the New Bridge, and had arrived at the Polish Street. Yosele would have gone even farther had he not been stopped in his tracks by a strangely sweet song sung by angelic voices, an unusual melody he had never before heard in his life. He paused to listen and couldn't seem to hear enough of it. He knew very well that up the hill, on the Polish Street, was a church. He also knew they played an organ in that church, but he had never heard it before, because there were dogs in every courtyard along Polish Street and, more important, it was forbidden for Jews to hear the organ played since the destruction of the Temple in Jerusalem.

At that moment he truly regretted the fact that Jews had sinned, and he was very sorry Jews no longer had their

Temple, their organ, and their Levites who used to accompany the singing of sacred songs with all sorts of instruments. And meanwhile the organ playing and the singing, apparently coming from the church, drew him like a magnet up the hill. From somewhere up ahead poured forth sweet, celestial voices, singing together in such perfect unison that it sounded like one voice ascending from the deepest to the highest notes, reaching him from above so that the very walls alongside him and the earth beneath his feet trembled. And rising above the incredibly sweet chorus of voices one lovely, smooth voice was heard that pierced the heart like a knife, stirring his soul and awakening the imagination. Yosele fantasied that this was the very way the Levites must have sung in the Temple in Jerusalem, playing on the organ and praising God, the Lord of Lords. And his heart became full and his imagination carried him far away to Jerusalem. He was now in another world; his eyes shone, his limbs felt light, he seemed to be lifted in the air, soaring upward, upward to the heavens. . . .

Suddenly the singing and organ playing stopped and Yosele heard another voice, a familiar voice coming from a different direction. He looked to see where the voice was coming from and saw before him a familiar-looking Pole with a fat, clean-shaven face. He recognized the priest, whom he had seen more than once buying goods at Zlate's shop. His round, smooth-shaven face, with its fat, red nose shaped like a pickle, had always seemed ridiculous to him, almost laughable. Yosele was startled—"Ai! Where am I?"— and started back down the hill.

At the foot of the hill a circle of men and young boys —Jews all—were commenting on the new bridge under construction. They were appraising the workmanship, exchanging opinions, and venturing critiques on how the

work was going, as Jews generally do when they get together to look over something new. Seeing Yosele running
down the hill, they stopped him and asked, "Where are you
coming from? From the church? Who are you, young man?"

"What do you mean?" one of them said. "Don't you recognize him? He's Shmulik's, Shmulik the cantor's son."

"A fine boy! You go to church, do you?"

"Look at him, that sissy standing there like butter
wouldn't melt in his mouth! And a cantor's son too!"

"Today's children! Fine times we're living in. Take him
home, Dovid-Hersh, he lives on your street. A fine story,
but a short one . . . !"

Gehenna itself with all its dreaded afflictions enumer-
ated in the holy books, including purgatory, which consists
of being flung from one end of the world to the other, all
the inflictions of pain from the beginning of time—those
were as nothing compared to what Yosele anticipated after
the terrible transgression he had committed, in total ignorance of how it had come about. He considered himself
finished, having forfeited not only *this* world but the world
to come. He surrendered to his fate, preparing to receive
whatever punishment would be meted out to him in utter,
abject silence, as if to say, "Flay me alive, destroy me,
devour me—I won't resist!"

Shmulik, as expected, punished him with a lecture; he
wanted to know only one thing: what was he doing in that
place? But Yosele was as mute as a wall, which was more
than the cantor's wife could tolerate. She fell upon Yosele,
attacking him with both fists, almost foaming at the mouth,
and braying like a wild donkey. If not for Zlate, who had
heard the uproar and the sounds of beating and shrieking
through the wall, Yosele would not have escaped from the
hands of the cantor's wife alive. Zlate tore him away from

her grasp and sent him off to her own house while she stayed on and berated Shmulik roundly for allowing a stranger to beat his own flesh and blood. The cantor's wife, for her part, also chimed in, but in the meantime Yosele was spared more abuse.

VIII

With Esther's Help Yosele Leaves for Tetrevetz to Become a Cantor

One warm look, one kind word from Esther was like medicine for Yosele, curing the ills brought on by his father's scoldings and his stepmother's beatings. When Esther, arriving home later from her Shabbos stroll, found Yosele cowering in a corner, looking as woebegone as a plucked chicken, his hat crumpled, his red cheeks swollen like dumplings, she approached him closely, took him by the hand, and asked him in a soft voice while gazing at him sympathetically, "What is it, Yosele? Your stepmother again?"

For the very first time Yosele broke down in tears like a small child and told Esther the whole story, not omitting any details, confessing as one confesses only before God. Esther was deeply moved by Yosele's confession. All the while he was talking she braided and unbraided her long pigtail as she looked straight into his eyes with her own luminous blue eyes. Then she tossed the braid behind her, drew even closer to Yosele, and said to him, "I'm going to tell you something, Yosele. You don't belong here. Your place is with a great cantor in a big city. So long as you stay here you'll get nowhere. Mark my words."

"Listen!" cried Yosele, and a spark reignited in his eyes that could be seen glowing in the dark. "Listen! That's exactly what I've been saying all along. I want to go to Tetrevetz, to be with Mitzi. There I know I'll learn something. I go around with nothing to do here, your mother's errand boy. Once I get there . . ."

"Wait a minute!" Esther said to him. "You said Tetrevetz, didn't you? I know someone from Tetrevetz. He's supposed to come to the market after Shabbos. I'll talk to him. I think something can be worked out."

"Do you mean that dry-goods salesman who has the stand next to yours?"

"Yes, a young man, a fine person, a good-natured man. I'll have a talk with him about you. Sha! Here comes my mother."

"A good week to you!" said Zlate as she entered her house. "Go, Esther, and recite 'God of Abraham,' and light the fire. And you can go on home," she called to Yosele. "I just had a big fight because of you. You're a fine one! Some people have children who sit in shul on Shabbos, but you, you go off to churches! Did you ever hear of such a crazy thing!"

"No, Mama!" Esther said, ready to defend him. "That's not the way it was. He was *near* the church, not *in* the church."

"Here's a new defense attorney!" Zlate said, cutting her off. "Go home, Yosele, they won't bother you any more. But please be more careful, and pull yourself together. Ach, if your mother were to rise from her grave, she wouldn't have too much pleasure from you."

After Yosele went home Esther began to think through various plans for getting him to Tetrevetz. With that voice of his, she thought, he should be studying with a great cantor. It's a pity, he's really suffering here.

If the three great fairs we talked about before—Yuria, Spaas and Pokrova—had been created for the Mazepevka hucksters alone, then surely they would have been the sole beneficiaries. The problem was that hucksters from all over the world, it seemed, also flocked to the fairs. They came from Makarevka, from Kashperev, from Bardichev, from Yamelinetz, from Tetrevetz, and from many towns too numerous to mention. They all came to Mazepevka for the fairs and they displayed such attractive wares on their stands that it dazzled the eye. And in addition, these visitors were so astute at turning a penny that the local merchants had to work hard in order to hold their own in that formidable competition. Terrible fights would often break out between the locals and the visitors; men fought and cursed one another, women made rude gestures and frequently came to blows. Still and all, on the holy day of Shabbos, when the market was closed, they made up with each other; yesterday's rude gestures and blows were forgotten. Everyone went to shul to hear the Mazepevka cantors.

The visitors were cordially welcomed in shul. The front pews were reserved for them and they were awarded the most prestigious roles in the service, not for the honor alone but for the donations these guests would make in response to the honors, thus netting the synagogue a pretty penny. On those Sabbaths, Shmulik the cantor prepared with special care; he extended himself for the visitors, and Yosele, for his part, also displayed his very best, giving them a performance they would savor. When they traveled on to other towns, the visitors would recount tales of the wonderful Mazepevka cantors. "You should hear! In Mazepevka there's a cantor with a remarkable voice. And his twelve-year-old son sings along with him in this soprano voice like a flute which is simply not to be believed! And most remarkable of all—it's in Mazepevka!"

Among the out-of-town vendors gathered in Mazepevka was a Tetrevetz merchant. Although knowledgeable about singing in general, he was a connoisseur of cantorial singing. While enjoying Shmulik's virtuosity, he would tap his foot in time to the music, holding his head to the side, eyes shut. After the services were over he would discuss the finer points of the music with Shmulik. The young man from Tetrevetz loved to discuss the Tetrevetz cantors, thereby displaying his great knowledge and appreciation of cantorial music.

"You should hear how they embellish their cantillations in Tetrevetz!"

The young man was friendly with Yosele, giving him a pinch on the cheek and telling him that as soon as his voice changed he would possess an exquisite instrument and that all he lacked was the ability to read music, and should he ever get to Tetrevetz and be able to study with Mitzi, that would really make something of him.

Shmulik would listen to the young man's words with a bitter smile, as if to say, "Yes, but where does one get the money to do it?" And Yosele, hearing such talk, was so thrilled that his heart nearly burst for joy. At that moment it was as if he were body and soul with Mitzi in Tetrevetz.

For Yosele the young man took on a different aspect; he looked upon him as a savior, an angel sent by God. In that young man's hands rested his fate and his very life.

But the fair was still in full swing; one had to toil, deal with the crowds, and make a living. Yosele worked, as always, in Zlate's booth, keeping an eye open for shoplifters, helping out wherever he could, running errands, and doing his job well. He never mentioned a word to Esther about Tetrevetz or the young man, as he was afraid of making too much of it. But when he saw Esther and the young man talking together, he turned away, his heart pounding. God in heaven, he thought, dear God! Please let him take me to Tetrevetz.

Using all her native intelligence, Esther persuaded the young man to take Yosele to Tetrevetz at his own expense. The task still remained to convince Shmulik. As much as he wished to ensure his son's future, it was nevertheless difficult for Shmulik to part from Yosele. "What is there to say— how can you let a child leave home?"

The stepmother added her opinion. She couldn't understand why anyone would want to waste his time with a brat like Yosele. The plan didn't appeal to Zlate either—sending off a boy not yet bar mitzvah to a strange place among who knows what kinds of people? . . . But Esther summoned all her best arguments and spoke so persuasively that she finally convinced her mother. Immediately after the fair Yosele packed his little pouch containing his phylacteries and his bundle of belongings. He was off to Tetrevetz! On that morning Yosele's heart swelled with happiness and gratitude to Esther. Had he not been reluctant to embarrass her in front of others, he would have embraced her and kissed her good-bye.

Who is capable of describing Yosele's feelings for his one true friend, for Esther? Such feelings could never be expressed in words; they could be expressed only through tears. When she said, "Go in good health," Esther noticed that Yosele was blinking his eyes, hiding his face, and coughing in a peculiar way, barely squeaking out, "Be well."

Yosele's eyes were moist with tears, with tears of happiness, as he looked far, far ahead along that great, broad road that now stretched before him.

IX

Mitzi the Cantor Listens to His Singing and Goes Wild with Enthusiasm

Not until they had crossed the Greblye River, the Mazepevka town line, did Yosele finally believe he was on his way to Tetrevetz. He kept rising from his wagon seat and looking back, afraid they might make him return home. Who could tell? His stepmother might suddenly decide he must go back. But now, drawing closer to the windmills on the horizon and seeing the woods fade into the distance behind him, Yosele at last believed he was on his way. He began to feel like a person who had escaped from a dark, stifling prison into the blessed open air. Glancing back at the woods, Yosele chuckled to himself as he remembered his onetime Garden of Eden from which he had so cruelly been driven. "Those woods! How did I ever think they were so special? They're nothing at all! Now, Tetrevetz—*that's* a whole new world!"

It was incomprehensible to Yosele that here, sitting alongside him, was a whole wagonful of Jews, all traveling to Tetrevetz, and what were they talking about? About the fair, about prices, about the Mazepevka customers . . . What kind of people are these? Yosele wondered. Tetrevetz, as he pictured it, was surely the sort of place where nothing but song and joy prevailed, where, free as birds, people strolled arm in arm. They never quarreled, never irritated each other, as in Mazepevka, they weren't preoccupied with such crass pursuits as fairs, buying and selling, prices and profits, but were pure and clean, their faces glowing, eyes shining, enjoying life as if they were in Paradise or on the island that lay across the Atlantic Ocean where it was perpetual summer and where people lived forever as in the stories he had heard from his friends at school. But more than all of that, Mitzi was there! Imagine, Mitzi!

These thoughts occupied Yosele's mind throughout the journey so that he hardly noticed the villages and towns they were passing. Yosele could absorb himself in his own thoughts, which had always set him apart from all the other boys his age. His daydreams could always carry him off into his own world so that everything he saw took on a different meaning for him than it did for others. He lived more in a dream world than in reality. His mind could transform what he heard or saw into wonderful images. Whenever he heard something, his thoughts would suddenly take wing and carry him off into realms of fantasy. When he used to sit in *cheder* bent over the Gemorah with all the other boys or at home doing some chore, he would be oblivious to anything going on around him. His mind was really somewhere else, and he would often fancy he heard voices raised in song. He would hear something being said three times over without understanding a single word, for which he would earn quite a few scoldings. Even Esther, who was as close to him as a sister, would often comment that he wasn't paying attention to what she was saying to him. So it is easy to see that because his imagination was so lively, when he eventually did perceive things as they really were, they appeared ordinary, trite, and often boring and tiresome.

Early in the morning of the third day Yosele felt the wagon shaking from side to side, clattering over cobblestones, and there, spread out before his eyes, was a breathtaking panorama of high white buildings, painted iron roofs, and fine courtyards planted with trees. So this must be Tetrevetz, Yosele thought, just as his heart had told him.

"Here, take your bundle," the dry-goods salesman said, handing him the large, knotted kerchief containing his *tefillin* sack, a little prayer book, his Sabbath caftan, a few white shirts, and a crust of bread left over from the journey.

"See, over there is where Mitzi lives. Get off here. Tell him I said he should take you on, and, God willing, tomorrow you can come to my house."

Yosele picked up his bundle. As the wagon drove off he remained standing in front of a large building, not knowing where to go.

"Whom do you want to see, young man?" a woman asked him, poking her bare head out of a window on the ground floor.

"I have to see Mitzi," Yosele answered eagerly, "Reb Mitzi the cantor."

"Just go down the stairs and turn to the right," the woman replied, smiling.

Yosele walked down a long flight of stairs, the longest he had ever seen, and after negotiating a dark corridor, he entered a pleasant room with painted floorboards, handsome chairs, and elegant mirrors. From somewhere came a full choir of sweet voices: deep basses, tenors, baritones and altos, and high, piercing sopranos blending beautifully and harmoniously together as he remembered having heard long ago in Mazepevka when Pitzi had conducted the services accompanied by his eighteen-member choir. After a while the full choir stopped and a single voice was heard, a pure, sweet singing that became quieter and deeper until it gradually faded away. Yosele stood in the middle of the room as if glued to the spot, not noticing that standing before him now was the woman who had pointed out to him where Mitzi lived.

"Go right on into that room—that's it," the woman said, motioning. Yosele opened the door and saw a group of young men and small boys lined up like soldiers, each holding a large open book. One of the group held a stick, and in front, on a bench, sat an ordinary-looking man with an ordinary yellow, pointed little beard, saying to him in an ordinary way, "What do you have to say for yourself?"

Can this really be Mitzi himself? Yosele wondered and said, "I want to see Mitzi the cantor. I have regards for him."

"Regards?" Mitzi asked. "From whom?"

"From a dry-goods salesman who lives here in town. He and I traveled here together."

"From a dry-goods salesman who lives here in town?" said Mitzi. "What's his name?"

"His name?" Yosele pondered. "Oh, my God! I forgot to ask him what his name was or where he lived."

Like a salvo of many cannon going off at the same time, the whole choir erupted into laughter, and Mitzi himself joined in as he observed a bewildered Yosele standing there, clutching his little bundle in his hand. His caftan was threadbare and patched, his shoes worn down at the heels, his cap had an old-fashioned visor, but his face was handsome, his hair curly, and his large clear eyes were bright and sparkling as if illuminated from within.

"Tell me, who are you and where do you come from?" Mitzi asked with a friendly smile.

"I am Yosel, Shmulik the cantor's son, from Mazepevka," Yosele answered him promptly. "A dry-goods salesman, a friend of ours, brought me here to Mitzi the cantor to apprentice me as a singer."

"So that's what it's about," Mitzi said. "So, put down your bundle and come closer. Let me hear you sing."

First Mitzi tested to see if Yosele could read music; when he saw that Yosele had no idea what notes were, he told him to go ahead and sing something. Yosele thought he was supposed to chant a portion of the liturgy and so he began singing a long passage from the Rosh Hashanah Shmoneh Esreh, the Eighteen Benedictions recited daily. At first the choristers muffled their derisive laughter behind their hands, but as Yosele sang on, the snickering subsided, the faces turned serious, and they began glancing at one another in surprise, amazed at what they were hearing. This was no ordinary voice! Mitzi at first cupped his chin in his palm, but then his jaw dropped and he gaped at Yosele as if he could swallow him whole right on the spot. As long as Mitzi had worked with singers he had never heard nor had he ever imagined in his wildest dreams such singing as he was now hearing. Yosele did not force his voice as others did, he did not bellow the notes or strain his vocal chords, but it was as if those sweet, glorious sounds were issuing from his throat of their own volition, pouring from his heart, from his very soul, and penetrating deep into the marrow of one's bones. At the same time Yosele displayed great ability, easily negotiating the scales from the highest to the lowest notes and back again, ornamenting his singing with such intricate trills that they were all stunned, unable to fathom how he could accomplish this feat. When Yosele finished singing, Mitzi stood up, and, clutching his head

71

with both hands, he ran around the room like a madman, crying, "Ai-ai-ai-ai-ai!"

"Tell me, who are you? Where are you from? Who are your parents?"

"I've already told you," Yosele said innocently, "that I am Yosel Shmulik's, from Mazepevka. I've come to apprentice myself to you as a choirboy."

"As a choirboy?" Mitzi exclaimed. "Ai-ai-ai-ai! As a choirboy, you say? Mirel! Come here, Mirel!"

On hearing the shouting, the very woman who had shown Yosele where Mitzi lived entered the room, and Mitzi, gesturing toward Yosele, shouted at the top of his lungs, "Do you see this little boy? This is the Mazepevker cantor's son. He wants to be a choirboy. As long as I've lived, as long as I've been a cantor, I've never heard such a voice. Mirel, it must be the end of the world, the very end, I tell you! Listen to me—they call you Yosele?" Mitzi said, slapping him on the back—"Yosele, I'm taking you on! You'll be staying with me! Mirel, he needs to have a new little caftan and other clothing. Maybe you want something to eat, Yosele? Mirel, give him some food! You should have heard him sing, Mirel. What can I say? It must be the end of the world—that's all there is to it!"

X

New City, New People, New Troubles

In the beginning Tetrevetz was a new Garden of Eden for Yosele. The first thing he did was to inquire about the synagogue, and upon entering it he imagined he was in the

Great Temple in Jerusalem. Gazing up at the awesomely high painted ceiling and the decorated walls, on which the artist had not spared his palette, having painted pictures of every kind of musical instrument and fruit—apples, pears, and sliced watermelon that looked real enough to eat—Yosele imagined these paintings were the ultimate in art and thought that nothing more beautiful could exist. And on that first Sabbath when Mitzi led the service, conducting his choir, Yosele among them, and they burst out with *Mah tovu*—How pleasant it is," in that inimitable style of all synagogue choirs, Yosele felt a chill pass over him, and his hair stood on end. Singing out in full volume, he could barely recognize his own voice, so different did it sound in that beautiful, high-ceilinged shul. Whatever he laid his eyes on struck him as a revelation. The first time he strolled about the city he had to hold onto his cap to keep it from falling off because his head was constantly tilted back. Everything astonished him. He regretted but one thing: that Esther was not there to see all those remarkable sights. His heart was full of gratitude and praise to the Almighty, blessed be His name, who had brought him there safely.

Naturally, with time Tetrevetz came to lose its luster and novelty in Yosele's eyes as he grew accustomed to it. He was also beginning to encounter some of the same problems as in Mazepevka but for different reasons.

As enthusiastic and devoted as Mitzi was, so Mitzi's wife was cold and unfriendly, looking disapprovingly at Yosele and in time behaving toward him almost as badly as his stepmother had at home. But that didn't compare with the woes he suffered at the hands of his fellow choristers, who were an odd assortment of young boys picked off rubbish heaps and plucked out of ratholes. Rarely could a decent lad be found among them, a well-brought-up child; for the most part they were empty-headed, lazy youngsters, and

73

talented troublemakers. Out of great envy, they could not abide Yosele, often going behind his back to Mitzi, undermining him, tricking him out of every groschen he might possess.

Yosele frequently obtained money from the dry-goods salesman who had brought him there—Bentzi Leibtzi's was his name. Every now and then he invited Yosele home for Shabbos or for a holiday, befriending him and bringing him warm greetings from home after his visits to the Mazepevka fairs three times a year. Those greetings were for Yosele more precious than a good dinner or money, and especially if Bentzi Leibtzi's also brought with him a letter from Yosele's father—that most precious of all gifts. He would answer the letters, reporting that he was, thank God, doing well and following the righteous path; he was obeying his father's exhortations not to stray from that path and was adhering to all the Commandments as he had at home, not deviating so much as a hair. He went to shul every day to pray and recited his Psalms, he performed dutifully at his bar mitzvah, and was even learning to write, thereby following every instruction his father had given him before leaving. He hoped that he would, with God's help, come home safely and that they would see each other once again in good health and full of joy, Amen! He then asked to be remembered to Zlate and to her daughter, Esther.

When he thought of Esther he felt his heart drawn to her without knowing why. Somehow Esther had become locked in his heart as if she were his own sister, and except for his father, he missed her more than anyone. His whole mood would change for the better when Bentzi Leibtzi's returned with a letter from Esther written in her own hand. Yosele would read and reread her words, pressing them hard against his chest as one clutches to oneself a small child who is dear and beloved.

As he was once drawn to Tetrevetz, so now he was beginning to feel drawn back even more strongly to Mazepevka. If Mitzi had not held onto him so possessively and had been willing to let him go, perhaps Yosele might have returned home. But Mitzi loved him dearly and showed him off like a precious jewel, boasting to one and all what an extraordinary little singer he had in his charge. "Only with me can you find someone like this!" Mitzi would crow. "If I want to, I can make a success out of anyone!"

One of Mitzi's former choir members, Gedalye Bass, was irritated by Mitzi's boasting. Gedalye Bass was by now a cantor himself. Once when he was passing through Tetrevetz he dropped by Mitzi's house—he was, after all, an old friend and had in the past broken bread with Mitzi—and there he heard Yosele singing. From that moment on he dogged Yosele's footsteps. Gedalye was always on the lookout for a chance to talk alone with Yosele; he shadowed him until finally he cornered him in Bentzi Leibtzi's house. He then set about trying to win over Yosele, first by patient questioning into every detail of his life, then by more insistently pressing his advantage, until he brought him to the realization that it was unheard of for him to work for Mitzi without pay and allow himself to be treated like a servant by Mitzi's wife.

"Who ever heard of such an outrage?" Gedalye protested to Yosele. "To take a child and turn him into a slave, an unpaid laborer, and on top of that to go around bragging to the whole world about someone else's voice until it makes you sick to your stomach just to hear it! And add to all that making you a servant to his wife—what nerve! To do this to a son of Reb Shmulik! Permit me a word. Don't I know your father? Who doesn't know Reb Shmulik the cantor? What a question! What's the matter, don't you have real talent? Don't you have a fine voice? Don't you read music? I'm not joking! Little fool, I have just the right position for you. Your own father would agree that you would be lucky to have it. But why do you need a position at all? With your talent, *you* are all the position you need. You know that, don't you? Little fool, ask me and I'll tell you!"

And Gedalye Bass began to describe to Yosele what marvels awaited him if he were to throw Mitzi over and go out into the world with him, with Gedalye, as had once upon a time those other young lads Arke Fiedele, the Vilner Balabeysl, and other such world-renowned cantors who had acquired great names for themselves. This invitation aroused in Yosele all the wonderful images from the past, and he was ready to commit himself heart and soul to Gedalye—such a trustworthy, fine, honest person!

"There's just one thing I wish to ask of you, Reb Gedalye," Yosele said to him.

"Just say it, my child."

"I'd like to go home first to see my father and my friends."

"Ach, of course, how else could it be?" answered Gedalye Bass. "Naturally! After all, how else? Honor thy father! Ach, listen, you're still a child, as I can tell from the way you speak. Who can be closer than a father?"

Those words of Gedalye Bass so moved Yosele that he decided right then and there he had to go home. Enough of this unsettled life among strangers. Three years—it was time.

Gedalye Bass made sure to be there when the moment came to bid farewell to Mitzi and all the choir members. Mitzi chided Yosele for throwing away such a great opportunity, and he advised him as his own father might, that after his visit home he should return to him, because that was where he belonged, that was where he had the chance to develop himself. Mitzi was as sorry to see Yosele go as if he were his own child. He embraced and kissed him, praying that he arrive home safely, and asked him to convey his greetings to his father, although they had never met.

How friendly! Yosele thought to himself as he climbed into the wagon and seated himself among the other passengers, preparing for the two- to three-day journey. "Be well! Be well!" he shouted in parting, sticking his head out of the covered wagon as the vehicle began to move, clattering and shaking over the streets paved with brick, the bells clanging, "Dzin, dzin, dzin!" Yosele was almost jumping out of his skin with excitement at the thought that he was actually heading toward home. The shaking, the clattering, and the clanging made him drowsy, and his reveries carried him away to Mazepevka—home, home!

XI

Yosele Returns Home, and Mazepevka Marvels: What a Difference a Big City Makes!

It never fails to amaze the Mazepevka Jews that whoever leaves Mazepevka for the greater world returns entirely changed. They look at him with delight and marvel, "Just look at him. The same person as before but really altogether different! Don't you remember how he used to go around barefoot? God's wonder! What a difference a big city makes!"

When Yosele returned from his three-year sojourn in

Tetrevetz all of Mazepevka was impressed with him. They could not comprehend how so young a boy could have matured in so short a time. Yosele the child had become Yosele the young man. He had become a substantial person, a *mentch*, fully poised, even though he was not yet sixteen. It was a pleasure to look at him. "What a difference a big city makes!" They all knew Shmulik had sent his son off to become Mitzi's choirboy, but no one could have predicted that Yosele, who only yesterday had run himself ragged delivering Purim platters, could turn into such a fine lad with such grown-up ways. And if utter strangers took such delight in him, imagine how Shmulik himself felt.

Shmulik was in the bathhouse that *erev* Shabbos when he learned the good news that his son had just arrived from Tetrevetz. He quickly tossed the besom and the small wooden wash bucket aside, threw on his clothes, and sped home. Although he had just thoroughly cleaned and besomed himself, he washed his hands before giving Yosele a hearty welcome, embracing and kissing him and then standing back to inspect him from head to toe. In three years Yosele had sprung up like a weed. He had never been a bad-looking youngster, smart and curious, having clear, bright eyes, but from great poverty and want he always bore an oppressed, downtrodden look like so many Mazepevka boys his age. But Yosele had flourished under Mitzi's tutelage, he had rosy cheeks and a contented demeanor. Moreover, he was better dressed than he had ever been when living with his father. Shmulik's heart was full of joy as he gazed at Yosele. He marveled along with the rest, "What a difference a big city makes!"

"So, how are you?" Shmulik asked him, seating himself alongside Yosele at the table and looking him over in his fine caftan with his rosy cheeks and nicely combed earlocks.

"How are *you*, Father?" Yosele responded with a question, as is the custom among adults. Yosele had never spoken so directly to his father. Shmulik looked at his son in surprise. Yosele's forwardness was a bit offensive to Shmulik and he was taken aback.

"What is there to say? Fine, as always," Shmulik answered him as he started to don his Sabbath caftan in preparation for going to the study house. "How is Mitzi doing?"

"How is Mitzi doing?"—Yosele drew out his words in that special intonation favored by adults. "May even half of his good fortune be yours!"

Yosele's heart wept when he noted that in the three years he had been away his father had become aged, gray, and stooped, his face wrinkled, his large, once bright eyes dimmed. At that moment he felt prepared to dedicate his life and soul to his father's well-being. As for Shmulik, he was so flustered that it was a struggle for him to find the sleeve of his caftan.

And when Shmulik's wife set eyes on Yosele, she stopped dead in the middle of the room, her mouth open as if to say, "What do you say to that? He's become a grown-up!"

Shmulik was so befuddled by Yosele's homecoming that as he conversed with Yosele he digressed into trivial subjects about Tetrevetz elders and about Tetrevetz streets and houses in which he really had no interest. Yosele thought his father wanted to hear about Tetrevetz, so he enthusiastically described the wide, paved streets, the high buildings that made one dizzy just looking up at them, and all the other wonders of that city. And Shmulik, watching Yosele as he embellished his words with gesticulations, drank in every word, nearly bursting with pride and pleasure. Suddenly Shmulik sprang up, "Oy vey, they've already

79

finished making the blessing over the candles! It's time to go to shul!"

The whole town, of course, soon heard the news that Shmulik the cantor's son had arrived from Tetrevetz. Right after the evening service people began to press around Shmulik, offering their "God love you and your guest" and extending a personal welcome to Yosele while carefully looking him over. Town elders and the rich men also stopped by to talk with Shmulik, inquiring about his son— where he had been, what he had been doing, how long he would be in town, and what his future plans were. One of the rich men, Reb Alter Pessi's, said, "It would only be fitting, Reb Shmulik, for your son to visit me, God willing, tomorrow after the Havdalah service and to sing a little for us. I hear his singing is quite extraordinary."

"What is there to say? To sing a little? With pleasure!" Shmulik said, still contemplating Yosele as he basked in the many greetings he was receiving from all sides.

"And I would appreciate it if your son would do a little Musaf service for us too," a young man added, "and chant the blessing in honor of the new moon. They say he does an excellent job of chanting the service. Berl-Isaac Feige's traveled with him in the same wagon and told us all about his singing, and he said his chanting is marvelous!"

"Really? Of course! Wonderful!" some of the elders chimed in. "It would only be right for him to chant for us. Tell him to, Reb Shmulik! How can it make a difference to you? Money it won't cost you."

"Done!" Shmulik replied, looking at his Yosele as the congregation dispersed after the service.

Zlate and Esther had worked late that Friday in the shop; when they arrived home the children, Ephraim and Menashe, told them the good news that Yosele had come from

Tetrevetz. "You should see, Mama, how Yosele's grown up!" Ephraim and Menashe said in unison. "He's gotten so tall, you won't believe it!" The news was indeed welcome to Zlate, but more so to Esther. She washed herself quickly and put on her Sabbath attire—a simple but immaculately white dress that sparkled and shone on her. Esther wasn't like the other Mazepevka girls, who loved to bedeck themselves in frippery, trying to keep up with the latest gaudy fashions. She stood out as the only one whose style of dress was not dictated by fads.

When they saw through the window that the crowds were dispersing from in front of the shul, Zlate and Esther went out to greet Yosele and to offer Shmulik their "God love you and your guest." It was a radiant, summery Friday evening, a few weeks after Shevuos, at that time of year when even the notorious Mazepevka mud has finally dried up, when even in Mazepevka the breeze wafts the sweet delicious aromas of green grass and fresh leaves together with the distant song of the nightingale warbling in the monastery garden. Esther recognized Yosele from afar and her heart began to pound, drawing her to him. Shmulik came over to them to wish Zlate and Esther a good Shabbos, and they in turn greeted him with "God love you and your guest." Shmulik told Zlate of the honor bestowed on Yosele by the elders, who wished him to chant the Musaf service the following day, God willing. Meanwhile Yosele edged over closer to Esther, gazing at her by the light of the half moon and the diamondlike stars that were reflected in her bright eyes. He was attracted to Esther with such force that he would have taken her by the hand had not his father and her mother been standing nearby. After a three-year absence from her Yosele wanted nothing more than to be there on the street on that lovely summer evening and chat a while with Esther. He truly regretted having to go home to make the kiddush blessing, eat dinner, and then rest afterward along with all the others. It was so beautiful outdoors, so radiant, so warm.

All of nature was in a Sabbath mood: the moon was shining like a silver candlestick, the stars were twinkling like Sabbath candles, and she, the lovely bride who is called the Sabbath Queen, was taking her ease and rejoicing along with all the Jews. The streets of Mazepevka were still. One really *felt* it was Shabbos. In all the windows the candles flickered. The men were by now at home, preparing to usher in the ministering angels, the *malachei hashares*, and to quickly accompany them back to their rest. From the kitchens emanated the aromas of freshly baked challahs and gefillte fish. Shmulik the cantor and his son were standing outdoors with Zlate and Esther, chatting about Yosele's homecoming. Shmulik's aging, dimmed eyes reignited with their former spark for a moment, his face shone and was radiant in the moonlight. His frequent sighs gave evidence of how happy and fortunate he felt. Zlate understood his feelings; she gazed at Yosele, almost bursting with pride, as if he had been her own child. And Yosele drew ever nearer to Esther. He looked directly into her eyes and saw how she lowered her thick lashes but could not understand why she was so shy this day. He wanted only to be with her, right there with her! But his father said, "Come, Yosele, time to make kiddush." And sadly, he had to go. As he was leaving, Yosele turned toward Esther and again his eyes met her lovely eyes, and that look lingered between them for a longer time than he had ever remembered.

All that night Yosele's parting gaze did not leave Esther's thoughts for so much as a moment, awakening in her heart all sorts of feelings, calling forth in her imagination happy thoughts and weaving wonderful fantasies that till now Esther had not known were possible.

XII

He Chants the Musaf in the Cold Shul and the Multitude Is Spellbound

The Cold Shul, where Shmulik had been the cantor for over twenty-five years, was not built to hold a townful of Jews. Considering that it was old and lopsided, it nevertheless provided sufficient space for its regular members. That is not to say they were always satisfied; each person had his own pride and had to have a seat by the eastern wall or, at the very least, in the front pew, where he could be seen by everyone. They were always at each other about who was to sit where, who was going to recite the blessings over the Torah, who would be honored at the Simchas Torah processions, and other such matters reflecting status. Consequently there was no reason to blame them for not wishing to allow the community at large into the shul that Sabbath morning when Yosele was to chant the Musaf services. They decided that right after the opening Shachris service they would lock the doors and let no one in, even if he were the *gabbai*'s own father. But then again, would that be fair? What sin had the Jews from the other synagogues committed? Was it not blasphemous to lock out the rest of the community from a holy place?

The crowds began to grow thicker around the Cold Shul; people were pouring in from all the other synagogues, most of them men and young boys, who caused such a din by pounding on the door that it finally opened a crack and a red beard appeared. It belonged to the *shamesh*, the sexton, who poked his head out, scolded them all soundly, and ordered them to quiet down. "Shoo, scoundrels, good-for-nothings, troublemakers!" he shouted, stamping his feet angrily and waving his fists in the air like a madman. "Get out of here, rascals!"

But his cries were in vain. They all pushed forward as one man, and the door gave way. The sexton was shoved aside and roughed up into the bargain, as he deserved. The shul became so packed that people appeared to be standing on top of one another. And outside a throng beseiged the shul. The whole town was in an uproar, the world was turning upside down. Yosele was going to chant the prayer for the new moon and the Musaf.

Yosele draped his large prayer shawl over his head and mounted the dais, glanced about at the crowd, and prepared himself to pray. His face glowed, seeming to radiate from within his *tallis*. The members of the congregation began shushing one another and the women, segregated in the balcony, leaned forward in order to see Yosele better. The crowd was growing restless, squeezing toward the dais, trying to catch a glimpse of the young cantor. The elders began stamping their feet, demanding silence. Voices in the crowd shouted, "Be quiet, everyone!" "Shhhaa!" Yosele straightened up, took his place, and cleared his throat like a full-fledged cantor. When the congregation finally quieted down completely, his voice rang out on a fine, resonant note, *"Yekum purkan min sh'maya!*—May salvation descend from heaven." A shiver swept through the shul, quick as lightning, passing over everyone's body, and they all remained as if paralyzed for a few moments, not moving a muscle. Only when he had finished the *v'nomar amen* —"and we shall say amen"—did they all mutter in unison, "Ach!" glancing at one another and nodding in approval, momentarily forgetting that they were in the midst of a service for the new moon and should be concentrating on prayer.

What prayer? Who could think of praying when the whole synagogue was alive with trills, exactly as if a nightingale were pouring out its song, suffusing one's body, soothing the heart as with balm, tugging at the soul, drawing forth a cry from the depths of one's being. Who could think of praying? Yosele chants and one imagines a choir is chanting; Yosele sings and one imagines a whole orchestra is playing. Now his voice suddenly rings out with the strength of ten voices, one louder and stronger than the other, so that the windows shake. Now his voice dies down, becoming quieter and quieter, still retaining such sweetness, such lightness and such liquid smoothness in its high register that it caresses the skin, calms the heart, cradles the soul, and soothes every limb.

And now another sudden blast of sound like many violins, trumpets, and flutes at once: he opens his mouth and the sounds pour out voluminously, filling the shul with a variety of melodies never before heard. No one had ever heard such a *mi sheberach* —"He who blessed"—no one! Even those who were considered connoisseurs had never heard chanting with so much heart, with so much warmth and passion. When it came to the words *"Hu y'varech es kol hakahal hakadoch hazeh* —May the Lord bless this holy congregation"—Yosele opened wide his hands, encompassing the entire congregation, and beseeched God on their behalf and on behalf of their wives and sons and daughters, an imploring expression on his face, articulating each word clearly and purely from the depths of his heart. And at the words *"v'chol mi sh'nosnim . . . ufas lo'orchim* —All who give bread to strangers," *"u'tzdakeh lo'anayim* —and charity to the poor,"— his manner conveyed to the congregation that there do exist Jews who are in need of bread, that there do exist the downtrodden who are in need of charity. He repeated the phrases several times, his voice full of supplication and compassion. Then he shifted to still a different musical mode, displaying all the while such vocal virtuosity that the congregation was utterly awestruck and unable to regain its composure for a long time.

Only after the blessing for the new moon, during the silent prayer of the Shmoneh Esreh, did the participants have a chance to communicate wordlessly, gesturing their approval and amazement while hurrying through the Shmoneh Esreh as if standing on one foot, as the saying goes, eager to hear what more would follow. They prepared themselves for the cantor's repetition of the Kedushah, or sanctification, by clearing their throats, blowing their noses, and perking up their ears in readiness for the next surprise. And Yosele delivered to the Mazepevka Jews a *Keser* (crown)—his original rendition of the first line of the Kedushah—that even their grandfathers had never heard. The Kedushah challenges the singer to reach the heights of his creative powers; at best he succeeds only once in a lifetime. This creation is not communicated through words or notes alone, but somehow the worshiper hears it; it is in a language everyone understands, it conveys a feeling everyone interprets according to his own experience.

'Yosele sang as if his voice were a free, unfettered spirit speeding upward to the highest octaves, downward to the lowest, and all the time executing the most daring variations, the most original twists and turns of phrase, weaving and threading together diverse melodic themes with consummate artistry. Those who heard him swore that with the words *"malochim hamonay ma'la* —angelic hosts of heaven"— they could imagine angels soaring and sweeping above the knot of Jews below who together were bringing into being, weaving and fusing, a Kedushah to God, angelic and mortal voices responding to each other sweetly: "Holy! Holy! Holy!"—*Kadosh! Kadosh! Kadosh!*

When Yosele ended the Kedushah with the words *"Heyn go'alti eschem*—Behold, I have redeemed you, tall and proud"—the words were those not of a cantor but of a prophet speaking in the name of God; he was reassuring, encouraging them, the Jews, not to despair because *"Ani adonai elohaychem* —I am the Lord thy God, a great and a powerful God!"

Yosele infused each word with fervor and passion. His voice was capable of producing the rarest of sounds, sweet as sugar, smooth as oil, elevated as the heavens, profound as the ocean depths, and pure as unalloyed gold. As from a deep, sweet sleep, as from an idyllic dream, the congregation awoke when Yosele ended the Kedushah and continued on, once again modulating his voice into another key. At the words *"Yehi ratzon milfanecha* —May it be Thy will"— Yosele raised his eyes to the heavens and implored God *"Sheta'aleynu* —Lead us joyfully back to our land," *"v'sitoaynu* —and establish us within its borders"—in a trembling, plangent voice, breaking as if in a sob, accompanied by such sorrowful, mournful wails, that everyone was moved to tears. Men wept, becoming like infants before God— beloved, pampered, delicate, favorite children. . . .

"Nnuu, Yosele! Nnuu, that was a Musaf!" they all said at the same time as they left the shul and pressed around Shmulik to wish him a good Shabbos. "Nnuu, Yosele! Aii, Yosele!! So long as we live we will never forget that Musaf! The memory of it will live with us forever—forever!!"

"This is not a human voice or a human throat!" they all proclaimed with great amazement as they sat at their dinner tables. "The only way to explain it is that he *has* to have some instrument hidden in his throat. He has a songbird, a real nightingale in his throat. That's the only way to explain it!"

XIII

Friends Send Gifts
in Honor of Yosele's Homecoming,
and the Nightingale Pours Out His Unique Song

Sending gifts in honor of a guest is a custom practiced in Mazepevka to this day. When someone has a special guest, all his good friends send over a bottle of wine or a flask of mead for the Sabbath table. That Shabbos, Shmulik the cantor's door was never shut for long: this one in, that one out; this gift from Abba-Meir the rich man, that gift from Mendel the tall one, this from Menashe the redhead, that from Yenkel the dark-haired.

Shmulik thanked the young messengers who delivered the gifts. "Listen, little girl, tell your father he should live to see his eldest daughter married, and then we'll reciprocate with a good wine!" Or "Listen, little boy, tell your father we'll send something for your bar mitzvah, God willing!"

Shmulik's face beamed with joy and his once bedimmed eyes were aglow with their old intensity; on that Sabbath he was happy as never before. Even his wife, from whom he had rarely heard a pleasant word as long as he had known her, shared his excitement. She demonstrated her delight with her guest by baking two kugels, a noodle kugel in honor of the Sabbath and a second, many-layered kugel dimpled with raisins in honor of the guest.

"Well, now," she announced with a sweet smile, "let's see if our guest will turn out well or not. We'll soon be able to tell by how his kugel turns out."

"Are you finished eating?" Zlate said, entering Shmulik's house with Esther. For the sake of the guest Zlate had patched things up with Shmulik's wife that day at the synagogue during the service for removing the Torah from the Ark. The cantor's wife had initiated the conversation, moving closer to Zlate: "Hmmm . . . we have a guest today! My husband, you should know, is very pleased."

Zlate threw her an angry look, as if to say, "Aha! Haman's surrender?" But out of civility she responded in a friendly way, "God love you and your guest!" They then engaged in a lengthy conversation touching on all kinds of interesting subjects: challah, fish, the cow, the neighbor, the neighbor's borscht, and the neighbor's daughter-in-law—that loose woman who refuses to wear a wig, the hussy—and so on and on.

"Remember now, Zlate," the cantor's wife said several times over, "don't make me keep asking you. Come over right after dinner, God willing, and without fail, bring Esther."

Zlate put aside her animosity toward the cantor's wife and came calling with Esther to pay her respects to Shmulik. The cantor's wife greeted them cordially, offered them kugel, and spoke in Germanic Yiddish, as they do in Bardichev. "Why don't you *enjoy*, please, a little of this, Zlatenyu—you haven't permitted yourself to *enjoy* this yet!"

Later they were joined by Zlate's younger sister, a close friend, a good neighbor, Tante Yentl and her husband, Beinish; also Reb Kalman the matchmaker made his appearance, his face reflecting his holiday mood. He gave them all a "Good Shabbos" and toasted a *l'chayim*, fervently hoping that Shmulik would derive great satisfaction from his son and that he would soon be present at the betrothal party, God willing.

"I have plenty of good choices," Reb Kalman said, rolling up the sleeves of his satin caftan to the elbows and clasping his gray beard. "Do you see this beard of mine? It hasn't got as many hairs as I have names of eligible brides right up here" —and Reb Kalman pointed to his forehead. "Do you hear me, Shmulik?"

"What is there to say?" Shmulik interrupted. "What do I care what you have in your head? It hasn't even entered my mind yet!"

Upon hearing those words Yosele and Esther exchanged glances. And the same thought occurred to both of them, a new thought, one they had never been aware of before, a thought that causes a Mazepevka girl and a Mazepevka boy to blush deeply, their hearts skipping a beat when they suddenly discover they have been unexpectedly linked together. This pairing of bride and groom calls forth in Mazepevka girls and boys fresh notions of romance—innocent, delightful, delicious—not arranged, not contrived or premeditated, without guile, without deviousness, as spontaneous as nature itself.

"And now let's get to what's left of the liquor!" Shmulik called out giddily after sampling the wine with the after-dinner benediction. "Here, Beinish, take a little, taste some!"

Beinish, putting on airs like a man of the world, began opening bottles, and the guests sampled each brand of liquor, toasting at each quaff and wishing one another health and wealth together with salvation and consolation for all of

Israel until they became quite tipsy. They all spoke at once, smiling groggily, the wineglasses bumping their noses on the way to their lips.

"Look at them, just look how they're nodding off!" the wives snickered, removing themselves to a corner. "It wouldn't do any harm for them to sleep it off a little!"

But this advice fell on deaf ears. They kept on drinking and toasting one another with good wishes for themselves and for all of Israel. The wives became involved in their gossip and household chatter, conversing quietly. No one noticed that Yosele had edged closer to Esther and was telling her all about what had happened to him in the past three years. Yosele had never been as elated as on that Sabbath; he felt as if he were a grown man, a *mentch*, who had already lived through his share of troubles. His eyes shone and his cheeks were flushed. His grown-up gestures, his long caftan and earlocks gave him the appearance, from a distance, of a young, adult Jew. Yosele told her how bitter those three years had been, how many difficulties he had suffered at Mitzi's until he was finally able to establish some degree of independence. At first Mitzi had taken him under his wing, boasting of his new choirboy to everyone. But Mitzi's wife had not been as enthusiastic about him as Mitzi—to her he was another mouth to feed; she had enough eaters without him. She herself was far from barren and presented Mitzi with a new "choirboy" every year—one of her own! Neither seemed to realize that all those children were a burden. "All right, it would certainly be better to have one child fewer, but as long as it's here, it will have to fend for itself," they would say. And many were the children who fended for themselves, rolling underfoot like so much refuse. Until they were able to stand on their own two feet the poor things went hungry, naked, and barefoot, languishing from great deprivation.

One could easily imagine that Yosele was not living in clover himself; among so many wretched creatures, he starved along with the rest of them, bearing his burdens in silence. Poor Yosele was fated to have a stepmother in Tetrevetz too; she exploited him for housework, wore him out running errands, made him follow after her carrying the market basket, had him take the chickens to the slaughterer, rock the baby, and perform other onerous chores, often rewarding him with a slap, a jab, or a pinch, as if he were one of her own. Not infrequently he went to bed hungry and thirsty. And as if all that were not enough, his fellow choirboys heaped new troubles on his head. Yosele had endured three very bitter years in Tetrevetz. But he had suffered them in silence, never bearing tales to Mitzi lest, God forbid, he jeopardize his position.

His position was precious to him. With great zeal he had studied the *Hilches m'shoyrer* —the art of being a synagogue choirboy—had completed his religious-school education, had pursued his cantorial studies, and had developed his singing voice. He could now confidently say that he no longer needed Mitzi's guidance. He could read music as well as any of the choirboys and was no longer obliged to carry Mitzi's wife's market basket for her or rock her baby. He was now eligible for the best positions offered by the most prominent cantors, and if he were to go out into the world, he would surely do well.

"I've come home now to rest for a few weeks," Yosele said, ending his story, "then I'll know what my next step is. I'm waiting for someone who promised to take me on at his own expense, to pay me a salary in addition to whatever I receive in gratuities. So you see, he'll help me make my fortune if I travel with him. This man himself was once one of Mitzi's choirboys, Gedalye Bass is his name. He heard me chanting the *Halel*, the Psalms of Praise, in Tetrevetz and was very impressed with me. He said to me, 'What do you need this choir singing for? You should be the cantor yourself, like that Balabeysl, the one everyone was mad about.' I owe it all to you, Esther. You and your mother made it possible for me to go to Tetrevetz. If not for you two I would still be wasting my life here in this forsaken Mazepevka."

As he spoke these last words Yosele wanted to take Esther's hand in his, to tell her how much he had missed her for three long years, how he used to pray to God for his father's and for her welfare, how she would come to him in his dreams, hugging him the way she used to do when they were children. Yosele felt they were both different now from the way they once were. It seemed to him Esther was not the same Esther she once was. She had changed completely in those three years, becoming taller and prettier, her face losing its childlike fullness. Although her eyes were the same bright, clear eyes as ever, it seemed to him that their expression was not the same as before, and her entire appearance was more that of a mature, developed person. Her way of speaking and many of her mannerisms were those of a young woman. He thought he detected on her high, pale forehead a small wrinkle, such as one finds in older people, and her laugh too was different. Formerly when Esther laughed, her voice would ring out so that one could hear it, but now her laugh was more restrained, as was true for older women. . . . Yosele gazed at her intently. He was eager to find in her the same Esther with whom he had spent almost all of his childhood years, but he felt she had changed considerably. And the more Yosele gazed at her, the more shy Esther became, the more attentive he was, the more distant Esther behaved toward him. Between these two children who had grown up together in the same poverty there had suddenly sprung up a wall, a division like that in the synagogue. Propriety and modesty had silently crept into their relationship.

"I wasn't fortunate enough to hear you chant in shul," Esther said with a friendly smile. "By the time I prepared the Shabbos dinner and set the table and so on, the shul was already so packed that I couldn't manage to get in."

"Oh, really? You went over to the shul?" Yosele cried, his eyes sparkling brightly. Suddenly he felt he *had* to sing: something in his throat was tickling, scratching, giving him no peace—he had to sing out!

Yosele loved to sing when the mood came on him, and the mood came on him especially when he was feeling very good or very sad. In a lighthearted mood he would pour out his song like a nightingale. And so now, sitting beside Esther, Yosele's heart swelled with happiness and the urge came upon him to sing. He stood up, planted himself in the center of the room, and began to sing. The guests, who were by now in their cups, aroused themselves as from a sleep and perked up their ears. The wives stopped in the middle of their conversations in order to hear Yosele's song.

Yosele sang without words. The Vilner Balabeysl used to sing in this manner, vocalizing on Friday night during the Slichos prayer before the High Holidays. It was said that Jews would drown in tears of sheer bliss! Yosele was now singing in this style. Rarely heard sounds and sweet melodies issued from his throat, filling the entire room. Now he sang out in a sorrowful, heartrending elegy full of compassion and entreaty, his voice executing artful runs and arpeggios as if it were diving deep into the ocean and emerging

94

again. Now his voice assumed an ominous resonance, and the windows reverberated with his booming tones, and now he modulated into a hushed, soft voice, lower and lower, quieter and quieter, as if he were singing from far, far away, from somewhere down below, deep, deep down, sending back gentle, pure, smooth vocalizations and at the same time scattering in the air the most delicate trills like the sound of many chick-peas tumbling and rolling over each other. And now he burst out with great force, crying out in protest against the enemies of Judaism.

The guests bowed their heads in deep contemplation, alternately inspired and troubled, woebegone, as Jews feel when they hear sad music. The women clasped their hands over their hearts, putting on pious faces as they do when they pray in shul, especially at the concluding blessings to God. And what could be said of Shmulik? He seemed to be in another world; the several glasses of wine drunk during the benedictions made his face glow, his eyes sparkle, and despite what appeared to be a smile, he looked as if he were about to cry. The quantity of liquor he had taken was small, but nevertheless it had made his head reel; he imagined his wife, Zelda, standing nearby, gazing tearfully at Yosele and taking great pride in her only son. "Nu, Zelda," Shmulik said to her, "did you ever think . . . your Yosele . . . what is there to say, ha?" His mind ran free, imagining great plans for Yosele; he had visions of his doors being battered down by people wanting Yosele for their cantor. The merchants are simply dying for Yosele, prepared to pay him twenty rubles a week besides gratuities, but the Tetrevetz Jews aren't fools either—they don't want to let him go under any circumstances. And from Yampele, from Kashperev, from Makarevka, and from all the towns for miles around he is bombarded with offers and letters: "Send him to *us*, Reb

95

Shmulik! We'll even offer you a gold coin in advance—just send him here, your Yosele!"

These pleasant, cheerful fantasies wove themselves in Shmulik's mind, cradling him and lulling him into a sweet, idyllic slumber. And Yosele went on singing, performing miracles with his voice, endless improvisations, like a songbird when it first feels the sun's warmth and then perceives its brightness. Yosele, enthralled, saw Esther before him as he expressed his rapture, not in words but in wondrous, divine song. The nightingale, sensing the fresh, newly awakened springtime, had burst forth in song, had loosed its throat and poured out its heart.

XIV

Gedalye Bass Comes to Take Yosele Out into the World

Gedalye Bass, the man Yosele was awaiting, arrived sooner, much sooner than Yosele had expected. Gedalye went directly to Shmulik the cantor's house, deposited his bag, and made himself at home, like a person who has come to do the world a favor. Shmulik was very flattered by his arrival, considering it a great honor that people stopped at his house first. Besides, the guest pleased him because he was such a respectable person.

Gedalye Bass was one of those people about whom it is difficult to say exactly what he was like. In some ways he was a wordly person, his traditional caftan had been discreetly shortened, his heavy, black earlocks were tucked behind his ears, and his thick, dark beard was artfully rounded and turned under, not trimmed, perish the thought. On the other hand, he prayed fervently, standing on his feet for one and a half hours straight, reciting the Shmoneh Esreh, the Eighteen Benedictions, during the evening prayers, bobbing his head to the right and to the left, accompanied by heartfelt sighs. Seems like a pious Jew, Shmulik thought, bidding his guest wash and join him for supper. During the entire meal Gedalye was silent, carefully observing Shmulik and his household and answering Yosele's questions about this or that choirboy sparingly. Only after grace, during which the guest rolled his eyes upward, pausing over every word, did Shmulik have an opportunity to sit down alone with him in a corner to discuss the matter for which he had come.

"You really do want, I understand . . . I gather that Yosele wants to go with you?" Shmulik asked, looking directly at him.

"What does it mean, 'I really want'?" Gedalye Bass answered, stroking his beard. "Is he the only one I have? I travel with seventeen people, thank the Lord. Do you think it's such an easy job to put up with a bunch like that, God bless them, Reb Shmulik? You are, after all . . ."

"Of course, that's understood," Shmulik answered, like a person experienced in such matters. "What I mean is . . . I'm talking about my Yosele. For instance, what can he expect to make?"

"What do you mean, 'make'?" Gedalye said, again sidetracking the discussion. "Making today and making tomorrow are always the same? Sometimes it happens you go into a town and you come out with what you went in with. How is it written, 'Alone he came and alone he departed,' and sometimes it's the other way around, you strike it rich. That's the way it is, Reb Shmulik, expenses bleed you to death—that's the way the wheel turns. Do you understand what I'm talking about? No one has to tell *you.*"

"Of course, what is there to say? That's the way it goes," said Shmulik. "But what I'm talking about is what a father wants to know: What are his possibilities—can he make it in his profession or not? Do you understand?"

"What does 'make it' mean? Can anyone say about a cantor it's paying or it's not paying? I ask you, Reb Shmulik, you yourself are obviously not just another cantor. A cantor is really like a miller, as long as . . . you understand? If not, that's the way it goes."

"Of course, you're absolutely right, but I've got to know about my situation, you understand? After all, you are the buyer and I'm the seller. What is there to say—you name a price, and I'll sleep on it and come to a decision. Do you understand?"

"What is this about a price?" Gedalye said, turning his palms up and smiling agreeably. "That depends a little on luck and on whether the crowd goes for you. With our Jews, Reb Shmulik, as I'm sure you know, this one they like and that one not. Now, take Pitzi. Here's a Pitzi all by himself, and nevertheless, may I have in blessings what he makes . . . !"

"That's also true! But I'm not talking about that much. I would be happy with half, with a third of Pitzi's. After all, my Yosele is only a child, what is there to say?"

"Oh, you say 'only a child,' Reb Shmulik? You think a child doesn't need anything? The extras are always there— you understand me—ten times as much as you can imagine!"

"No, I'm not talking about that!" said Shmulik, feeling he had somehow been led around by the nose. "I had in mind something altogether different."

"What? Do you mean how he'll behave himself? You can believe me, Reb Shmulik, that—"

"Perish the thought!" cried Shmulik. "That's not what I mean! I'm talking about something altogether different!"

"Ah! I'm at your service, my dear friend. I want to help you work out exactly those matters you're concerned about—I mean, about children . . ."

That's how the two of them sparred late into the night, and Shmulik went to bed empty-handed. In the morning Gedalye Bass began hurrying Yosele to get under way; he put pressure on him and dogged his footsteps. As for Yosele, although it had been very agreeable to spend time with his near and dear friends, he was drawn toward that greater world. He realized there was no future for him in Mazepevka, where he would be limited and dependent. He had not yet attained his goal. Those marvelous tales and sweet dreams about the young Balabeysl, Canarik, and others began to surface again in all their grandeur and drew him away from Mazepevka. He persuaded Gedalye to allow him three extra days, no more, to spend with his family, to bid farewell before embarking on his journey.

"When do you suppose he'll be coming home again?" Shmulik asked Gedalye on the day he was leaving, and one could hear in his voice the trembling of a person about to cry.

"What do you mean, 'home'?" Gedalye Bass answered him in his usual manner, parrying the question. "It isn't as if he were going to one place. We're world travelers—today we're here, tomorrow we're there, like people who travel with fairs. Do we know if something will work out or not? Not at all—we go, and that's it."

Shmulik's spirits sank; on the day of Yosele's departure he became upset and sick at heart. The thought, Exactly who is this Gedalye Bass and what is there about him? flitted through his mind, too late. On top of that, Zlate was needling him, making him feel he was, alas, a sheep, not a father. Who ever heard of a father not asking ahead of time, the way proper people do?

Yosele prepared for the journey. There was a great stir in Shmulik's house—Yosele was going off! Food was prepared to eat on the way—*kichel*, corn bread, and honey cake. Since his arrival from Tetrevetz his stepmother's attitude had changed entirely; she had begun to treat him with respect; there was no limit to her generosity. That whole morning she didn't step away from the stove, constantly cooking and baking, roasting and frying—all for Yosele's journey. Her face was flushed, her kerchief knotted in the back to keep her hair in place; with her own hands she packed his bundle for the trip. Feeling such devotion on her part, Yosele forgave her for all the vexation and beatings he had suffered at her hands. Then and there he was ready to embrace her as his own mother. As the moment of leaving approached, Yosele's heart softened, and he felt devoted and tender toward everyone. Everything took on a festive appearance. The people, the streets, and the houses appeared to him bright and joyous. Mazepevka, with its dark, muddy alleyways, its squalid, lopsided hovels, its gloomy burdened inhabitants, appeared in his eyes like a Garden of Eden, where everything blossoms and shines, thrives and rejoices, and he felt like hugging and kissing each and every one. His fantasies so carried him away and he was feeling so exhilarated that he imagined he had wings; he wasn't walking, he was floating; he wasn't simply happy, he was radiant; he wasn't speaking, he was singing. In sum, Yosele's time in Mazepevka was spent in a state of exultation—he was finally going away! With *tefillin* bag and walking stick in hand, Yosele started off for the synagogue to pray. But on the way he dropped by at Zlate's house to say goodbye to Esther.

XV

Yosele Bids Farewell to Esther Several Times

Esther had one bright happy day in her life—the day Yosele was leaving. It was still quite early when Yosele, his *tefillin* sack under his arm, entered Zlate's house to say his farewells. Zlate was at the shop, the children, Menashe and Ephraim, were still asleep, and only Esther was up. She was standing at the stove preparing the fire, brewing chicory for breakfast. On seeing Yosele she turned down her sleeves, which had been rolled up to the elbows, exposing her slender white arms. Her face was flushed from the heat of the fire, her hair hung loosely about her shoulders, barely held in place by a hairpin, which added all the more to her charm. Her short white apron sparkled, enhancing the light reflected in her radiant, lovely face. Clasping her hands over her heart and staring pensively into the fire she heard Yosele out as he spoke on and on.

Yosele began by describing how far away he was going

and how he would be seeing the entire world, God Almighty! He would be everywhere—in Makarevka, in Kashperev, Gnilopiatevka, in Glupsk, in Dneprevetz, in Tuneyadevka—everywhere! Gedalye Bass had promised him they would go together to Chmelnitz and to Gontoyarsk as well. He would take him to the theater where Pitzi's tenor sang every night, and people said he was happier than he'd ever been. He sent large sums of money to his father, who was the cantor at the Makarevka Butchers' Shul. The father had once been a wretched pauper, but today, since his son had become so famous and popular, he was prosperous. . . . Yosele said that if God were to grant him but half of what Pitzi's tenor made, even a tenth, he would be able to support his father in his old age so that he would not need to ruin his health conducting the services all by himself. "He's toiled enough, he's entitled to a rest."

Those words were spoken with passion, his eyes blazed, his face glowed. Yosele was still only a lad of almost sixteen, not more, but a tall boy, one of those young Jewish lads who grows up and matures quickly. Because of the hardships he had endured since childhood Yosele had developed early, already behaving like a sensible adult, walking like an adult, talking intelligently, conducting himself like a man.

Listening to him speak, Esther was impressed. He acted as if not three years had passed but ten. Observing his sober demeanor, she had to restrain herself from laughing. Esther was a year and a half older than he was and had always thought of him as a child, a youngster, but hearing him speak now, she looked at him intently and let him go on without interrupting until he had finished. And Yosele spoke without a stop, with increasing enthusiasm, setting forth his golden dreams and his ambitions to conquer the world. When he paused for a moment Esther said with a tender smile, "Be careful now, don't forget later on what you're saying now, like Zalman-Hersh, my Tante Breine's eldest son. Do you remember him? Before he left for Brod he promised her the world, and no sooner did he arrive there than he sent maybe two letters and then stopped writing to this day. I'm saying this to show that promises are easy to make."

Those words gave evidence of Esther's unhappiness with Yosele's leaving, for some reason her heart was uneasy. But what she said apparently hit home, and Yosele became even more animated. "Are you comparing me, Esther, to that rogue, to Zalman-Hersh? Zalman-Hersh was always a good-for-nothing, insolent and impudent. A day didn't pass that he wasn't flogged for his nasty tricks. How can you compare me to him? Don't you worry, I will never forget my father. I will be away, but my heart will be here, with my nearest and dearest. I'll write often. I'll write you every week, Esther. Will you answer my letters?"

Esther felt the blood rise to her cheeks, and she lowered her eyes. When their eyes met they understood each other completely; words were superfluous. There was no need for explicit commitments. Since neither of them read romantic novels they didn't know how one was supposed to conduct oneself in these circumstances. And they didn't have to know—nature can manage without romances. Yosele and Esther had been together from early childhood, and it would be unthinkable if they were to be parted forever. Till now they had harbored one secret in their hearts. Now, having expressed their feelings, not through words but through the meeting of eyes, through exchanged glances, it was not a secret anymore. But it wasn't necessary to put those feelings into words, nor would it be easy. It was already decided between them—bride and groom—what was there further to talk about? They were both still young. First Yosele would go out into the world, then he would return, and he would . . . she would . . . it would work out!

"So meanwhile let's say goodbye," Yosele said, offering Esther his hand like a person from the big city who knows his way. "Be well, Esther!"

"Go in good health!" Esther replied, extending her hand to him for the first time in her life. Esther felt that Yosele was squeezing her hand very, very hard, but she made no effort to remove it from his. Is there anyone who has never experienced such a handshake? Is there anyone who doesn't know the meaning of that kind of farewell? Yosele and Esther were floating on air. For a moment they forgot themselves and tacitly pledged their lives to each other. Their eyes met again, speaking in their own language, mutely, in that language familiar to all young people at that moment when the springtime of the heart awakens, the happiest time of the first true, inspired love.

Standing on the threshold, Yosele again turned his face toward Esther and again said, "Be well." Esther responded, "Go in good health," and Yosele again repeated, "Be well," and was finally about to leave when suddenly Zlate appeared behind him and said, "Oh-oh, just look at him! Why this 'Be well' so early? Hold on a little. Until Lazer the coachman pulls himself together and hitches up his three old nags, you can say goodbye six times over. Why don't you go to shul, Yosele, and then come back here for lunch. The last hot meal should be eaten with us. Anybody with any sense will tell you that's the way it should be. Do you hear, Esther? Frume-Blume brought me some fish to the shop, do I have to say any more? Go on over there, I left the helper all alone. Business is so good, blessed be His name, it almost pays to close up the shop, may it happen to all the enemies of Israel! To spend such a day, sweating and roasting in the sun—and for what? Remember now, Yosele, be sure to come for lunch! I'll tell your father and stepmother myself—it's Rosh Chodesh, the new moon, almost a holiday. They can come too."

That day was the most blissful, the happiest, the brightest day of Esther's life. There is a time for everything. There even comes a time for the solitary flower growing in a corner of the woods, ignored, hidden, forsaken. The best time comes for the neglected flower when one bright ray of sunshine reaches it, reviving it, and the refreshed blossom raises its head for a moment, opens wide its petals, and in full bloom, looks up into the fair heavens and offers a thankful greeting to a benign nature that has not forgotten her.

Part Two

XVI

He Leaves and Quickly Forgets His Promises

Like a bright comet flashing through the dark sky, flaring incandescently for a brief moment, leaving behind it a long, bright afterglow, and then vanishing, so too was Yosele the Nightingale's career in the cantorial world. On one day he would arrive in a town, making a great stir among the Jews, appearing before them, captivating and amazing his audiences with his extraordinary, wondrous, uncannily sweet voice, with his divine praying and chanting—and the next day he would vanish, leaving the townspeople dazzled and astonished, talking about him, telling of his remarkable prowess, praising him to the skies, convinced they would remember him and his chanting all their lives. Even before his arrival in a new place the excitement would start to mount. A week ahead of time could be heard: "He's coming! Yosele the Nightingale is coming to us for Shabbos!"

And when Yosele Solovey would arrive, the very ground

seemed to shake—who did not want to hear the Mazepevka Nightingale? Most of the time Yosele the Nightingale performed for paying audiences that snapped up the tickets before you knew it. It was rare for the Nightingale to stay more than one Sabbath in a town, even if he were to be showered with gold, as there were many towns and it was necessary to go everywhere. Right after his departure the townspeople would begin to buzz about his visit, one telling the other his reactions with great enthusiasm: "What do you say to the Nightingale?" "What do you say to that voice?" "Did you get a look at his face?" "What do you say to his choir?" "Nu, Mazepevka! Nnuu, Soloveychikl!!" Avid fans followed him from town to town in order to hear him again. When Yosele went out in the street, gangs of boys, young scamps, would chase after him, shouting, "The Nightingale! The Nightingale!" And not only youngsters but also bearded Jews paused to take a look at the Mazepevka Nightingale. One wonders what there was to see: a young lad in his teens, with rosy cheeks and combed-out earlocks, wearing a long caftan reaching to the ground and a rabbit's-fur hat— that's what Yosele the Nightingale amounted to. But his reputation was so widespread, his voice was so wondrous, his chanting so unbelievably sweet that his face took on a special charm, and those who could see him felt privileged.

As happens with every famous person, there were stories enough about Yosele Solovey. Endless legends sprang up about him. For example, it was told that he carried an instrument in his throat, a little harmonica or a fife, with which he performed those feats—that was the only way to explain the humanly impossible vocal feats he performed. Others said it wasn't a little harmonica, not a fife, but that he was born with that voice, because when he was still an infant in his mother's arms, he sang out so beautifully that people became frightened and brought him to the rabbi, who peered down his throat and then blessed him, saying that he hoped Yosele would find as much favor in the eyes of the world as he had found in the rabbi's eyes. They also said that Yosele didn't eat anything—no bread, no meat, no fruit—but hot milk beaten with an egg and honey, that was what he lived on; he drank sixty eggs every day, and that explained why his voice was so pure and smooth. "He is exceptionally pious," they said about him, "and is an outstanding student." In fact, no one had actually ever tested him, but they could tell from his face that he must be a refined boy. "He's so handsome, you don't dare look at him," they all said. Community leaders, gentry, the aristocracy and nobility all proudly reflected themselves in his glory and beauty.

These stories eventually made their way back to Mazepevka, where for Shmulik, for Zlate and Esther they were a balm, a compensation for pain he had been causing them. They assumed he would come home for Sukkos to rest up a bit before traveling on; but Sukkos came and went, as did Pesach and Shevuos, and no Yosele. Another Sukkos passed, and Yosele wasn't there; another Sukkos passed, and still no Yosele! He wrote, "I'm on my way! I'm on my way!"— but he didn't come. If they had known where to find him they would have written or visited him, but he was dashing all over the country—here today, there tomorrow. Go find him! It was fortunate that he at least wrote letters. For a half year they received fine, happy letters, at first fairly often, then afterward not so often. But they did hear good news about him, that he was touring far and wide, creating a sensation, pleasing the crowds, making money and continuing his travels. Several times Shmulik received from Yosele a thick envelope containing rubles, and Mazepevka was agog. "What do you say about our Shmulik the cantor? His Yosele is sending him heaps of money. He'll become a rich man in his old age!" The following year Yosele not only stopped sending money but wrote only one brief letter of only a few sentences every three months: "I want you to know that I am, praise God, in the best of health. May the Lord let me hear the same from you, Amen Selah!" And after that the letters were even fewer. Soon the letters stopped coming altogether, and they lost track of Yosele. He was gone as if he had dropped like a rock into the sea. No more Yosele!

Poor Shmulik the cantor suddenly plummeted from the heights to the earth. He lamented his beloved son, the apple of his eye, the comfort of his old age and became embittered. He was beside himself with grief, not knowing what he could possibly do. But great as his anguish was, the humiliation was greater. More than once Shmulik would pour out his bitter heart to his good friend Zlate the shopkeeper, asking her advice. "What can I do and where do I begin?" But what kind of advice could Zlate give him, being a woman and a widow besides? As usual, she threw the entire blame on him, rubbed it in, and said that if she were a father, she would behave differently with her child, and if Zelda, may she rest in peace, were alive today, everything would be entirely different! These talks between Shmulik and Zlate, which took place in front of poor Esther, made her sick at heart, but she was unable to confide her secret to anyone.

Thick clouds darkened Esther's bright sky, and the world, which for one moment had been bright and beautiful, again became gloomy and empty, worse than ever. Until that time Esther had been in her own narrowly circumscribed world, naïve and innocent, like an unborn chick in its egg, unaware of what the world was like outside. Esther would surely have met an appropriate mate and would have made a happy marriage; whether or not she would have lived happily ever after is another story, but she would not have complained, just like the other Mazepevka girls. But now that her heart had tasted that secret emotion, now that she had for a brief moment considered herself blessed in her Yosele, her intended bridegroom, and not having told anyone and having waited so long—now she had to abandon her dream and had to withdraw herself, hiding from people, to bear her sorrows alone. For the longest time Esther could not reconcile herself to the fact that Yosele had behaved in this fashion, had forgotten his promises, forgotten them forever! How could he! How could he do this to her! What of his loyalty? Where was his devotion to his father? If Yosele can do this, Esther thought, anything is possible! But what Esther was suffering now was nothing compared to what awaited her. . . .

XVII

Yosele the Nightingale Causes a Sensation and Falls in with Bad Company

There are two kinds of wanderers in this world: for one kind wandering is an affliction, wrenching him from home and loved ones, uprooting him; for the other kind it is a source of pleasure that warps him, intoxicates him, making him lose his bearings and his sense of reality. The second kind of wanderer was our Yosele. Traveling about from town to town, he himself hardly knew where he was on any given day. Yosele didn't have to worry about where to go next or how to get there. That was no longer his concern. For that there was a Gedalye Bass, who managed his affairs as his own father would. Gedalye had taken on the name Bass when he was a singer, but once he began touring the country, he hardly used the name, because he was now doing other kinds of work: traveling from town to town "arranging Sabbaths." While Yosele the Nightingale was chanting in one town, Gedalye was already in the next, bargaining with the *gabbai*, the synagogue administrator, down to the last groschen, arranging a Shabbos for Yosele, making sure to receive the money in advance. Once Yosele arrived, Gedalye would go off to the third town to arrange another Sabbath, and so it went. Gedalye was shrewd in these matters, and Yosele could rely on him for everything; he was in charge, hired the choir members, made travel arrangements, working everything out by himself. All Yosele had to do was arrive on the scene, chant the Shabbos service, and move on. To Gedalye, Yosele was as important as his own child; he protected him as he would his own eyes. Yosele prospered under Gedalye's care, as he wrote to family and friends in his first letters. But Yosele could not at that time fully understand the reason for Gedalye's benevolence.

The choirboys, one had to admit, were a wild bunch, most of them lively, happy-go-lucky boys recently freed from their dark classrooms and cruel rabbi's switch or from the boss's wickedness. Out in the big world these young boys were like frisky colts: they didn't know what to do first. They were for the most part boys who till now hadn't had so much as a crust of bread to eat, had been religious-school students, tailors' apprentices, or errand boys. Whatever they once were, they now became fast comrades, saw eye to eye on everything, ate together, and had great times together. Naturally, their adherence to Jewish law was forsaken and they did as they pleased. No sooner did they arrive in a town than they took to eating; that was the most important thing in the world to them. Like hungry wolves, like locusts, they would fall upon the owner of the inn and fill his coffers with money. In their free time they would saunter through town, smoking cigars, clowning, and causing mischief. In a word, they lived it up!

While Yosele was with Mitzi in Tetrevetz, he had his responsibilities and was occupied with his singing. His father's letters sustained him and reminded him that he had to maintain his Jewishness: he should not forget to put on his *tefillin* every day, should observe all the Commandments, avoid foolishness, and remember he wasn't like all the other choirboys but was his father's son. . . . The letters Yosele received from his father were for him the best counsel, and he obeyed his father, observed the Commandments, and had little to do with the rest of the choirboys. In addition, he was kept quite busy; when he wasn't singing, there was other work to do—rocking Mitzi's wife's baby, carrying her market basket, polishing the brass, and so on. For Yosele it was a labor of love—so long as he could sing for Mitzi. But later on, when Yosele the young singer became Yosele the Nightingale, having come into his own, he fell in with a different crowd, a band of lively, fun-loving boys who had seen it all and knew it all, and Yosele's character changed.

At first, when he observed their antics, he couldn't countenance them and complained to Gedalye, who heard Yosele out and answered him with a little smile. "You're still just a child, Yosele. You have to know these fellows.

They're a lively bunch." Later Yosele noticed that Gedalye himself sometimes cut a corner here and there in the prayers or skipped an evening service altogether, among other things. "A Mincheh prayer isn't a goat, you can't lose it," Gedalye would say, quoting an adage, and he noticed Yosele was shocked by it. It also surprised and dismayed Yosele that such a refined Jew as Gedalye Bass, a Jew who wore traditional attire, should permit himself to sit down and play a game of Okeh all night with the choir, listening to their jokes and going along with their loutish behavior. But little by little, as Yosele grew more accustomed to the group and became more friendly with them, he found himself going along with their whims. He began, like them, to skimp on his prayers and play an occasional game of Okeh, nibbling sweets, sometimes even bending the elbow with them. He shortened his caftan, trimmed his earlocks and tucked them behind his ears, pomaded his hair, devoted a good deal of time to his appearance, and turned into a regular dandy. But when it came to money, Yosele Solovey was not as attentive; the choirboys were always cadging change from him, but Gedalye took the lion's share.

At no more than sixteen, Yosele lived like an adult. When he arrived in a town he especially enjoyed how the people would run after him, pointing him out, marveling at his good looks and telling him so to his face, mostly the young girls and young women. Yosele was lionized as a celebrity, and he could boast afterward that people pursued him, kissed the ground he walked on, and threw themselves at him. A handsome face can be a liability. Had Yosele not been so handsome, he might not have gone astray so quickly. His good looks, one could say, were his downfall. It would have been far better for him, for his father, and for others as well if he had not been such a celebrity, if people hadn't pointed him out and had not turned his head with juvenile nonsense. . . . Because of that Yosele lost his innocence, his honesty, and his devotion to family, along with his earlier fine qualities, and with time he lost his magnetism, his fervor, his honor, and his appeal in the eyes of God and of the people.

A cantor is not an actor. Jews certainly love to hear good singing, admire virtuosity and vocal feats in the synagogue; however, the cantor must never forget he is called *shaliach tzibbur*, a messenger of the congregation, an advocate, a representative, and consequently the congregation demands of him that he be a person of impeccable virtue, a respectable Jew, not a profligate. A house of worship is not a theater. When Yosele Solovey was conducting himself as a Jew, virtuous and pious, as one should, his chanting on the pulpit possessed a special sweetness and he himself was supremely attractive. But later, when he changed his ways, the congregation gradually found him flawed, unfit.

"Some prayer leader," they said of him. "All he does is play cards, eat unkosher food, and promenade with girls—a proper prayer leader! . . ."

Jewish people react the same as everyone else in the world: as long as they think well of someone, they don't spare their praise—they glorify him and extol him to the skies; but as soon as he falls from grace in their eyes they begin to find fault with him, heap blame on him, and discover things about him that would make one's hair stand on end. That is what happened to Yosele the Nightingale. When he was good, he was infinitely good, beyond all measure. But once his downfall started, ugly tales began to surface about him. One said he saw with his own eyes how Yosele the Nightingale was walking through the inn courtyard without a hat on, singing bawdy army songs, carrying on a love affair. . . . Another told how he had heard Yosele ate fresh pork, fried in butter, on Yom Kippur. A third told he had heard how in some town Yosele was removed from the pulpit for some terrible deed. . . . And so Yosele finally earned such a bad name for himself that he might well have stepped down from the pulpit and quit being a cantor, ignoring Gedalye, who tried to persuade him not to pay attention to what was being said about him. "Let our Jews gossip till they burst, so long as the money keeps coming in!" Gedalye said.

Gedalye's permissiveness toward Yosele was not without a motive. Yosele Solovey was for him a good piece of property from which he made a respectable profit. Beyond that Gedalye had a far-sighted plan; that plan was a match. Gedalye had a daughter, not anyone remarkable but a bright enough girl, small in stature and getting on in years, over twenty—that is to say, almost thirty. "She has no luck!" Gedalye would lament to his choir and to Yosele too. "No luck, and that's all there is to it! She's such a capable girl, and it's so hard to find the right one for her; what we want she doesn't want, and whomever she wants is not to be found, naturally. Your modern girls!" So Gedalye would often hint obliquely, as was his style, always talking in fragments, half sentences, with a wink, leaving the other person to divine his meaning. One would have to be dense not to surmise what Gedalye had in mind in talking to Yosele about his daughter.

Yosele understood it full well but pretended ignorance. He was used to those things by now. In every town where he went to sing for Sabbath he would be besieged by matchmakers afterward; he was offered proposals, one more extravagant than the next—ten thousand, fifteen thousand, twenty thousand. . . . Among the wealthy were many ea-

ger people who were willing to pay handsomely to obtain
Yosele the Nightingale as a son-in-law, and especially before Yosele's downfall, when he was still conducting himself
like a Jew. Of course they didn't go directly to him but to
Gedalye Bass, because he was an older person. And
Gedalye, for his part, talking in half sentences, with a wink,
did everything in his power to discourage them, to dissuade
them, sending them off with a wave of the hand, since he
had his own designs on Yosele. But there came a time when
Gedalye realized these designs on Yosele were no more than
empty dreams that he had to drive out of his head and
forget; he couldn't continue to entertain such foolish notions. Yosele told him right out that he had no thought of
marrying. He wanted to go home, and there, among his
own, he would find his intended. Gedalye realized that his
game might be up.

Meanwhile, an unforeseen turn of events caught Gedalye
by surprise, dazzling him with the prospect of a fortune,
which Gedalye was always eager to acquire. And this is how
it happened.

XVIII

Perele the Lady Is About to Leave the Town
of Strishtch But Remains on Account of Yosele

Between Yampele and Makarevka, exactly midway, one
finds a certain town, Strishtch by name, which is renowned
for its old families, their descendants, cabalists, simple ordi-

nary people and poor folk who go about, each with a copy
of his family tree attesting to the remarkable fact that he is
the grandchild of his grandfather and hence is entitled to a
coin or two. What those Jews lived on is hard to say; if you
should ask a Strishtcher how he managed, he would answer,
"Just like this, as you see"—and he believed he had fully
answered your question. Their principal occupation was
brokering; a stranger would be astounded by the multitude
of middlemen: grain brokers, moneylenders, real estate and
employment agents, would-be cantorial impresarios. Almost every Strishtcher was a middleman. There were plenty
of idlers too and all kinds of societies—a Mishnah Society
for religious study, a Psalms Society for devotions, a
Shomrim L'boker Society for alerting the community to
danger, and other societies, seemingly without number.
You could also find several large synagogues, small
prayerhouses, a home or two where little more than the
required ten men gathered for worship, a bathhouse, and
two cemeteries, an old one and a new one, and they were
thinking of buying land for a third.

You could count the wealthy people on one hand; they
were called "the Strishtcher Aktziznikes." Apparently this
name stuck with them when they bribed their way out of
Aktziz. The brothers Aktziznikes were famous, not so much
for their philanthropy as for their great wealth. "They are as
rich as Korach," is what they said of them in Strishtch.
"They live like royalty but don't give so much as a groschen
to anyone. The blessed God apportions to this one everything and to the other nothing. . . ." Nevertheless when
one of the brothers died, all the shops were closed and the
whole town mourned Reb Moshe-Wolf the Aktzizniker, as
was fitting when the richest man in town dies. Reb Moshe-
Wolf died childless and left almost his entire fortune to his

two younger brothers, Meir-Hersh and Pesach-Leib. He also left a tidy sum to his third wife, the young bride he had brought from Bardichev a few years before his death. People said that this young widow had managed to salt away some two hundred thousand rubles, which, so the story ran, she was planning to take with her to Bardichev, where she would find a young man to marry, not another old codger like Moshe-Wolf. But at that very moment Yosele Solovey came upon the scene, and Moshe-Wolf's young widow, Perele the Lady, stayed on.

She was called Perele the Lady in Strishtch because she was almost the only one who dressed like a princess, drove about in a carriage, kept a dog, and played the pianoforte. While Moshe-Wolf was still sitting *shiva* for his second wife they were already whispering in Strishtch that he would now marry a young, modern woman, and why not? Money he had—he could allow himself anything he desired. The townspeople hit it right: Moshe-Wolf, after observing the appropriate thirty days of mourning, drove off to Bardichev (where else?) and soon brought back with him a "lady." As long as Strishtch had been a town, a woman had never kept a dog or played the pianoforte. The first time they heard her play, people crowded into her street and exclaimed, "My! A woman who's a musician!" and gossip began to fly about the dog and the piano. From that time on, "The Lady" or "Perele the Lady" stuck with her. People rubbed their hands together in anticipation of collecting some extra money from her—"After all, a Lady! It would be beneath her dignity to bargain. Of course she'll give a donation. People like that love to do such things!" But they quickly saw that they had fooled themselves from start to finish. Perele the Lady, who had grown up in Bardichev, a trading center, could bargain better than all the Strishtcher fish-wives, and she hated giving a donation even more than her husband did. "Of course you have to know how to tinkle away on the piano," the Strishtch wives said sarcastically. "Of course you have to act like a grande dame in order to push us around!" Or "Perele, may you be well! Give us some bread. Pretend you're giving it to your dog."

While he was still in Makarevka, Yosele had been invited to perform for Shabbos in Strishtch. He had turned up his nose at the invitation, not wanting to waste his time in such a place, a town known mainly for its poor people. Moreover he had planned to make a short visit to Kashperev and from there go home to Mazepevka. The traveling was becoming tedious; he was forever on the road, far from home. He was even thinking of writing a few words home (it had been so long since he had written!) when in came Gedalye, cursed be his name, and with his doubletalk he persuaded Yosele that it was far better to stop first at Strishtch to chant the Sabbath and from there go on to Mazepevka, in order to avoid Kashperev, saying in his usual elliptical way, "Because Kashperev is so hospitable to cantors, may it burn to the ground three times over, may it be cursed!" So reasoned Gedalye, and so it was decided, without objection.

In Strishtch for Shabbos, Yosele the Nightingale and his company presented the town with a service that threw it into an uproar. People besieged the inn where Yosele was staying in order to get a look at the Mazepevka Nightingale, if only from a distance. Among those who were curious to see Yosele was Reb Moshe-Wolf's young widow, Perele the Lady, who had heard him sing and came home from the synagogue in a state of excitement, disquieted, quite agitated. "I am so eager to see his face," Perele the Lady said to those close to her. Saturday afternoon she put on her silk outfit, adorned herself with her most expensive jewelry—pearls, diamonds, and other precious gems—and promenaded through town with her personal maid, making sure to stroll right past the inn where Yosele and his company happened to be lodged. It was summertime and the windows were open; leaning on his elbows at one of the windows, with a silver-bordered, gold-embroidered yarmulke on his head, was Yosele the Nightingale. His hair, worn in the turned-under Russian peasant style, fell over his shoulders; his face was pale, and his smiling eyes, large and shining, gazed out from under full brows. Around him stood the choirboys, mocking and laughing at the town of Strishtch and its people.

"What do you make of this 'Trishtch?'" joked the boys among themselves. "This town is at the bottom of the heap!"

"Who is that young woman dripping with jewels from head to toe?" asked Yosele, scrutinizing Perele the Lady as her large eyes met his. Perele was not a bad-looking woman, still young, with a round figure, a fair complexion like a fresh pastry, a full chin, and a fleshy neck hung with large pearls. Her fingers were adorned with rings, her wrists with bracelets and bangles, her neck with many-stranded necklaces, her figure expensively attired in silk and velvet in the latest Bardichever fashion. Strutting like a peahen, she made sure to pass the inn several times, each time catching a glimpse of Yosele. When she came home Perele felt her heart stirring with passion.

Even while Moshe-Wolf was alive she had decided that if she were left a widow, she would take a young man who would be handsome and fair-haired. Since Moshe-Wolf was old and infirm, she had certainly expected to be left a widow. He had married her only for her beauty. The marriage contract for over a hundred thousand left her well provided for. He had promised to make her happy for a hundred and twenty years and not to forget her in his will. Perele was still a very young girl then, but like all Bardichever girls, she loved to dress up, follow the latest fads, while always keeping an eye open for a rich husband. Naturally, when Moshe-Wolf came calling, he didn't make her heart skip a beat, but the hundred thousand rubles and his carriage and his fine furniture so turned her head that it seemed the right thing to do. There was, however, one thing she could not abide and that was the name of Strishtch—"What kind of name is Strishtch! A fine name! Feh—disgusting . . . !" Perele brooded, and it rankled her. But Moshe-Wolf did her a great favor, right after the wedding he took ill, lingered several years, and finally died, liberating Perele the Lady. Nonetheless she conducted herself as a devoted wife, as a Jewish daughter, should: she sat *shiva*, observed the required thirty-day mourning period, and then, together with her maid, Leah'tzi, packed her clothes and prepared to leave. As you would expect, she was besieged by matchmakers from all over pressing upon her favorable matches, but Perele the Lady wouldn't hear of it—she wanted no part of that dull Strishtch and couldn't wait to be out of it. She had already written to her parents that after Shabbos, God willing, she would be coming home to Bardichev. But as it turned out, she remained in Strishtch. And on account of Yosele the Nightingale!

"What do you think of this Yosele?" Perele the Lady asked Leah'tzi, her maid, as they were strolling by the inn, casting a glance in that direction.

"What can I say?" answered Leah'tzi. "He's surely as handsome as the morning star, just like that Solomon, the character in the romances—tall, well built, and golden-haired."

Leah'tzi the maid loved to read romances, the first page of which always carried the inscription "A Most Interesting

Novel, Reprinting Forbidden." Leah'tzi would read the romances aloud to Perele the Lady while Moshe-Wolf was lying ill. Even though Perele ridiculed her for her silly stories, she nevertheless enjoyed them. Perele had brought this maid with her from Bardichev. Her duties consisted solely of dressing her mistress, strolling with her, and making sure to be always at her side; she also was her only confidante and, like her, looked forward with all her heart to her master's early demise, although they were both ashamed to say so openly. They understood each other implicitly and were both eager to go home.

Even though Leah'tzi was no beauty and had a pockmarked face, she had a fiancé in Bardichev. His name was Levi-Mottel and he was in the "tobacco business," meaning that he sold cigarettes. No matter what others thought of him—he might have been an old, pimply bachelor with ugly red hair—in her eyes he looked like an "angel, tall, well built," and that was why she was "in love" with him, exactly as described in those "romances" she read. Leah'tzi loved her betrothed and was faithful to him, entirely devoted. She sent Levi-Mottel every last ruble she could scrape together; she didn't allow herself so much as an extra dress, a shawl, or boots. "I have to send it off to Levi-Mottel, who really needs the money!" In return Levi-Mottel sent her appreciative letters every week, one the identical twin of the other, as if born of the same mother.

"And I greet you," Levi-Mottel would write every week, "and I thank you, my dear, for the gift and I've had new boots and galoshes made and I beg you to write how your health is and if your master is still alive and I am, thank God, well and there is no work; cigarette rollers are not cheap and there's no work and I'm not making any money and send me, my dear bride, money for a new suit and the other suit is old already and write me how your health is and if your master is still living."

These letters were to Leah'tzi the most precious things in the world. She lived with the satisfaction that Levi-Mottel was dressing well with her money and was wearing her suit and her boots and galoshes.

"Fool, fool!" Perele the Lady would say to her. "Foolish girl! He'll end up putting a fancy headstone on your grave, that fiancé of yours! Don't you see?"

Leah'tzi had no reply to that; she had her mind made up. She counted the minutes, the seconds, until she would finally go home to Bardichev and stand under the wedding canopy with Levi-Mottel. "Who cares what she says, the madam, or what she thinks! If I could show her what is in my heart, then she would know not to make fun of such things. . . ."

But the time came when Perele the Lady would speak differently; the time would come when she would discover that "true love is not a servant," as Leah'tzi used to say, "whom you can dismiss with a wave of the hand," as Perele had once thought. After coming home from her stroll, Perele flung herself into an armchair, summoned Leah'tzi, and asked her to feel her brow.

"You have a headache, madam? What shall we do?"

"A headache, you say? It's my heart, silly goose, it's my heart that's aching. I'm beside myself, I'm burning up, I'm in pain, I'm fainting, and you say *that*!"

"What's the matter then, madam? Tell me, so I'll know too."

"Oy vey, Leah'tzi, what can I tell you? It's awful, it's the end of me! There's a fire burning right here, in my heart! From the first moment I heard him singing and ever since I laid eyes on him I feel it's the end of me!" Perele the Lady wept from great heartache. Leah'tzi stood by in deep thought, trying to figure out what might be done. As she was not given to subtleties, she didn't have to think long.

"Do you know what, madam? Listen to me. You're a free woman now, thank God, and a rich one too—would that I had your worries. Now, listen to me. Grab him and marry him!"

Perele the Lady almost leaped from her armchair, greatly excited, and burst out laughing, tears in her eyes. "Foolish girl! What do you mean, 'grab him'? Doesn't he have a say in it too?"

"So what are you afraid of? That maybe he won't want you? Is that it? You think you're ugly? Or that you are, God forbid, common? Or that you're a widow? Some problem! A lot of women would love to be in your place! Or maybe it's a sin for you to take a young boy? Even a lunatic wouldn't say that! What is it, then? The wonderful life you had with your husband? Wasted three and a half years in this God-forsaken Strishtch. The great joys you had here? Seems to me, living in the same house with a sick man, you've earned your reward. No one knows how somebody else's shoe pinches, and you don't owe anybody an explanation!"

"Ach, Leah'tzi! My soul! My heart!" Perele the Lady said and threw herself into Leah'tzi's arms.

In a big pond one finds all sorts of fish; in a city like Bardichev one found all sorts of people. Perele the Lady's origins were not of the highest: her father, Meir Zeitchik, was what we used to call a speculator. He was ready to buy whatever was for sale but never had any permanent business of his own. Should an old plant, a factory, a house to be repossessed, an estate, or a broken-down shack come on the market anywhere, Meir Zeitchik was ready to buy. If someone discarded an old carriage or old furniture, Meir

Zeitchik was on the spot to make an offer, just so long as he could make a ruble on the deal. You could find anything at Meir Zeitchik's, whatever your heart desired. Is it iron? There's iron. Brass? There's brass. Feathers? There's feathers. If it's everything you want—there's everything, everything! He never had any capital of his own but always managed with other people's money. As with most merchants, business was sometimes good and sometimes bad. All in all, he led the life of a tolerably successful businessman, borrowing here, grabbing there, giving a little, taking a little—managing!

Although Meir Zeitchik raised his children to be good Jews, he never thought of educating them or teaching them to play the piano and other such worldly things, as Jews do nowadays. Meir said, "For my daughters a dowry is all I need. What good is all that other nonsense?" As luck would have it, he had bought up a pianoforte, quite cheaply, from one of the gentry who was selling out and leaving town. Try as he might, he couldn't find a customer for the piano, and it remained unsold for quite a while, covered with a sheet, till one day it occurred to Meir: "Here's a piano. Perele's growing up. She's as pretty as a picture. Why shouldn't she learn to plunk on the piano? Anything can happen these days. Maybe it can help her get a finer husband. What do you say, Malke, ha?" Meir's wife, Malke, agreed to it. The only problem left was where to find a teacher for Perele who wouldn't cost too much.

With time Perele learned how to play, exhibiting a real talent for the piano, even though, when it came to other matters, she was shallow-minded and not too bright. Her piano playing caused quite a stir in Meir's neighborhood. "They know how to play the *piano* over there!" the neighbors said. For that reason Perele gained more respect in the house. While her younger sisters were busy with housework Perele would sit idly by, her hands folded, or would dress up in her Shabbos best and go out strolling, acting as if the middle of the week were the Sabbath. Everyone had to wait on her hand and foot, treating her with respect. "Imagine, she knows how to play the piano—that's really something!" Even Meir and Malke fussed over her, while Perele looked down on them all condescendingly, counting herself their better. To strangers the Zeitchikes, as Meir and Malke were called in town, bragged constantly of their Perele's playing.

"Play a little something for us on the pianoforte, Perele," they would ask when a stranger visited, and they beamed with pride as she did so. "Perele can play the piano!"

But later, when Perele was a little older, her piano playing became a liability. She wasn't just another girl, she had to dress elegantly, had to have a pretty hat, a parasol, gloves, and all the other accessories that a "mamselle" requires. And didn't she have to attend the theater? How would it look if a girl who plays piano failed to go to the theater? But that was nothing compared to what her parents went through when it came time to arrange a match. Only then did they discover how much the piano had cost them. The bridegrooms they could afford Perele spat at, and the ones she desired, alas, they could not possibly afford because the bridegrooms Perele wanted demanded big money. Meir and Malke realized how God manages His world! Their daughter treated them badly, not at all like a cultured mamselle who plays piano but like a common Bardichev girl who can talk back to her mother and father. God knows what they would have done with her if the match from Strishtch hadn't materialized—such a happy, fortunate match! Meir raised his hands to God and said, "*Boruch sh'ptarni* —Thank God

I'm rid of her," swearing never again to keep a piano in the house.

Although her parents sent their daughter to Strishtch in fine style, they did not receive from her a single groschen in return, although she wrote them happy enough letters. Once there, she did not provide them with so much as the worth of a glass of water. She did not behave at all decently toward her family.

That's the kind of "madam" Perele the Lady was.

XIX

A New Character Is Introduced—Berl-Isaac Is His Name—and Yosele Rides in a Carriage

The rich man is lucky in all things. It's not enough that he is rich and can afford any luxury he wants, he is also always surrounded by a multitude of hangers-on who are willing to serve him for nothing, hoping they will gain some favor by doing so. The rich, attended by so many hangers-on, come to believe they are entitled to be waited upon—they must be worth it—and as a result they look down on these followers, as befits a master looking down on his slaves. That describes the kind of rich people the Aktziznikes of Strishtch were. Each of the three brothers had clustering about him his little clique of Jews, his followers—meaning his unpaid servants. Each hanger-on strove to be closer to his benefactor. If that benefactor showed the least preference for one, the others would redouble their efforts, turn themselves inside out, groveling in the dirt. One of the most dedicated and persistent hangers-on of Moshe-Wolf's, may he have a bright Paradise, was a certain Berl-Isaac. Who this Berl-Isaac was and what he did was hard to say exactly, because he had no particular occupation; he hung around Moshe-Wolf, made himself useful, and in that way scratched out a living. He was, in fact, distantly related to Moshe-Wolf, but he knew Moshe-Wolf wouldn't want to be reminded of it, so he set aside his kinship. What did it matter if he was or wasn't a relative, so long as Moshe-Wolf was rich.

Berl-Isaac had a way of walking slowly, looking sideways at people, speaking softly, suavely, sparing words, not being forward, as others were, and always turning up exactly when and where he was needed. For these reasons he gained Moshe-Wolf's favor more than anyone else in his household. If it ever happened that he was called to account and berated, Berl-Isaac would accept it, tuck it away in his pocket, and—sha!—quiet! "All rich people are like that," Berl-Isaac would say afterward. "Sometimes they have to get mad, so you have to let them get it out of their systems."

The entire time that Moshe-Wolf lay ill Berl-Isaac never left the courtyard; like a loyal dog, he guarded the house, on the alert, sniffing out and checking into everything quietly, walking slowly and inspecting every little corner. He had been told by Moshe-Wolf's two brothers to inform them immediately should Moshe-Wolf's condition worsen, God forbid. After all, he was old and sick and had no children; they weren't about to trust his young wife. . . . Berl-Isaac was quick to understand; he didn't need to have any diagrams drawn for him, and he did what he was told. When Moshe-Wolf was at the point of death both brothers were already in the house. As expected, Berl-Isaac didn't neglect his duties. After Moshe-Wolf died, Berl-Isaac remained on. When the master is dead the mistress becomes rich. Isn't that the way it is?

The entire time of sitting *shiva* and the following thirty days of mourning Berl-Isaac was always to be found in the courtyard, not leaving his post for a moment in case he was needed. But Perele the Lady had little need of him. Every Strishtcher person was revolting to her, despised and loathsome. Leah'tzi the maid hated him as well. "That young man," she would say, "with his quiet talk and his sideways glances, makes me sick just looking at him. I can't stand him!" Berl-Isaac was fully aware of this, and he tried in every way he could to placate her, to find her soft spot. "If not today, then tomorrow"—thus he consoled himself. "The time will come—*Preyde koza doh voza*, as the Russian saying goes—'The goat will come to the cart'"—and the time did come. That Shabbos evening, after Perele the Lady had bared her soul to her maid, Leah'tzi came upon Berl-Isaac as he was walking about the courtyard, dressed for the Sabbath, a kerchief around his neck, softly humming a tune, as is the custom on Sabbath evening.

"When were you figuring to leave?" Berl-Isaac said, sidling up to Leah'tzi, glancing at her slyly.

"Leave?" Leah'tzi answered, irritated as usual. "You're all ready for us to leave!"

"What, then? Not done packing yet?" he asked, his face crinkled with an ingratiating smile.

"What packing?" Leah'tzi said angrily. "He can't wait, can he? There are more important things than that! Listen to me, Berl-Isaac! You're pretty sure of yourself. I know you. I'm going to tell you something, but first you have to swear by your wife and children that it will remain between us."

Berl-Isaac's face, which till then had been smiling, turned earnest. Bit by bit Leah'tzi disclosed the whole story and again made him swear that no one else would know of this. Berl-Isaac heard her out, thought a moment, his squinting eyes darting about, and said to Leah'tzi, "Trust me. It's done. Tonight after the Havdalah service, he's here."

"Remember now, Berl-Isaac, you swore by your wife and children to keep it a secret."

"A secret, a secret!" Berl-Isaac echoed and slowly went off to the inn where Yosele and his choir were lodged.

The negotiations that took place between Berl-Isaac and Gedalye Bass were highly diplomatic. They were very cautious with each other, sparring like two veteran boxers, until they had worked out a mutually acceptable plan.

First Gedalye saw to it that without knowing the real reason, Yosele would agree to meet Perele the Lady. "There's this rich woman, they call her Perele the Lady," Gedalye said Saturday night after Havdalah, "who really wants to meet you. She knows all the big cantors and loves singing and she herself plays the piano. It wouldn't hurt to go visit her." Yosele obeyed him. He and Gedalye went over to Perele's home, where they beheld a large, brightly lit house with richly furnished rooms elegantly decorated with velvet divans, soft armchairs, crystal and bronze chandeliers, dizzyingly tall mirrors, flower vases, and all kinds of pictures in gold frames.

Upon seeing all this for the first time in his life, Yosele's head began to spin. "If you play your cards right," Gedalye whispered in his ear, "all this can be yours." Yosele stared at Gedalye in amazement. It finally dawned on him that his visit had been arranged with a match in mind. Yosele was ready to make an about-face and take off; he felt like sinking into the earth out of fright and embarrassment. "Run,

Yosele, run away!" he said to himself. "Run as fast as your
feet can carry you! Run home, run away as far away as you
can get, the sooner the better!" But it was too late. Ap-
proaching him was Perele the Lady, an attractive young
woman dipped in gold and heavily bejeweled. As he took in
this "Lady," Esther came into his thoughts—the devoted
Esther whom he would soon be seeing, God willing. He
had to laugh to himself when he compared Perele to Esther.
"Could I? Could I do such a thing? Could I exchange Esther
for this one? How can you compare them? No comparison!"
Perele the Lady gave him her hand, a small, white, cold
hand, and he felt that cold little hand scorch his flesh. A
mist seemed to settle over his eyes, his ears were ringing,
his head felt as if it were splitting open—he was lost. . . .

For almost the first time in his life Yosele heard piano
playing. He had heard it from a distance many times, but to
be sitting so close to a beautiful woman as she played, her
small, white fingers seeming to draw from the instrument
such soft sounds, such tender melodies—that he could
never have imagined. The room was soon filled with beautiful sounds, and Perele became even more charming in his
eyes than before. As always happened with him, things
quickly took on an entirely changed aspect: the house was
transformed into a palace and Perele into a princess; in a
state of ecstasy he arrived to the sound of miraculous, divine
music that melted his heart, caressed his soul, renewed his
vitality. He passionately desired to join her; he longed to
blend his voice with the sounds of the piano. Yosele the
Nightingale began to sing, following the same rhythm, the
music pouring from his throat, his rare, accomplished voice
forming such sweet, tender melodies that Perele the Lady
stopped playing to listen to him sing. But Yosele insisted she
keep on playing. As she accompanied him, his exquisite

voice poured forth sublime supernatural sounds like a nightingale's.

Gedalye Bass, who was reclining in a comfortable easy chair off to the side, had not heard such singing from Yosele as he heard that Saturday night at Perele the Lady's. Even Gedalye's corrupt soul, which understood only money, was elevated, sublimely satisfied as he heard Yosele singing. Nevertheless he reasoned it would be wiser for him to return to the inn and leave Yosele alone. Leah'tzi the maid had with great condescension served him a glass of tea on a silver tray, but Gedalye refused the tea, muttering that he had to be off, and slipped out.

Not till midnight, when he was getting ready to return to the inn, did Yosele look around and realize that Gedalye was gone. Perele, Yosele, and Leah'tzi enjoyed a laugh together, and it was decided that they would wake the coachman and have the carriage hitched up. But waking the coachman proved unnecessary; coachman and carriage were already in attendance at the door. Just outside the door Berl-Isaac was nodding off. Leah'tzi looked at his half-asleep face and said to him, "So you're the one who made sure the carriage was ready, Reb Berl-Isaac, eh? You really are something!"

"So, what do you think, Leah'tzi, is he mine?" Perele the Lady later asked her maid, standing almost naked and then flinging herself onto the bed.

"Of course!" Leah'tzi answered, covering her mistress with a soft satin blanket. "Of course! Couldn't you tell by his sparkling eyes that he's completely smitten?"

"Leah'tzi, dear heart, dear soul!" Perele exclaimed, embracing the maid and pressing her tightly to her heart.

And Yosele Solovey, sprawled out in the comfortable carriage taking him from Perele's to the inn, felt a new life beginning for him, and Perele's visage appeared before his eyes. He forgot where he was; he could think of only one thing—to visit again tomorrow, again to see Perele and again to hear her play. Another thought also flew through his mind: he imagined seeing before him the two hundred thousand rubles Gedalye had mentioned in passing . . . a plan was forming in his head. He pictures himself driving into Mazepevka in a carriage drawn by four spirited horses. The town stops dead, sees him, and is stunned. His father runs out to greet him. "Welcome home, Yosele!" Yosele takes out a bundle of bills and says to his father, "Here, Father—ten thousand, twenty thousand—forget about being a cantor, it's high time!"

And Esther? At that moment Yosele forgot there was an Esther who had been waiting for him so long, and when he did think of her he dismissed the question forming in his mind, "Why am I so troubled?"

XX

He Falls into the Net and Realizes It Too Late

It had been much harder to persuade Yosele to visit Perele that first time than it was to have him sign the betrothal agreement and then stand under the wedding canopy with her. Gedalye Bass made all the arrangements with the rabbis, cantors, and synagogue officials. He himself did the running around, the organizing, and making the preparations for the wedding. Naturally, Berl-Isaac, his partner, helped out. It was a considerable task Gedalye took upon himself. He also had to do battle with Perele's two brothers-in-law, the Aktziznikes. They absolutely opposed the match, adamantly vowing that, come what may, blood would flow in the streets before they would allow such a disgrace to take place in Strishtch. "Let her go, for all we care, to Bardichev," they said, "and throw herself at whomever she pleases. We won't allow such a humiliation of our dead brother, whose body isn't yet cold in the grave. What is going on? What kind of wantonness is this?"

Gedalye was not silent. He had the ability, with his half sentences, to dissuade anyone. He convinced them that it was an honor rather than a humiliation, God forbid, for their brother, may his soul rest in peace. Who knew into whose hands such a rich woman with so much money might fall these days? Yosele was, first of all, a properly brought-up son of a respectable father; he came from a long line of rabbis, and this very day two rabbis and three rabbinical assistants could be counted in the family. And second of all, he didn't need her money, he had money enough of his own. It was no small matter, the way Yosele could spin gold; a ruble was as dear to him as his own eyes! Gedalye, one can say, knew how to handle these Strishtcher snobs. Along the way he found out that the Aktziznikes had a grievance against the widow, something about a partnership entered into with a rich landowner. Gedalye set to work and persuaded her to give the brothers the contract—who needed it! This rankled Perele, but she reluctantly gave it up, and on the third day after signing the betrothal agreement they were married; afterward the guests returned to wherever they had come from. Gedalye paid off his choir and returned home with a sackful, more than enough money to marry off his daughter and some to put away for the future. All in all, it had worked out well for him.

Gedalye Bass had been worrying that Yosele's voice was beginning to lose its pure timbre. He might even lose it altogether, because he was at the age when the voice undergoes changes, and until he would establish his mature voice a year or two could go by. Now, Gedalye figured, he can have the voice of a hyena or sing like a fish for all I care, I won't waste any tears over it. Still, he parted from Yosele as from his own child, wishing him a long life of honor and riches with his wife and no further need ever to chant on the pulpit as long as he lived.

And Perele the Lady clung to Yosele, not leaving his side for so much as a second. Leah'tzi, humming a song, packed the bags for the trip. Her heart was trembling with anticipation, because in a few days she would be with her Levi-Mottel. Berl-Isaac helped her pack, ran errands, did odd jobs, and worked hard, as if he belonged to Perele. "Nothing is ever lost on the rich," Berl-Isaac reasoned. "I maintain 'The goat will come to the cart.'" But, alas, this time Berl-Isaac had made a grave miscalculation. When the time came to take leave, Perele the Lady didn't so much as spit in his hand. Like a plaintive kitten, like a timid wretch, Berl-Isaac stood by, his head to the side, grinning obsequiously, trying to be of service, waiting on everyone hand and foot, a pitiful expression on his face, and wishing them "Go in good health! Go in good health!" But in his heart a raging fire was burning. That bitch, that cheap tramp—may she break her neck on the way, God in heaven!—"Go in good health! Go in good health!" Berl-Isaac said for the last time, doffing his cap and bending over double while his thoughts went to the roll of bills Gedalye had given him as his share of the matchmaking money, which warmed his bosom and comforted him like a priceless possession.

And so our three heroes—Perele, Yosele, and Leah'tzi the maid—sat in a large, comfortable coach drawn by four horses as they rode from Strishtch to Bardichev with happy hearts. Leah'tzi pretended to sleep so as not to appear to be looking at how her mistress was hanging on Yosele's neck and how they were laughing and kissing each other, acting like lovebirds. That I've lived to see such a sight! Leah'tzi said to herself. The grass hasn't even grown on the other one's grave, his soul hasn't even reached the Other World yet, and already she's hanging on a new one! And how she ran after him—my God! Couldn't she wait a little? And she got herself a cantor, hee-hee-hee! If my Levi-Mottel were here, he would get a good laugh out of this! What these rich folks will do!

My mistress is also a good one with her sweet talk—"My soul, my heart, my love"—so long as it pays off. I lay out her clothes—dear God, may I have half of them. Does she ever say, "Share a little bit of my luxury, take a pair of stockings for yourself, for appearance's sake, or a shirt or an old dress, whatever you want"? Does she ever say, "Here, Leah'tzi, have a little something to remember me by"? Not a chance! Would anyone else in my place have put up with it? Anyone else would have broken her bones, not so much as a shred would have been left. So, is it better to be a stupid fool like me? For all I care, let her burn with her whole fortune, with all her *shmattes*. As for me, may God help me get home safely and start planning to get married.

These musings filled Leah'tzi's head as Perele and Yosele were kissing, embracing, and fondling each other. And the horses drew the coach with its three passengers onward, leaving behind fields and forests, villages and small towns. Not one of them noticed how time was passing. All three were preoccupied with their own thoughts, all had their own fantasies, their own gratifications. Perele had never been as happy as she was at that moment, traveling with her handsome "hero," her "angel." He was hers, hers! The very thought that such a "hero," whom one reads about meeting only in romances, that such an "angel" was hers, made her head spin, intoxicated her, and delivered her into a sweet, blissful sleep.

And Yosele?

Later on, when Yosele the Nightingale would come to his senses and look around at where he found himself, he would swear that he absolutely could not remember what had happened to him since first meeting Perele. When, where, and how he had married Perele the Lady—he could not for the life of him recall. He could remember only a thick fog settling around him, gold coins, diamonds and gems glittering before his eyes. Stretching out invitingly before him were several bright, happy, festive days. People were waiting upon him as if he were a prince. The princess, Perele, was sitting at his side, not leaving him for a moment, hanging on his neck, kissing him, fondling him. "Yosele, Yosele, my sweetheart, my soul, my hero, my angel!" And his head was spinning, spinning. He had felt as if he were in a cloud—confused, dazed—in a connubial Garden of Eden, in heaven itself, redolent with all manner of spices, where wine and oil flow and almonds grow, where birds sing and people go about without a care. And he is singing beautifully and sweetly and will do so forever. Perele is playing the piano and he is singing and the whole world resounds with voices, with music. He can go on forever this way, without a care, in this Garden of Eden, just singing and singing . . .

The journey from Strishtch to Bardichev in the comfortable carriage, the air so sweet and fragrant, with Perele close by him, seemed to Yosele like a delightful dream. He didn't want to take into account where he was going or why; he simply wanted the dream to last forever. But here on earth, where life lasts but a minute, a mere second, a dream cannot last forever. A dream must come to an end; the time must come to wake up, there is no use in wishing otherwise. . . . And when he did wake up and begin to look around at where he was, like a drunkard waking up sober after a drinking bout, he wondered what he had done. God in heaven, he thought. What am I doing here?

He saw around him a sprawling city, dingy, bleak, muddy. Men and women streamed through the streets. Coachmen shouted, shopkeepers hawked their wares, fish-wives cursed. The stench of the mud was so strong that one had to cover one's nose. Where had he landed? In Bardi-chev. The coach had come to a halt in front of a dirty, square outer wall, and after passing through a dark alley with mud-covered steps, they came to a house. Yosele saw standing before him a tall, thin, wrinkled man wearing a cap and, alongside of him, a short, fat woman wearing a large bow under her chin and a headband on her forehead. The tall man greeted him, kissed him, and the fat woman spoke to him with the familiar "du," congratulating him, and both stood back to look him over. These were his in-laws. Perele had informed them by letter that she was bringing home a fine inheritance and an even finer husband. Something to celebrate! Joyous occasion! Their daughter had come back, thank God, thank God! Her late husband's death excepted, may every Jewish girl have her good fortune! . . .

All of Perele's parents' friends gathered to give a mazel-tov and to inspect Yosele, staring at him constantly. He looked all around him like a small boy who had just been brought to *cheder* for the first time. He was trembling, and everything appeared new and strange. He looked at his bride, at Perele, and she wasn't at all the same Perele as in Strishtch but an altogether different woman! There she had possessed infinite charm for him, there her eyes had had a different life to them, there she had spoken to him in a different way. The former Perele seemed to have vanished and another one had appeared before his eyes. Then there was the little matter of living in Bardichev! He wasn't used to this kind of life, to their talk, to the customs. Everything, everything was alien. He felt utterly out of place. What was he doing here and what on earth had brought him here? What did he have in common with Meir Zeitchik and what did he care about his business? What significance did Perele's loans and banknotes and interest rates and all her other dealings have for him? Perele, upon arriving home, had quickly become involved in investing her money profitably. All he wanted was to be free. Ach, God Almighty! He had not realized before marrying Perele that he would wind up stuck in this hell, among total strangers, never seeing the light of day, not to mention singing or playing piano.

Yosele would wake up in the morning, drink his coffee, and look out the window—dark, dreary, muddy—may God protect him! Then he would listen to a long harangue about business, again business, again percentages, again money. After lunch Perele would go shopping with her mother, cheating the salespeople and hunting out bargains. Yosele looked on astonished, listening to Perele talk to the women in their own slang, swearing and scolding like an experienced fishwife. Day and night an unholy racket, swearing and cursing. Perele quarreled with her sisters, screaming at them, trading insults. Her mother and father always took her side—after all, she was the aristocrat in the family! More and more Yosele somberly recognized his wife for what she was. Observing her as she quaked over a groschen and noting all her unflattering, unpleasant gestures, he thought to himself, Is this the Perele I imagined to be so refined and gentle, so decent, so beloved? Now look at her! He tried again to talk to her about his previous plans—to travel abroad, to study, sing, perform. She would have none of it! "You want to be a cantor?" she cooed, putting her arms around his neck. "What good will that do you, silly fool? Just wait a little and I'll invest my money properly, and then we'll both be able to travel in style to the spas, to the vineyards, for the 'cure'—you know, where all the rich people go, silly. And you're talking about being a cantor, studying, singing! Feh, dear heart, forget it, my sweet life, forget it and let me kiss your bright eyes and your wonderful golden hair, my angel, my wonderful hero!"

As time went on Yosele realized what he had done, that he had placed himself in bondage, fettered himself forever, for always. Like a bird locked in a cage, he tried thrashing about to free himself, and saw it was no use struggling. All those sweet dreams he had once dreamed were now vanishing like mist. Gone were those golden, precious fantasies of his, blown away like smoke, and in their place came other fantasies, other thoughts. Gone were the sweet sounds of yesterday, gone were the beautiful images he once saw before him! The carriage, his homecoming to Mazepevka, the wonderment of his acquaintances and good friends, the joy he would give his father—gone, gone! Other images took their place, another kind of life. In place of that former sweet-smelling Garden of Eden now stood before him the dreadful Bardichev mud. In place of palaces, a dreary house with dreary people. In place of singing, talk day and night of trade, percentages, profit, money, costs. In place of a comely wife, a vulgar woman who was always hanging on his neck, hugging and kissing him, not allowing him to leave her side. And everything was so commonplace! So ordinary! He was bored, the world and his life were tiresome, stultifying. Behind his back he could hear them talking about him—"That's him, Yosele, the one who married the rich widow. . . ," and it pierced him to the quick. When he looked at Perele he was reminded of Esther, and he began to fully comprehend the fact that he had committed a grievous mistake, that he had ruined his life, that he had behaved badly toward Esther, toward his father, and toward himself. He sank into a depressed, distraught frame of mind.

"Yosele, my soul, my sweetheart, my dear little nightingale," his wife, Perele, said to him when they were alone, she playing with his long, thick hair, "what's the matter? Why are you so distracted? You go around looking so preoccupied and pensive. Tell me, what do you need? Don't I deserve to know the truth? What's the matter? Are you tired of me? Bored?"

Bored? Yosele thought. Bored to death! But he restrained himself, gritted his teeth, and told her a big lie. "Bored with you? God forbid! What can you mean, 'bored' with you?" And as he said these words his thoughts, his mind, his heart, and all his feelings were far away in Mazepevka.

XXI

Mazepevka Talks—
and Poor Esther Has Her Troubles

Smart people have often wracked their brains trying to figure out how Mazepevka learns what is going on in the world. Mazepevkers certainly don't hold much with newspapers—that everyone knows. But let there be talk in the highest quarters of war, it is immediately known in Mazepevka. A new edict, even before it is proclaimed, is known there and the people study its significance, pinch it here and there, discuss it thoroughly, each person in his own way. The Mazepevkers have a remarkable knack for sniffing things out, because they rely on a richly intuitive sense for the natural course of events and for what is reasonable.

No one knew how the rumor had sprung up that Yosele Solovey had gotten married somewhere, had accepted a hundred thousand rubles as a dowry, and was no longer a cantor. One person reported that a rich man had heard him chant, invited him to his home, and had given him his daughter as a wife. Another person reported that Yosele had married a fifty-year-old wealthy widow. Still others insisted it was quite otherwise: he had married not a widow but a divorcée, and there was an interesting story to tell about it: Apparently Yosele had been invited by a rich man to a Sabbath evening meal. The rich man was married to one of those modern women, a self-styled lady, quite educated. In short, when she heard Yosele sing, she became infatuated with him and wanted to run off with him to the ends of the earth. The rich man thought things over and said to the wife, "What good will it do you to run away and humiliate me? Here's a divorce. He's yours." What do you think she does? She's no fool either, and so she says to him, "If you give me a hundred thousand, I will. If not, I won't, and I'll really give you something to remember me by!" They argued back and forth, others got involved. They finally settled for eighty thousand. And now, the story goes, our Yosele is a somebody. But the fact that he doesn't send his father any money, that is unforgivable! . . .

When the rumor spread through town, everyone said it was the way of the world, it stood to reason that Yosele had to make an important match; everybody knew that even beforehand; how could it be otherwise?

"Are you to be congratulated?" people asked Shmulik the cantor as they approached him in shul. "They say your Yosele has gotten married." "What, you don't know about it?" "Is it true?" "Of course, of course—they say he's very fortunate. A hundred thousand, they say, two hundred thousand!" "How did it happen? We hear he doesn't even write you any letters, Reb Shmulik." "Modern children! Go kill yourself for a child, sacrifice yourself! They repay you with stones." "A fine world it's become. What's the use of talking—a proper little world!"

Shmulik, when he heard, was crushed by these comments. "After all, how can Yosele do this to me, his own father?!" It had been a shame, a disgrace for people that he hadn't heard so much as a word from Yosele for almost a year, hadn't known what to think, and now—to hear this kind of news! Imagine! Imagine! To marry, become rich, and forget a father! It can't possibly be true! That was Shmulik's only consolation—it couldn't possibly be true! If not for the hope that one day Yosele would come home,

Shmulik could not have gone on. He had enough troubles as it was; recently, as the result of a severe cold, his voice, alas, had been ruined. Shmulik's once famous throat had become infected, and his "lion's roar" of a voice sounded dull and hoarse, like the sound of a cracked instrument. Where Shmulik could once sing in the highest registers, improvising in his purest falsetto at the top of the scale, now he could render only an ugly-sounding gargle like that of a slaughtered ox or the crowing of a young, immature rooster. Shmulik's chanting sounded labored and, forgive me if I say this, very artificial; no matter how hard he tried, no longer could he rely on his old powers! No more voice, no more sweet chanting, no more, no more Shmulik— worse than dead! The only thing that kept him on the lectern was his seniority.

To allow a fallen man to fall even further, to take his last crust of bread away, to cut off a man's livelihood—that the Mazepevka Jews, who were by nature soft-hearted, compassionate people and, above all, pious and honest Jews, could not bring themselves to do. Nor could one say they were saints either, but ordinary folk, for they didn't deal with Shmulik in the most decent way. They taunted him with snide comments and insinuations, asking him how Yosele was doing, complaining about his chanting and his singing. True, one couldn't altogether blame the members of the Cold Shul; they were, after all, very spoiled in these matters. They had gotten used to having superb cantors, excellent prayer leaders. But what could they do? They had to put up with Shmulik's chanting in spite of themselves.

For Shmulik his life as a cantor had become a life of torment and toil. But as if these travails and heartaches were not enough, once the rumor had spread in town that Yosele had married, Shmulik the cantor's wife returned to her old opinion of Yosele and began nagging and carping at poor Shmulik, rubbing salt in his wounds, as only she knew how. "A fine way to behave toward a father! Not for nothing does the world say 'You can't make a *chasid*'s hat out of a pig's tail!' Your Yosele was a charlatan and remains a charlatan! Now I understand why I didn't like him from childhood on. You can say I'm a good judge of character, I can tell right away what a person is like; he probably was the devil-knows-what from birth! I could never understand why Zlate praises his mother to the skies and says that such a saint as your Zelda is not to be found on this earth, may she forgive me, wherever she is now."

Shmulik heard her out and swallowed her words, each a bitter pill. It would be far worse for him when he had to see his good friends Zlate and Esther. What could he tell them when they would ask about his son? But he didn't have to worry about that. Zlate had once again quarreled with the cantor's wife and was busy with her own affairs, had worries and troubles enough of her own: a daughter had to be married off, and Esther was already, *keyn eyn horeh*, a full-grown woman in people's eyes, and there was no dowry. Without a dowry no one would take a girl these days; any ordinary man at all, a nobody, demanded several hundred besides gifts, and in the meantime Esther was getting older, she was almost out of her teens, God in heaven! There had been a possible match, nothing to brag about, but it would have brought with it a pot of gold. But how could a poor widow with tiny orphans make the arrangements by herself?

As for Esther, when she found out Yosele had gotten married, what could she have thought? Who could imagine what her poor, offended, sad, abandoned heart felt? She thought she had known Yosele thoroughly, and had always believed whatever he said was sacred. But in the end he had deceived her in such an ugly way, lying to her from start to finish. Esther had always felt that a son as loving and devoted to his father as Yosele was nowhere to be found. She could still picture him vowing as he was leaving home that he would never forget his father and would make him happy. She could still hear his sincere words and those sweet songs in which he poured his heart out to her and in which she imagined he was promising always to remain the same Yosele who would never forget his true loved ones. Now two years had passed and no one had heard from him, no one had seen him, and suddenly, out of the blue, this shocking news arrived! Yosele married! And married to whom? To a widow, a divorcée—for money! And he had done it secretly, ruining his life! . . . "My God, my God, that Yosele could do such a thing!"

Esther resolved not to tell a soul; she was reserved as usual, busy with the shop, keeping house, quiet, controlled. But what was going on in her heart? That no one knew, just as no one knew of those golden dreams that had sustained her for two whole years since Yosele had left home. One might say that those two years were for Esther one long sweet dream. Yosele's image never left her thoughts, and wherever she went and whatever she was thinking, it was of Yosele and only of Yosele. More than once Zlate had noticed that Esther's mind seemed to be somewhere else. "What's happening to you?" she would complain: "You've become so absentminded. You measured out thirteen lengths and only charged for twelve. And you called Gedalye-Meir the shopkeeper Meir-Gedalye, turning the shlemiel's name around." Another time, sitting on a bench near the shop with some work on her lap, she sank into thought and started to sing to herself, at first quietly and then louder and stronger, imitating the way Yosele used to

149

sing, without being aware that not far from her some men were sitting. Her reveries carried her far off to her Yosele, and there she would be with him, gazing at him and hearing his sweet voice, his heavenly singing, exactly like that Shabbos afternoon in Shmulik the cantor's house.

And sometimes she would imagine that they were coming to tell her the news: "Esther, guess who's here! Yosele Shmulik's, Yosele the Nightingale has arrived!" Then an unwelcome thought would flit through her mind, a cloud would pass in front of the sun, hiding it momentarily, blocking its radiant light, and Esther's thoughts would take a different turn and she would begin to worry, become apprehensive, and she would let out a deep, deep heartfelt sigh. But the cloud would pass, and the sun would again shine in all its glory. The bad thought would be banished from her mind, and those blissful thoughts would return— her heart would again be stirred with happiness and pleasure. The sweet dreams would reappear, spinning their golden fantasies, and again she would sing in Yosele's style. "What's happening to you, daughter?" Zlate would say, breaking into her daughter's reveries. "How does it look, I ask you, to sit in the middle of the street and sing? And in front of strangers . . ." Esther would jump up with a start and ask, surprised, "Sing? Who's singing?"

When Yosele stopped writing letters that last year, Esther suffered greatly, but she trusted in him so implicitly that she wouldn't allow herself any doubts. She defended him to herself: "When a person travels constantly, is never in one place, why should anyone be surprised?" And she hoped against hope. Then suddenly this unforeseen blow! A blow that Esther had not counted on! The news struck her like a bolt of lightning. She seemed to awake from a long sleep and realized that all her happiness and all her hopes were nothing more than a dream she had been enjoying for two years, the best two years of her life. All at once she was made aware of the deception and evil in the world, all at once she saw before her a horrid, bitter, bleak existence! But who could have guessed what she was going through? And who would have cared? Who in Mazepevka paid attention to a poor girl who one moment was as happy as a lark and the next plummeted into the depths of despair? Esther cried quietly in her bed at night, not once but many times. But her weeping didn't ease her bitter heart at all. To her misery was added a new misfortune to afflict her young years. That affliction was the rich man, Reb Alter Pessi's.

XXII

Alter Pessi's Becomes a Widower, and Reb Kalman the Matchmaker Puts Ideas in His Head

Alter Pessi's was a successful businessman. He made an easy living in Mazepevka as a moneylender. But he wasn't like others living off interest who barely survived. A Mazepevker moneylender existed in a constant state of worry and sleeplessness, dreading that one debtor or another would default. He soon became overly suspicious, imagining that everyone was out to cheat him, to take away what was rightfully his, rob him outright, take over his very life. In short, everyone was out to get him. And what would become of him if he were to go broke? He might as well sling a sack of goods on his back, heaven protect him, and peddle from door to door! When in the grip of such anxieties the Mazepevker moneylender would start cutting back expenses, squeezing every coin, doing entirely without, scrimping on the crust of bread for his own table. No, Alter was not of that ilk. He knew his Jews and knew full well that he could always get from them what he needed. Though he was much talked about with contempt behind his back, referred to as Esau, leech, Haman, and other such insulting names, to his face, as you might imagine, he was treated with respect. They addressed him as Reb Alter. What choice was there for his clients? He had what they needed, and everyone had to come to him.

So Alter lived a good life, making sure that his pot contained a succulent chicken and rich broth, that his stomach was full, and that nothing disturbed his tranquillity. Like the worm that has burrowed itself into the juiciest apple and lies there unseen, contentedly sucking and draining the juice slowly and methodically, indifferent to what is happening outside the apple, that was how Alter conducted his business in Mazepevka. What did he care what others said of him? Let them talk! As long as he was comfortable . . . If you would complain to him, "Reb Alter, you'll have to forgive me, but what good will it do you to take another ruble out of my hide, for God's sake? What will you gain from it? Will it make you rich? You don't have enough? Your wife and children are bankrupting you?" he would hear you out quite cold-bloodedly, and as cold-bloodedly, with a smile, answer, "I can't, honestly!" and after that you could talk as much as you pleased. Try to get a charitable contribution of more than his usual three groschen and he'd answer you so pleasantly, so amiably, "I don't give more, honestly!" and he would mean it, you can be sure of that. That's the kind of person Alter was.

Alter Pessi's was a fine, well-dressed Jew, compactly built, in good health although well on in years, with a prosperous look about him. A small beard gave him the appearance of a younger man. He had a substantial paunch—bloated, they say, with Jewish blood. His small mouth was drawn and puckered, his lips red and thick, ready to suck, like a leech; his cheeks were always florid and puffy, like dumplings. On the whole, Alter was an impressive-looking man, except for his eyes, which were decidedly unattractive; one eye was much larger than the other, and when he looked at you with the smaller eye it made your blood run cold. His gait was measured, his speech subdued, with an occasional squeak; a little smile always played on his face. Alter required everything around him to be spotlessly clean; his silk hat, his caftan of rich, lustrous material, his mirror-bright shoes were elegant and always brand-new; he didn't allow so much as a speck of dust to alight on him.

After lunch he would take a long nap and then stroll over to the market, for no other reason than to see this one or that one, have a little chat, "borrow" some tobacco from someone. "Borrowing" was his greatest pleasure, and though he knew quite well that behind his back he was despised for it, that didn't faze him at all. What do I care! he would think, smiling. When people came to his house on business he put on his best face, greeting each and every one with the greatest politeness, eagerly offering them the most comfortable seats and never sparing kind words to anyone, ever. But in spite of that he was profoundly disliked in Mazepevka; they could not stomach his unctuous ways. From all outward appearances they had no real reason to dislike him. He didn't so much as harm a fly, but nevertheless he was hated in town more than the Angel of Death himself; they could easily have done without him. But do you think he didn't know all this or that it bothered him? Not the least bit! That's the kind of person Alter was.

He was called Alter Pessi's after his mother, may she rest in peace. Pessi was a capable person, an attractive woman who in her youth, they say, was quite a beauty. Because of her beauty and ability she completely overshadowed her husband, Reb Chaim-Yeshaye, who sat all day in the synagogue studying and serving God. Pessi ran the household herself while she made a living from a small tavern. "It's a little place, barely earns me a piece of bread," she would say. But that "little place" brought in a substantial income for Pessi, enough so that she eventually built herself a house, bought a few shops, accumulated some jewelry, and occasionally lent out a few rubles, if you insisted on it. She especially loved to do business with priests. "The devil take them!" she would say. "Three Jews for one priest, forgive my saying the two in the same breath." There were even rumors around town that—but you know what those Mazepevkers can think up!

"What an amazingly capable woman, that Pessi!" they said of her, looking at Reb Chaim-Yeshaye, whom many envied. "A good woman, your wife!" people said to him in the synagogue. "A good woman—she's equal to three men, your old lady." Reb Chaim-Yeshaye wouldn't answer but would stare at them over the top of his spectacles, raising his thick eyebrows and heaving a sigh. He would sink back into thought, scratch himself under his small prayer shawl, and go back to the Gemorah. And in that way, sitting in the synagogue, Reb Chaim-Yeshaye once fell asleep for good. No one knew the cause of his sudden death in the midst of prayer. "Seems he was a strong, healthy man, and suddenly—there you are!" "Nu, likely his time had come, may he have a bright Paradise. He was a worthy man, an honest man!" they said in town. And Reb Chaim-Yeshaye had the kind of funeral many people would be proud to have after living to one hundred and twenty. "Well, well, he was a good man, very quiet and a great scholar. It's likely he was an ascetic." "Whether he was an ascetic or not, he was an honest Jew, certainly a kosher Jew, though not too clever, may he forgive me." That was the kind of praise they gave Reb Chaim-Yeshaye in town for a short time, and then they quickly forgot him.

Pessi continued with her business as before, doing very well with her priests, one can't complain, and no one could tell she was a widow because she never bemoaned her bitter luck the way widows usually do. Pessi sat *shiva* for her husband, honored him with the thirty days of mourning, as he had earned of her, wore a black apron as a sign of mourning the required year, and remained the same Pessi as ever, having in mind only her business, her priests, forgive me, and her son, Alter, long life to him. Pessi was a devoted mother; Alter was precious to her, the apple of her eye. From childhood until the day of his wedding he was tied to her apron strings. Pessi brought Alter up in a way envied by all the women. "She plumped him up, that son of hers, may no evil befall him!" Pessi invested all her love in him alone. "Like my own eyes," Pessi said, "and I had plenty of trouble having him. For more than seven years after the wedding I had no children. I thought I was barren. What didn't I do until I finally lived to see him born, and with him my happiness was complete."

Pessi didn't let him out of her sight; she would visit his *cheder* several times a day to see how the child was doing, bringing him a little something each time: some food, a snack, a treat. All the boys in *cheder* envied him, swallowed down their saliva, and wished they were in Alter's place. The rabbi didn't dare flog Alter; if anyone so much as lifted a finger against him, Pessi would claw his eyes out. In winter frost and summer heat Pessi didn't allow him out of the house. "The Torah, I daresay, will still be there," she would say. For learning, Alter had little aptitude, nor was he very industrious. Pessi knew he would surely never become a rabbi, but she didn't worry much about it. "So he won't be like his father," she said, and when he was sixteen years old she removed him from *cheder*, supported him for a few more years, and then made a good match for him.

Pessi's choice of a wife for him was a genteel, quite ethereal child. Pessi was an even better mother-in-law than she was a mother. Feigel, as Alter's wife was called, was treated like Pessi's own child; she followed Feigel about everywhere, not letting her out of her sight. "Feigele, is there something you want? Maybe this? Or perhaps that?" For Feigel life was marvelous; she was quite fortunate, but her luck didn't last long. Nothing can be altogether good. God punished Feigel and didn't bless her with children. Alter so yearned for a child, and Pessi so desired a grandchild, a blessing from Alter, that they both made Feigel's life miserable. At first, it started with a word in passing, just a remark: "Are you a woman with children that there is something to talk about with you?" And then Alter began to pout and Pessi, on her part, began to goad Feigel to try one or another remedy, to seek out help wherever it could be found. "I also couldn't have a baby for a long time, my daughter," Pessi said, trying to sympathize, "and when I realized nothing was happening, I tried everything, I went everywhere—to the devil, to the rabbi, to that Gentile woman I told you about, and in those few years I drank plenty of root medicine, God in heaven! What else? Is it better this way? What is a woman, after all, if she can't have children? If you have children, your husband loves you, and if not, God forbid, he loses interest or he even turns up his nose or spits on you. . . ." As time went on, Pessi became even more persistent and made Feigel's life a living hell, drained her very life away. "What do you need her for, the barren she-goat?" Pessi asked, badgering Alter. "Divorce her and be finished with her!" Feigel heard it all and it hurt her deeply, but she bore her sorrows in silence, her hurt buried deep in her heart. She began to ail, tried to cure herself by drinking root medicines and vials of powder, until she finally died.

It was not fated that Pessi should live to be blessed with a grandchild. There was talk of quite a few other matches for Alter. Negotiations dragged on, but nothing ever worked out. When it came to matches Alter didn't seem to have any luck, and so he remained a widower for a long time. Pessi had long since left this world and still Alter remained a widower. But did it bother him to be living alone? Not at all! Should a good match happen to come along—well and good—why not? But to pursue it, run after it—that it wasn't worth!

Reb Kalman the matchmaker wasn't about to take this in silence and persisted in his self-appointed task assiduously: He wrote letters, moved heaven and earth, frequently bursting into Alter's house shouting, "How long can you drag this out, Reb Alter, this torment, how long? It has to end sometime, it has to!"

"Why are you in such a big hurry?" Alter said to him with his usual smile.

"At least give me a few groschen in the meantime, a few, Reb Alter!"

"Groschen? Feh!"

"For expenses, Reb Alter, for expenses!"

"Who needs it!" Reb Alter answered and didn't say anything more that day.

That's the kind of person Alter Pessi's was.

XXIII

Alter Is No Fool After All,
and Tante Yentl Gets Involved in the Matter

Everything has its time. So it happened that Alter had a meeting with Reb Kalman the matchmaker at his house, in that little room where the money chest stood—the very spot Alter used if he wanted to talk to someone in private—and there they talked for a long time. When Reb Kalman left, his face was red and he kept snorting, nodding his head, and mumbling to himself, "Fine, fine . . ." And whatever else he might have muttered under his breath, no one knew.

Reb Kalman lifted the hem of his caftan and made haste to Zlate's sister, Yentl. Reb Kalman talked to her in secret a long time, snorting and coughing like someone who has something important to say. Yentl stood in the center of the room the whole time, cupping her head in her hand, listening to Reb Kalman babbling on as he dropped hints and repeated his words, until he finally came out with what he wanted to propose.

Yentl slapped her thighs with both hands and cried out so angrily that Reb Kalman, quite startled, reeled backward. "Are you crazy or just plain out of your mind?" Yentl exclaimed, heaping scorn on him. "May the nightmares I had yesterday and the day before and all of last winter fall on my enemies' heads! Some match! All along I thought you were talking about Zlate, and it turns out you're crawling off in another direction. What do they say—'Slowly thought out, but cleverly brought out.' He's no fool, your Alter, it seems. I can't believe my ears! Are you mad? Such a young thing, a baby, still wet behind the ears! Some match—summer and winter! Such a fine girl for such an old dog, a radish, please forgive me, a radish!"

"A radish, you say, Yentl, a radish? But a juicy radish—meaty, firm, I tell you, stuffed with money! May I have such a year, may I. What a stroke of luck this would be for your Zlate, a stroke. Here I want to hand her a pot of gold, make her rich, and she's angry yet, angry. You don't want to, so do as you please. I've said my piece, I have, and the choice is yours to choose."

"A pot of gold, you say?" said Yentl, now softening some. "The gold disappears while the pot remains. I also tried to rely on a pot of gold, as you know, and—how is it said—But never mind, if you want me to speak to my sister, I'll speak—a word isn't a slap. But I tell you right off, Reb Kalman, it won't work. Esther is a different kind of child, not like your ordinary Mazepevka girls."

"If it's no, it's no. So what? Are we forcing anyone, God forbid, like the police, are we? A girl is a hand towel—everyone wipes his hands on her, everyone. And what is Esther, what? A female. Here's a groschen, here. Naturally, if you play your cards right, there'll probably be more, probably."

"Yes," said Yentl, pondering all the possibilities in this deal, "but don't you think there will be objections on his side?"

"Are you talking about Alter?" said Reb Kalman, stepping closer to Yentl. "Not a chance, believe me. That one is dying for it to happen, fainting for it, and she says objections, she says!"

"That's not what I mean," said Yentl. "I'm talking about a dowry. Zlate, you know, can't get together even a hundred rubles for a dowry. It's enough she has to marry off a daughter and doesn't have with what, poor thing. How do they say—'It's easier to lift up a drunkard than a poor man.'"

"I don't know what you're talking about, Yentl, what. Do you think Alter is interested in your Zlate's money, is he? Too bad there's no one here to laugh, too bad!"

"If that's the case," said Yentl, putting a finger in her mouth and thinking it over, "if that's the case, we'll see. We have to give it a try. If you can't get over the top, you go around!"

"Make up your mind: if it's yes, yes—if no, no!" said Reb Kalman, opening his hands wide and bending his head to the side. "But certainly if you want it, it will definitely work out, no doubt about it. You have a way with words, praised be God. You just have to push it and not let it cool off, really give it a chance!"

"Yes, give it a chance!" answered Yentl. "I'll talk it over with my Beinish, and we'll hear what Beinish thinks about it—two heads are better than one!"

"Right again!" answered Reb Kalman. "If you want to talk it over with him, do as you see fit. After all, he's a man, and they say . . . really give it a chance!"

"Good, good! See to it, Reb Kalman, that you don't say a word of this beforehand, not to Zlate, not to my Beinish. We don't want it to fizzle out, do you understand?"

"Fine, fine!" said Reb Kalman and left Yentl, very satisfied, talking to himself all the way.

But promising to consult her husband was merely a diplomatic tactic on Yentl's part. It was proper for her to say she had to talk it over with Beinish. Truth to tell, she didn't dare divulge the matter to him. Beinish would ruin it rather than help. As a young man Beinish once considered himself to be a Maskil, a devotee of the secular Enlightenment movement in Mazepevka. He himself was from the big city of Kashperev, and Basya had obtained him as a rare find for her younger daughter, Yentl. As a bridegroom Beinish was considered a prize, a young man of learning; but after the wedding it turned out otherwise. He put aside his religious studies and devoted himself to other kinds of "learning"—mainly to antireligious pamphlets. In time the family found out about it and tore him away from the pamphlets. Basya was on the warpath; she wanted Yentl and her husband to get a divorce, and that was that. She argued that Beinish had been misrepresented in the prenuptial agreement, and she didn't want damaged goods. Basya summoned Beinish's parents from Kashperev, and together they managed to stand Beinish on his feet and make a decent person of him, like all the other Mazepevka young men. From that time on Beinish became a respectable merchant who never had anything more to do with pamphlets, while Yentl took over completely and taught him a harsh lesson: he should know what a wife means and remember that a wife has to be obeyed. In the privacy of his heart, however, Beinish remained a Maskil; he loved Maskilim as his life and couldn't bear the Mazepevka people, especially those fine Jews the moneylenders, who walked about the market, cane in hand, badgering the poor, sucking out the craftsman's lifeblood like so many leeches.

"Oy, how I hate them!" Beinish would say. "One God in

heaven knows the truth! I would like to string them all up on one rope, and first of all that potbelly Reb Alter, may he sink into the earth!"

"What has he ever done to you? Just look at him, how he's gotten so hot under the collar!" Yentl would say, throwing cold water on his ardor. "Don't you be so smug, Beinish. The time may come when you'll need a favor from him, and then we'll hear what you have to say! How do they say— 'He who flies too high has far to fall'!"

Alas, Yentl hit the mark. When Beinish became a merchant he needed to come to Alter for a loan, and from that day on he despised him even more. If anyone spoke of Alter in his presence Beinish would tremble with rage. Yentl was delighted by this turn of events and would often make a point, especially after Reb Kalman's visit, to needle him about Alter's wealth, inflicting verbal barbs: "And without pamphlets and without Talmud," Yentl would say, letting him know in no uncertain terms that she was onto him.

"I ask you, please," Beinish would say, "don't talk to me about that Haman, that enemy of the Jews. I can't stand to hear his name!"

"What did he ever do to you?" Yentl would ask him, twisting her mouth to the side. "Just because he's rich, whose business is that? A lot of people could be as rich as Alter if they had his brains. Interest grows without rain, stupid."

"Please, I'm begging you, Yentl, don't mention his *traif* name! Do me a favor, don't remind me of him!"

"Look at him, this holier-than-thou, how he's talking! He sounds off and everybody is supposed to listen. Why are you so critical? We're talking about Alter, and I say he isn't as bad as they make him out to be. Everyone has enemies, how do they say—?"

"Who cares what they say? Tell me better, Yentl, why are you suddenly going on like this about Alter? Something has to be up, something's fishy."

"What fishy? Ridiculous! It's true what they say—Once a fool, always a fool. What it takes a mute a year to say, you can say in a minute."

"No, Yentl, I know you better than that. Something's going on."

"You know what, Beinish? Better be quiet. How do they say—Talk less and mean more. An ox, you understand me, can have a long tongue but still can't blow shofar. That's the same with you. Even if someone tries to work something out with you, right away you bring in your high-flown words. They found a sage—Beinish! Big blowhard! The geese are frightened! Go, go, get out of my sight!"

Some discussion! Beinish loved his wife, and it was especially when she insulted him through and through and cursed him out that he would become soft as dough and let himself be kneaded. And Yentl kneaded him, doing with him what she wanted. "Listen, Beinish, I'm only asking one thing of you—listen and shut up, because even a kitten can wreck a good thing."

XXIV

Yentl Does Her Job
and Things Naturally Go Alter's Way

Meddling in other people's affairs, giving gratuitous advice, offering an uninvited opinion, and sticking one's nose in another's pot are all activities every Jew enjoys. But meddling in matters that concern the heart, keeping in mind this one's son or that one's daughter, finding for each his or her intended, making this match and arranging that match—at that, you see, the Mazepevkers were great experts, the best in the world. Every Jew there was a matchmaker—not, perish the thought, for the commission; if a matchmaker's fee happened to work out, well and good, who would turn down an extra ruble? But there were many who didn't even consider the fee—they did it, plainly, for the love of God. They would spot a boy and a young girl, a widower and a widow, a divorced husband and a divorcée, and immediately it would pop into their minds: "Ay, that would be perfect! Truly, a perfect match!" And they would get right down to business, entirely for the other person's good—the widower was matched up with the young girl, the boy could take the divorcée, and the divorced husband was made to measure for the widow. They weren't lazy when it came to these matters; they set aside their own affairs, devoted themselves entirely to the task, and threw themselves into it, doing everything possible to make sure the match would work out, as if it were essential to their very lives and livelihoods. It galled them to see an old bachelor or a girl getting on in her years. "What are they waiting for," they complained, "till their hair turns gray?" Worst of all to them was an unmarried girl; she was an embarrassment to people, men began to treat her too freely, as if she were a man, and women looked at her as if she were moldy horseradish, something disagreeable, and they turned up their noses. Everyone had pity on her, and it was a big *mitzvah* before God to put the bridal veil on her.

"You may get angry, Zlate, but you can't set the truth aside. How is it said in Russian, *Za pravdu byut*—'For the truth you get beaten'? I'm an older sister so I can say freely what's in my heart. Your Esther is certainly a wonderful, a dear and honest girl. May the year ahead be as wonderful! May my problems in making a living be as great as yours in finding a match for her. But you still mustn't forget that she isn't a young girl anymore. You in her years already had two or three children. . . . May I have such a good life as she has a good name in town! But of course, when I hear them saying of your daughter 'There goes the old maid,' I feel a knife turn in my heart. What more can I say? What is that saying, 'Bother me it doesn't, it only boils and burns me up.'"

These were the reproaches of Zlate's older sister, Breine the bead-seller. Breine was a stout, earthy woman with a man's voice and an asymmetrical pockmarked face with black whiskers on her upper lip. In town she was known as a wise, honest, pious woman, devoted to poor people, for whom she frequently served as an advocate. Together with another woman, she would go from house to house collecting donations in a large handkerchief for poor pregnant women, dowries for poor orphans, bread for paupers, and so on. One couldn't say she was greatly beloved in town, because she was constantly hounding people with her frequent charity campaigns. "Here she comes again, the female *gabbai*, with her kerchief," they would say when they saw her coming from a distance. Her husband, Moshe-Abraham Zaliaznik, had his own business—an iron foundry—and Breine, who was, after all, raised by Basya the wholesaler, couldn't sit idle without employment, so she invested her money in beads. Her husband derived little benefit from her business dealings, as all of her meager earnings went to the poor—the poor pregnant women and the poor brides she would marry off. But what could he do about it? Basya's daughters didn't appreciate advice from their men. Breine's words of reproach had a profound effect on Zlate.

"What can I do, a widow with three little orphans?" Zlate asked her. "How can I help it if the right one doesn't come along for her? I can't make it happen if it won't happen. You can imagine, life is bitter enough for me, and when I look at Esther, *keyn eyn horeh*—" Here Zlate broke down in tears, and Breine consoled her as much as she could, maintaining that Esther wasn't a "lost cause" she had to cry over. "When the time comes, she'll find a match. He'll find her himself, because there aren't so many Esthers in town. Let's not fool ourselves. God helps if only He wants to. Believe me, God willing, you will have plenty of *naches* from her."

But that wasn't the way Zlate's younger sister, Yentl, handled the situation; she took the matter equally seriously but used a different approach. She knew how to achieve her goal one step at a time, and she had plenty of time. Yentl was a housewife, not a businesswoman like Breine or Zlate. She was the youngest of Basya the wholesaler's three daughters, the *mizinka*, and had been brought up by Basya in her later years when she hadn't had the same time to devote to her youngest daughter's proper upbringing as she had had for the older daughters. As a result Yentl was always the lazy one. She preferred to gossip and meddle in other people's lives and especially in matters concerning matchmaking, husband and wife, brother and sister. She loved to stick her nose into these matters, throw in a word, stir up some trouble, and afterward, when others were tearing each other's hair out, Yentl would stand off at a distance, quiet, polite, innocent as a lamb.

Understandably, where they knew Yentl for what she was—and they knew her everywhere because she turned up like a bad penny—they were careful to avoid her. If two women were speaking together in the market and Yentl would come by, they would both immediately stop talking. "Sha, here comes that troublemaker. Who needs her?" Even between her own sisters Yentl had caused so much trouble that Breine and Zlate often would not be on speaking terms for years. Yentl had a knack for telling something so convincingly that one had to believe her. Her gift lay in her choice of words, in her facial expressions, in her eyes. Time she had plenty of—there were no children to raise. Beinish was busy at work—he was a grain dealer—and all doors were open to her because she was Basya the wholesaler's daughter. Yentl was no fool. Reb Kalman knew whom to choose for his business concerning Alter. Yentl threw herself into her task so assiduously, so cunningly, that Zlate, who was herself not born yesterday, did not detect so much as a hint of manipulation or of anything underhanded. When she talked to Zlate about Alter, Yentl ridiculed him and put him down for the way he conducted his life.

"What a way to live!" Yentl said in passing. "All alone with the four walls! Eats and drinks and counts his money. He's rich as Korech, I imagine. What does he lack? A headache, I suppose? If he were only a little younger, they would arrange a bride for him even if she came without money."

"That's what you think!" Zlate answered her. "That one would sell his soul for money. How can you say that?"

"You're very wrong, Zlate. Kalman swore to me that he's looking for a match for Alter and especially among ordinary people, as long as they're respectable, even if they don't have money. It just has to be someone worthwhile, and he'll even throw in something extra himself. I'm telling you the truth, Zlate, if I had children—not like God punished me—and especially a fine daughter, I wouldn't waste any words. Who cares if he's a scoundrel so long as a child is provided for, eh? Listen, Zlate, call me a fool as long as you give me a honey cake."

Yentl passed the time of day quite often conversing with her sister and would so ingeniously bring up the topic of Alter that Zlate never so much as suspected Yentl's plan. Once Zlate let it slip out. "Do you think, Yentl, there's a chance my Esther would want him?"

"What are you talking about? Are you crazy?" Yentl protested. "What's the matter? Is your Esther such an ugly girl that you want to get rid of her? What are you talking about? Just words!"

"Ay, don't say that, Yentl, God alone knows my suffering. You think it's so good to hear what they're saying?"

"What exactly are they saying, I'd like to know," Yentl said, feigning ignorance.

"What do you *think* they're saying? It's enough that they're talking about Esther, that she's already grown up, *keyn eyn horeh*. They say—"

"*They* say! *They're* talking! What do I care, Zlate, about 'they'? '*They*' don't mean a thing! Let them talk about death and destruction, for all I care. Better they should bother about themselves and stop bothering their heads about others! No, I really mean it, I just can't stand it when some people meddle in other people's business. I could tear them to pieces, all those who are talking! What is it to them that Esther isn't a bride yet? Why should it bother them? Why doesn't it bother me that Leah-Tziporah's daughter is as full of years as a sackful of thatch? Why don't I worry myself sick that Mintzi's old maid reeks of the grave? Why don't I talk about Ben'tzi the Redhead's three daughters who are well past the marrying age and not even a crazy bridegroom will so much as stick his nose in there? Why don't I raise a fuss about Malkeh Henni's daughter-in-law who suddenly cast off her wig? Really! Just because her husband got some money? Don't worry, he certainly won't go bankrupt. And Golde the bead-seller's daughter—didn't she sneak a kiss last week from that errand boy under the pushcart at the fair? I can't stand it, it burns me up, it drives me to distraction when I hear how they're always backbiting and tearing down other people, only others!"

Yentl had flared up so angrily that she left boiling mad, seeming to forget what she had come for. A few days later she again visited Zlate's shop, sat down on a bench outside with some mending in her lap, and remarked, "Listen, Zlate, I've had a chance to think it over at home. I had a long discussion with my Beinish about what you said the other day. I decided it's not as out of the question as I thought at first. How do they say, 'Straight as a poker, straight to the mark.' They do say about him that he's rich, stuffed with money, and since he has no children . . ."

"Really, he never had any children?" Zlate asked, deep in thought, scratching her head under her wig with a knitting needle.

"What are you talking about?" said Yentl, laying aside her work. "They tried to have a child. His wife was sickly. Don't you remember Feigel? She was always frail, may she forgive me, from who-knows-what, always doctoring herself. She miscarried a few times and stopped trying to get pregnant."

"I had a talk with Esther," said Zlate with a sigh, "and she had nothing to say. Do I know what she means by her silence? Today's children—try and guess what's going on with them! But Esther is the kind of child, *keyn eyn horeh*, who realizes her circumstances and has never gone against me."

"Nu, and that one really wants her, do you think?" Yentl asked innocently.

"Does he want her, you're asking? You make me laugh, really! He can't sit still! He's sent Kalman over several times and he himself has been to my shop a couple of times already, just when Esther happens to be standing near me— and you ask if he wants her! That one is ready to make her rich, and she says that!"

"Is that so?" said Yentl, pretending not to know anything, and she changed the subject to everyday matters: geese, jam, well-baked challah for Shabbos, and things of that sort.

Zlate never sat down with Esther with the aim of talking about a match or marriage, but the subject would come up between them often enough. Zlate's greatest satisfaction was putting by a groschen or two spared from her expenses in order to enrich her daughter's trousseau. In Zlate's hope chest for Esther were accumulated over the years a half dozen shirts, beautifully worked borders and lace yokes in the latest fashion, embroidered sheets, a few piqué quilts, cotton for making stockings, and more. The chest was for Zlate a kind of a safe, a bank where, little by little, one item at a time was laid away from her earnings for Esther's sake.

"Why are you squirreling things away?" Yentl once said to her, seeing Zlate busying herself with the chest.

"Why am I squirreling things away?" Zlate answered resentfully. "Maybe for the sake of her future husband—can't you figure that out?"

"Not thought out but well brought out!" Yentl answered her with a newly minted aphorism, as was her style. "May I have what I wish you, do you hear? I see you gathering things, so I ask for whose sake. For a word you shouldn't get a slap, right? Let's agree on that."

"You know very well—why fool ourselves—that this is

Esther's hope chest for her wedding, may God make it happen soon—Lord Almighty, it's time already!"

Esther, who was sitting nearby, had to turn her head away toward the window so as to hide her blushing face.

Once, on a winter evening, Zlate sat at the side of the stove working over a feather sorter while Esther sat at her side on a bench sewing little *arbe-kanfes*, ritual garments, for the children, Ephraim and Menashe. The conversation between Zlate and Esther had long since run out, and they sat silently absorbed in their work. Not a sound was heard in the house or outdoors. Only the old gray tomcat would occasionally wheeze as he sat purring on top of the stove. Suddenly Zlate let out a sigh, almost like a hiccup, with a catch in her throat, "Vey, vey, vey!"

"What's the matter, Mama?" Esther asked, alarmed.

"What 'What's the matter'?" Zlate replied.

"Why are you sighing so deeply?" Esther asked, laying aside her work.

"Why am I sighing?" said Zlate. "A sigh came, so I sighed. Of course, if I were feeling good, I wouldn't be sighing. I'm not sighing out of happiness, am I? Once you start to think things over from every angle, all kinds of thoughts come into your head. But it's nothing. You worry, you want to solve all the world's problems."

"What good will worrying do?" said Esther amiably to her mother. "You see that it's God who prevails over us, as with all Jews. Soon the farmers will be paying us their bills. With God's help, we'll take in some money."

"Money-shmoney!" said Zlate, "I have more important worries than that—I'm talking about children. They grow up, and something has to become of them, and I can't even begin to help them. I'm talking about you. What, I ask you, what good, in fact, is Zalman's coming around here? For pity's sake, there's no dowry, and without a dowry you can't get anyone, but he thinks there's a possibility, so he hangs around. Go tell someone what's going on in your heart! And in the meanwhile time doesn't stand still and a day stretches into a year. May I never live to hear my child called 'a gray-haired spinster—'"

At that moment the door flew open and Ephraim and Menashe burst in from *cheder*, their faces flaming from the frost, wearing feather-filled jackets and round little embroidered hats, paper lanterns in their hands.

"Good evening!" they said at the same time, throwing off their jackets. "Let's eat! Let's eat!" cried Menashe, pulling at Esther's dress.

"Sha, sha, it's coming, it's coming!" said Esther, getting up and serving the children a supper of dumplings and beans.

Ephraim was only one year older than Menashe but he was more reserved, more mature-looking than Menashe. Pale, with a thin, soft-featured face and two long, thin earlocks, he truly looked like a scholar. "He's just like *him*, altogether *him*, may he rest in peace, but may he have more years than he had," Zlate would say of Ephraim, thinking of Levi, her dead husband. Menashe was a short, compactly built lad, mischievous, lively, who would eagerly ride the goat. He was a big eater, a gabber, a nosybody who was ready to turn the world upside down—but to study, not a lick!

"Mama, Mama, you know what?" said Menashe, gulping down his words with the dumplings and beans. "You know what, Mama? Ephraim can read a portion of the Torah by himself! The rabbi gave him a portion to read for Thursday—and Pinni-Meir Pinni's is a pretty smart boy, isn't he? Well, he didn't know anything at all about *his* portion.

Nu-nu, did he flog him! Just Pinni-Meir's luck, Reb Kalman came in to talk to the rabbi about a match. The rabbi is arranging a match, and Reb Kalman comes there every day and sits for three hours straight with him, and we boys choke with laughter, and in the meantime Pinni-Meir Pinni's has wriggled out of the rabbi's hands and knows as much Gemorah as a wolf."

"Nu, and do *you* know the Gemorah?" Esther asked him, clasping her hands over her heart with pleasure at the young children enjoying their supper after spending all day and part of the evening sitting in a crowded *cheder* lit by a three-groschen candle. And Zlate swelled with pride looking at her treasures; her heart was full of gratitude to Him who lives forever for His great compassion for her, a lonely, miserable widow. But suddenly Zlate's joy was marred. Ephraim, who till then had been sitting quietly, said to her, "Mama, the rabbi asked for money."

"That's true, Mama," Menashe chimed in, "the rabbi and the rebbetzin really asked for money. They need it for rent and for wood and for the market. Berl-Moshe Abraham's brought two rubles yesterday, and the rabbi was very pleased with him, and he told Pinni-Meir Pinni's probably ten times over that without money he shouldn't dare cross the threshold. The rabbi and the rebbetzin really want you to send our *cheder* money."

"Again *cheder* money!" exclaimed Zlate, and her heart grew heavy. "I owe him about fifteen rubles, so I have to send him at least ten. Tomorrow the farmers will pay their bills at the market. Any money we get has to go to buy merchandise to restock the shop—you can't remain empty-handed! But you still have to pay *cheder* money." And Zlate's face looked anguished. She went to bed distraught, her head throbbing. All night Esther could hear her mother groaning and tossing in her bed. A thousand different ideas went through Esther's head about how to help her mother in her need. Understandably her first thought was of Yosele; the two of them together would think of a solution all by themselves. As soon as she was married it would be easier for Zlate in every way. They would work hard and see to it that both Zlate and Shmulik were provided for. . . . But those bright fantasies were short-lived. Like a dark shadow, a dismal thought flitted through her mind: If not, God forbid, if it isn't my fate to have him, I'll work for my mother's sake. I'll leave this place and go somewhere else. Everyone says I could get the best position in a shop or in a business. Immediately this thought seemed outlandish to her. Who ever heard of a respectable Jewish girl hiring herself out? Well, just words. So what's to be done, she wondered again. Get married? She turned cold and hot at the thought. What! Marry someone other than Yosele?

The following morning, preparing to go to the shop, jingling her keys, Zlate let out her bitter heart on Ephraim and Menashe, who didn't leave her side for a minute, reminding her, "Mama, money, Mama!" Zlate cursed them out and Menashe even received two slaps for being insolent to his mother. "Good-for-nothings, pests!" Zlate screamed at her children, yesterday's "treasures," and with an agitated heart, handed them the *cheder* money with their lunch and shipped them off to *cheder*. Esther couldn't tolerate it and said boldly, "I don't understand. If you did give them the money, why did you have to punish the children for no reason at all?"

Zlate could not contain herself any longer. She lashed out, knowing full well her children were not to blame. But her heart was tormented from Yentl's and Kalman's pestering her day and night. Once and for all, let bad come to

174

worse, let the bubble burst, there was nothing for it, she had to blurt out to her daughter what was in her heart: "Listen to me, Miss Bleeding Heart, my dear, dear daughter! You're sticking up for the children? You feel sorry for them? Why don't you feel sorry for me, a lonely, miserable widow, the mother of three children? A daughter like you, grown up, thank God, who should long ago have been married so I could also enjoy my life a little, ha? Pity you have? Why don't you have pity on me who is breaking my back, drying up the marrow of my bones to provide for you, raise you to be something, not sit and wait for the Messiah to come and have everyone point a finger at me? What, just because your father was Levi Reb Abrahaml Slaviter's? I tell you, I still don't know what golden chair I'm supposed to have for that in Paradise! I just know that in the meantime I'm worn out, my life is blighted, and when it comes down to it your family connections are worthless. What's so terrible? Here's a man who's a widower—a very fine person, I imagine. What does he lack? Really, would he make me such a terrible son-in-law? A rich man, may all Jewish children have what he has, an honest person, and no kith or kin. He wants to make a match, he's dying, dying for it, and she stands around here with her pity! What's wrong? The pearls aren't beautiful enough? Did you ever hear of such a thing?"

For a long time Zlate went on, blazing, cursing, ranting and raging at Esther, who, of course, did not say a word, her only answer two rivulets of tears that ran down her lovely cheeks, slowly, down, down. . . . Zlate would afterward have given anything in the world to undo all she had inflicted on poor Esther, who was entirely blameless that dreadful morning. For several weeks in a row she tried to placate her daughter, gazing into her eyes and trying with all her might to make up for that awful outburst. More than once Zlate woke in the night, went to Esther's bedside as she slept soundly, stood over her as one stands over a tiny baby, and murmured to her quietly, "May all I wish you be yours, my soul, my bright star, my precious treasure."

Esther had long forgotten her mother's blistering outburst that dreadful morning; she had become used to such scenes. Besides, Esther was plagued by other thoughts and in her heart she harbored other worries. Her mother had not mentioned who this widower, this fine, honest person was. Zlate had not specifically named Alter to her daughter; she found out from her Tante Yentl. Zlate had kept it to herself until another one of her early-morning outbursts, when again she was angry about something, and she blurted out everything that was in her heart to Esther, this time not bothering to disguise anything but stating things quite openly. Indeed, Esther preferred having it out in the open to the previous hints and insinuations. Gradually she got used to the idea of marrying Alter.

Zlate herself was torn by two contradictory feelings. The first feeling was: Since when do I have to ask her at all? I'm her mother, and what I say goes! Since when does she have a say? What is she, the pharmacist's daughter who promenades with young men openly on the street, that she can say, "This one I want and that one I don't"? She isn't like the others, thank God. She is Reb Abrahaml Slaviter's granddaughter! The second feeling was: What if she really doesn't like Alter? He is, after all, an older man and a widower. It might be hard on her to marry him. Why should I ruin the child's life, a young person, for no good reason? And such a dear, devoted child as Esther is, may she live long years! Then a still different thought ran through her mind, a very different one: "What is there to talk about with her, with a

176

child, when it's for her own benefit? It's really a stroke of luck—so rich, and without children. What does she have to lose? What can she expect from me? The big dowry that I'll be able to give her? The trousseau I can make for her? Who will take her, a poor orphan, these days? And one getting on in years at that? And here is Alter Pessi's, who has become so warm and attentive . . ."

Alter, in fact, had never in his life been as warm and attentive to anyone as he had suddenly become toward Zlate the shopkeeper, even offering her a loan without interest. "It's a pity, a widow," he would say to people, who carried this back to Zlate. She was quite astounded by Alter's generosity. Normally Zlate wouldn't think of going to Alter's house to ask for a loan, and to send Esther—certainly not—he was a widower, it didn't look right. But meeting him once in the street, Zlate stopped to talk with him and confided in him a little.

"Really?" Alter replied with a kindly, earnest expression, "I had no idea you were so short on money, no offense. Why don't you turn to me sometimes? Your Levi, may he rest in peace, and I got along very well. A fine thing! How come, how come? And how are your children? You have three, don't you?"

"Three, may they all be well," Zlate answered, "but till now, not too much *naches* from them."

"*Naches*?" Alter said with a friendly smile. "What's your hurry? Or is it that you're having trouble making a match for your daughter? You'll get the right one. They say you have a very fine young girl."

"Praise God. You have to have money, Reb Alter, for that young girl. I'm talking about a dowry, and where can I get that?"

"So," Alter said, "*that's* your problem? Nu, at any rate, I mean this for the future. If you really need a loan, send someone over. After all, how do they say—Old friends are good friends!"

From then on Zlate began receiving many favors from Alter—a small loan one time, a low-interest loan another time, and no written agreement necessary, simply her word, as it is done between friends. But for these favors there was a price to pay, and she soon found out what a favor from a Mazepevker moneylender means.

XXV

Esther Feels Like a Guest
at Her Own Betrothal Party

It sometimes happens that a demon in the form of an outsider insinuates himself into a Jewish home, may it not happen to you. Only the devil himself knows where it springs from. The household peace is destroyed, and no one knows why people have become angry, sullen, and offensive toward one another. Just such a demon insinuated himself into Zlate the shopkeeper's home in the form of Alter Pessi's, may he never find peace.

As if Esther's unabated sorrow over Yosele were not enough, a new Gehenna began for her: Alter! Wherever she went, every step she took, all she heard was Alter, Alter! But it was still much easier to hear her mother speak openly about how she desired and hoped for a match with Alter than have to bear her mother's barbs and insinuations. Her mother would go on and on about her getting married and providing for her, about becoming a housewife in her own home, taking a wealthy husband, and living the good life, which meant eating and drinking well, dressing richly, bearing his children, and enjoying life to the full, not like herself, Zlate, the great Reb Abrahaml Slaviter's daughter-in-law who daily had to labor like a mule, harnessed to the business while her children must go without.

"Ay, daughter," Zlate would say, heaving a sigh, "may God help me! Be luckier than I was, don't rely on family pride alone the way my mother did, insisting I become Reb Abrahaml Slaviter's daughter-in-law. Nothing else would do."

"Better an ounce of gold than a pound of pedigree," contributed Tante Yentl, who seemed always to arrive just as these discussions were taking place.

One early morning Esther was sitting alone at home, busy with some work. Zlate was at the market and the children were in *cheder*. Yentl appeared at the door.

"Good morning to you, Esther, my dear!"

"A good year! So early, Tante Yentl? Sit down."

"Thanks, I've already sat enough and run around enough; I am completely hoarse from talking, and all with you-know-who."

"With whom, Tantenyu?"

"With whom, you ask? With that mother of yours, I think you know her? And entirely about you."

"About me, you say?"

"Who else is there to argue with her about if not you? Do I always argue with my sister? No, I truly mean it, Esther, a person can spit blood to see what's going on! 'Seems you have one daughter,' I say, 'and not a bad one at that, so what's the hurry, what's the rush to get her married? And married right away! All right, getting married is fine, but with someone suitable instead of chasing after money,' I say, 'and to be so stubborn about it!' 'I want my daughter to be well off. Go do me something!' says she. 'But I can't afford it. The times,' she says, 'are terrible—not only no dowry, not even enough to sew up a shirt! The child is getting older,' says she, 'and it's getting late. I'm already at the end of my rope,' says she. 'What can I do?' Of course, she wants to talk to you herself, but she can't bring herself to do it. She so much wants that match for you. Why shouldn't she? Let's not fool ourselves. First of all, it's a stroke of luck for you, and second of all, how do they say— around a tub of fat you should grease yourself!

"She asks me—I mean Zlate—what I think of it. Do I know what to tell her? I tell her, with you she doesn't have to hurry—the right one will come along. 'Where, where is the right one?' she hollers. 'Bring him to me!' 'Take your time, Zlate,' I say, 'he'll come on his own.' 'Without money, without clothing,' she says, 'without a thing to her name, naked, barefoot, poor, and getting older into the bargain! After all, Reb Abrahaml's granddaughter, oh my, is so much in demand.' 'Nu,' I say, 'if he does want her so badly—Alter, I mean—let him wait a little. What is it? Is he standing in the rain?' 'No,' says she, 'he's waited long enough!' He won't take just anyone, you know, and because you are you, it seems he wants to make you rich, you and your mother and your children and your children's children. 'I don't give a groschen for all his fortunes,' say I. 'It isn't everyone who has such a wonderful daughter,' say I. 'So the parents are hungry, so what? Oy, oy, oy,' say I, 'I should have such blessings!' So she gives me a for-instance about Bluma's children, because Bluma's children support their mother, a wretched widow. 'Where do you find such children?' say I. 'Esther,' says she, 'is the kind of child who would sacrifice herself for her own.' You would, says she, for your mother's sake, drown yourself. The sad part is, she says she can't talk about these things with you. 'That,' say I, 'is ridiculous. What's there to be ashamed about? Who can be closer than your own child? Make up your mind—'"

At that point Zlate arrived and a bit later Reb Kalman, and the three of them, Yentl, Zlate, and Reb Kalman, spent the entire day in talk, arguing with one another, insinuating, citing examples and counterexamples, telling stories without end. Finally Zlate burst into tears. "I'd rather go where my Levi went before his time than live such a life! I tell you the truth, I really envy him for being spared the hardships I have to live through day after day."

"Be careful what you say," Yentl interrupted. "Thank God you have children who know and understand what's good for them at least and aren't at odds with you, as many of today's girls are."

What could Esther have replied to that? Could she tell her mother she had been waiting for Yosele and he had deceived her? How would that look? Was it fitting for a young Jewish girl to have such things to tell? Could she find fault with Alter? Who was she to differ with a mother about a match? How could she even bring herself to say the words? And if not Alter, it would be another shlemazel. No one had to remind her of her bitter lot; she herself knew the fate among Jews of a poor girl—and a Jewish convent doesn't exist. But what affected her most were her mother's tears, which were always difficult for her to tolerate. She gave herself into the hands of those who wanted, more than anything in the world, to provide for her future, to make her forever happy, so that she would never forget them.

Meek as a lamb, Esther let herself be bound hand and foot. Whatever they asked of her, she agreed to, not voicing any complaint—sha, quiet, fine and proper.

Alter, on his part, was magnanimous with his future mother-in-law, offering to pay for the *knos-mol*—the betrothal party—and cover all other expenses. Overnight he became soft, gentle, and good-natured. "Butter wouldn't melt in his mouth," Yentl said of him as she rushed back and forth, burning with a demonic fire, as if she herself had accomplished who knows what marvelous deed. Zlate inspected the wedding presents Alter had sent over in advance of the betrothal party, turning them this way and that way in her hand, appraising them with Breine's and Yentl's help and that of other such experts on pearls and gold. Never had Alter been so talkative and so extraordinarily affable. He would bear the cost of the wedding and the bridal gown; he would take care of all expenses. "Zlate has struck it rich, no bad luck to her!" That's the way they talked in town and said outright that they envied her. Every Mazepevka Jew would wish himself the good fortune Zlate had arranged for her daughter.

"What are you talking about? That's more than a stroke of luck!" they said. "It's a *miracle!* And not every Purim does a miracle like that happen! To take a girl as is, cover her with fine clothes and jewels, and make her into a lady overnight! A miracle! That's *really* a miracle!"

Gathered together at the betrothal party at Zlate's were her whole family and good friends, men and women. Shmulik the cantor took it upon himself to draw up the engagement contract. When Zlate saw how sorrow had aged Shmulik, her heart ached for him. She couldn't bear to go over to him and ask him about Yosele. She busied herself with her guests. The women were having a wonderful time chatting with each other, as usually happens among women when they get together, especially at a celebration. They all talked at once, each telling a different story, but nevertheless they were able somehow to follow one another's accounts. The men, as usual, poked fun at the women: "Look at them! Just like geese!" They themselves talked more than enough, drinking and toasting l'*chayim*, wishing Zlate and Alter the best, as well as salvation and consolation to all of Israel, as they sighed, turning glazed eyes toward the ceiling. Shmulik the cantor, while offering a l'*chayim*, began to toast Zlate with the wish, "May God grant— Oy!" and broke down right in the middle of the toast, letting out the "Oy!" from the depths of his heart. Zlate understood that "Oy!" and answered "Amen." She left him quickly to go to the other guests, who were sitting with filled glasses, waiting for her to join them so that she could offer the customary response to their l'*chayim*s.

The one and only Reb Kalman was walking about the house a bit tipsy, his hands clasped behind his back, talking to himself, as was his habit, wrinkling his brow and shaking his head like a person concentrating on important matters. Reb Kalman was never one to refuse a little drop; on the contrary, he was hardly against taking more than a drop. A wise person knows when to drink and when not to. There is a time for all things; at a wedding, quite appropriate—then Reb Kalman can indulge himself, as one should, be lively and act up a bit. But at a betrothal party, when the time would soon come for both sides to talk about the matchmaker's fee, for which a matchmaker should have a clear head to bargain over his share—then one has to have all his wits about him. The guests may drink as much as they can hold, why not? The matchmaker has to keep his head on his shoulders and know what has to be done.

In the midst of all the excitement at the betrothal party the bride went unnoticed. Esther sat in a corner with Breine's daughters, five quite grown-up girls, not overly attractive but all ripe to be led to the canopy. They were all chattering, giggling, behaving coquettishly, telling funny stories in order to cheer up the bride. But, alas, it was difficult to cheer her up! Esther seemed strangely pensive, her eyes gazing somewhere far off, hardly hearing what was being said to her or what was happening around her. She was present not as a bride but as a guest, a stranger. . . .

Zlate brought her the pearls the groom had given her, as well as other jewelry: an expensive necklace, a costly brooch, a watch on a precious gold chain, a pair of diamond earrings—really exquisite!—two valuable bracelets and be-jeweled rings, though previously worn and apparently pawned, but nevertheless of great value. Esther, along with the others, looked at all the bridal gifts Alter had given her; she regarded them as if she were an outsider, as if they had nothing to do with her. As she stared at her gifts her mind was elsewhere; she could not yet grasp their consequences for her young life. She was leaving her youth behind, and soon, too soon, she would be going from under her mother's authority to that of her husband, and soon there would be an end to her dreams, those golden, happy dreams she was still enjoying.

Truthfully, even though the whole town had talked about Yosele's marriage, Esther still did not fully believe it. She tried to convince herself that it was a made-up story, a rumor invented by Mazepevker gossips. She still dreamed that at any moment the door would open wide and in would come Yosele, the same as ever—and then she wouldn't be ashamed before anyone. She would immediately inform her mother that Yosele and she had pledged themselves long ago to be man and wife—it was a settled matter. . . . These were her fantasies as she stood, along with the others, admiring the bridal gifts Alter had sent, while Zlate stood at her side, beaming at her daughter and thinking, Thank God for all this. It seems the child is happy. May God grant her a good life and much *naches* and much joy! Esther felt completely out of place at her own betrothal party, as if it were not in her honor. But at the loud sound of the customary smashing of pots and dishes Esther had the sensation of something giving way inside her. The bridal gifts fell from her hands and suddenly she grasped the full significance of that loud noise. From that moment on she knew it was the end, the end of her free life, the end of those happy, precious, sweet dreams; a new world, a new life faced her now.

Part Three

XXVI

The Story of Jephtha the Gileadite's Daughter Is Told

Do you remember the story of Jephtha the Gileadite's daughter?

Va'yidar yiftach neider—"And Jephtha vowed a vow"—as it is written in that portion. *Vayomer*—and he said, "Dear God, if Thou without fail shall deliver into mine hands the enemy, the children of Ammon, then it shall be that whosoever cometh forth of the doors of my house to meet me when I return in peace shall surely be the Lord's, and I will offer it for a burnt offering." And so it came to pass: Jephtha fought against the children of Ammon and smote them and they were subdued. And Jephtha came to Mizpeh unto his house and, behold, his daughter came out to meet him with timbrels and with dances: and she was his only child; and it came to pass, when he saw her, that he rent his clothes and said, "Alas, my daughter! Thou hast brought me very low, and thou art one of them that trouble me, for I have opened my mouth unto the Lord, and I cannot go back."

And she said unto him, "My father, if thou hast opened thy mouth unto the Lord, do to me that which thou hast promiseth forasmuch as the Lord hath taken vengeance for thee of thine enemies, the children of Ammon."

And she said unto her father, "Let this thing be done for me: let me alone two months, that I may go up and down the mountains, and bewail my virginity, I and my fellows."

And he sent her away for two months and she went with her companions and bewailed her virginity upon the mountains. And it came to pass at the end of two months that she returned to her father, who did with her according to his vow which he had vowed. And it was a custom in Israel that the daughters of Israel went yearly to lament the daughter of Jephtha the Gileadite four days in a year.

That custom has long been forgotten, and Jephtha's daughters have other customs today. I am referring to the nuptial feast that is made in Mazepevka before every Jewish wedding in honor of the bride and her friends so she can dance her last dance with them and take leave of them. This celebration takes place the Sabbath before the wedding at the bride's home. The girl friends sing as others dance a *sher*, a quadrille or a polka; they crack nuts and regale the bride one last time. She bids farewell to her maiden years and to her young friends, as she will soon become a wife among wives. This leave-taking ritual is repeated the day before the wedding, also in the bride's home. Girls who are invited consider it a good deed to dance a last dance with the bride, and the wives stand along the side clapping their hands. This custom has always been observed in Mazepevka, and, of course, for Esther's wedding all the customs had to be observed; not one could be omitted or overlooked.

Esther danced the last dance. The Mazepevka girls couldn't take in enough of her lovely face, though she was frightfully pale, white as a sheet. It was, however, expected that a bride would be pale, because she was fasting, and as everyone knows, a bride has reason to worry. For the last time her Tante Breine combed and curled her lovely hair while talking to her about connubial matters, gently preparing her for her wifely duties. These curls so accentuated the charm of her pretty face that Breine couldn't help but plant a kiss on her forehead as she said, "What a shame to cover up such a beautiful face and such magnificent hair. But it's all right, Esther, you're lucky, you've fallen into a good thing. Between us, I don't need to tell you about your mother's circumstances—you know them better than I do. Of course, a mother wants to see her child happy. A mother puts up with a lot of pain. Her eyes practically creep out of her head till she lives to see a child brought under the canopy. When you're a mother yourself, God willing, you'll know what it is. . . . And your mother, I must tell you, has earned it of you that you should help her out and go to her with a generous hand occasionally. One should always lean up against a sturdy wagon, as they say, and rich people, Esther, breed little rich people. . . ."

There were many other words of wisdom that Breine imparted to Esther while she was combing her hair for the nuptial feast. After the feast, when Esther had danced her last dance, her Tante Breine brought her the *Korben Mincheb*, the prayer book, showing her what was and what was not to be said.

"At the *al chet*, the confession, my child," her Tante Breine said, "at the *al chet* you must cry. As the bride cries at the *al chet* she prays to God for a good life with her husband and for healthy children. Today, my child, is a Judgment Day for you, just like Yom Kippur, forgive me for saying it in the same breath. You must cry before God so that He may show you mercy, inscribe you for a happy lot in life, forgive your sins . . ."

Esther stood up to pray the Mincheh service with heart and soul, as one should, and she wept copiously, though not for her sins, as her Tante Breine had instructed her, for Esther felt she had committed no sin, either against God or against man. But Esther wept because the wellsprings of her tears had opened; the tears came of their own, pouring out so easily! Esther had reason to cry. No matter how she looked at it, her life appeared to be bleak, desolate, and dreary. Nor did she have anyone to complain about or to blame. Was her mother to blame for wanting Alter as a son-in-law? Zlate was her mother, and her sole desire was to see her daughter become a rich housewife. Could Esther have told her mother she didn't want the match? How could she have! Esther wept because her luck had so swiftly run out, because her happiness had so quickly ended once Yosele had vilely deceived her. Who would have taken it upon himself to tell Esther a few years earlier that it would end this way?

Esther beat her breast as she recited the atonement prayer, and the hot tears poured down on the prayer book as she contemplated not her sins but Yosele's. Of all people, Yosele, in whom she had trusted implicitly, in whom she had placed her deepest faith, and whose word had been so dear, so sacred to her. He had treated her abominably, going off and forgetting his promises, not sending back so much as a word to explain himself. How badly he had behaved toward her! Only now did she realize how dear, how beloved, how ingrained in her heart Yosele had always been. She beat her breast in atonement, confessing to herself that she loved him, she had loved him always, as long as she had known him, from childhood on—and now she had to part with him forever, drive him out of her mind, tear him out of her heart, and forget, forget! . . .

Her thoughts turned from Yosele to Alter, and her blood chilled: not a person in town did not hate him for no other reason except that he was Alter—and this Alter was to be her husband! With him she would have to spend the days and years of her life, with him she would have to grow old, bound to him forever, forever! Alter would soon bring her to his house, would soon turn over to her all the keys, and Esther herself would become the mistress of a household. He would give her money for the market, she would buy fowl, throw them into a cage, fatten them up for slaughter, and prepare a broth for his sake. All week long she would stare at the four walls, hear people coming to him to borrow money with collateral, make sure he had everything he needed on time, waking up very early, running to the market to buy good fish and fat-marbled meat with a bit extra attached and a calf's foot for Shabbos. On Shabbos she would don her satin dress, put on her jewels, drape herself in her velvet cape, go to shul, and sit upstairs in the seat where Feigel had once sat.

With a start Esther remembered that while still a child she had heard people in town saying that Alter's first wife, Feigel, had left this world on account of him. She remembered the stories about Alter's poor wife, and her blood froze. They said that Alter had driven her mad because she couldn't have children, and his mother had forced her to do unthinkable things: kept her for days on end in hot baths so she would sweat profusely, made her drink huge amounts of hops, tortured her to death. Before the wedding Esther had asked her Tante Yentl if it was true what they said about Feigel, and Yentl swore to her that it was an utter falsehood, not a true word in it. "Don't you know what they can think up in Mazepevka?" Yentl had said to her. "Why do they make up these stories that I'm driving my Beinish into the grave? Do I know? How can they say that? As I see it, may all my loved ones have the life Beinish and I have together. God Almighty! What they can think up in Mazepevka! I tell you, I'm surprised they haven't come up with anything yet about your husband wanting to convert. What won't these gossips think of next? This is some town! May it sink into the earth! Day and night all they worry about is other people's business, slandering others, finding fault with everything though they themselves are so far from perfect. Only such fools knock their brains out slandering others. I tell you, this town makes me sick, it makes me aggravated. Feh, an abomination of a town! Imagine, if they can think up such tales when that one has been lying in the earth for so long! What kind of world is this? Thank God you have a mother, may she live to a hundred and twenty, who can look out for you so you won't lack for anything. Our family, thank God, is still around. So what's there to worry about? You're still a child, Esther, really, you're a little lamb, may I be so well off."

As she remembered her aunt's words Esther grew dizzy, and when she remembered about Feigel, Esther almost felt she would faint. People were pressing all around her, musicians playing, women dancing, her head began to spin, and she felt she might fall to the ground in a faint.

"Why does the bride look so ashen?" one of the relatives asked. "Is she having a difficult fast?"

"Don't worry," another relative replied. "Let her fast and pray to God above for a happy life with her husband."

XXVII

The Poor Bride Has a Difficult Fast

There is another nuptial custom in Mazepevka: it is the blessing of the candles by the bride before the wedding, which is observed as if it were a Commandment. It is fitting for the bride to get used to the rites she must perform. Let her know that soon, in a few hours, God willing, she will become a woman and, according to the Commandments, must perform the rites that pertain to women. Let her partake of the rite of the blessing of the candles and let her learn what it is like.

Esther's Tante Yentl brought her two candles in silver holders, and her Tante Breine, with an affectionate glance, placed in front of her a *T'chinah*, the women's Yiddish prayer book, which had Esther's name inscribed in it.

"First, my child, pray from this prayer book and then afterward say the blessing Shehecheyanu. It doesn't do any harm to cry, my child, when you light the candles for the first time."

And Esther began to pray silently from the prayer book, whose ancient text lacked all punctuation. She did not understand a word of it: "Thou Lord of the world and of the universe and the reincarnations above and the deep abyss below incline Thyself from Thy sanctuary and have mercy upon the head of Thy servant who stands here before Thee together with all the beloved children of Israel who are deeply committed to abide by all Thy wishes as a King abides by his Queen or as a bridegroom abides by his bride as I Thy servant have kindled the lights for the first time two

195

candles Thy sages told us and forewarned us of all encounters and also of all events and may Thy candles that I light burn brightly and clearly to drive away the evil spirits and devils and imps born in sickness all those who come from Lilith so they will fly away and Thy servant who stands before Thee shall be worthy of the merit of our Mother Rachel who when her children were driven into exile they were driven not far from the Mother Rachel's tomb where Rachel lay buried and did cry Mother Mother how can you witness that we are driven into exile the Mother Rachel rose up to the Blessed Name with a bitter cry and so spoke to the Lord Almighty Thou art a merciful and compassionate God which means Thou showest more mercy than the people thus had I more compassion for my sister Leah who did weep day and night so as not to suffer Esau's fate thrust upon her till her eyes did darken from great weeping today all the more so Thou God . . ."

Esther recalled the sorrowful story of Leah, which her mother used to read to her on Shabbos afternoons from the women's Yiddish version of the Pentateuch. This time she wept, not over Leah's fate but over her own bitter luck of having fallen into the hands of Alter, another Esau who was blighting her young life. And she wept, her face bathed in tears. But who cared that she wept? A bride was supposed to weep, have a good cry before the *bedekns*, the veiling ceremony. Musicians were playing, girls were dancing, men and women were frolicking, relatives were running in and out. Breine and Yentl, the matrons of honor, each took Esther by one arm, seated her in the center of the room on a stool, and began the custom of unbraiding her hair. The bride sat among all the wives in a white silk dress like a princess, her braids now undone. The women gathered round. Each woman took a strand of Esther's beautiful hair in her hand.

The musicians began to play a sad tune for the traditional seating of the bride on the bridal chair, and there ensued a mournful weeping among the wives. They looked at the bride's flowing hair, blew their noses in their aprons, squinted their eyes, and cried.

Zlate gave way to tears completely; her heart was breaking for her poor child. God knows in whose hands she was falling, such a child, such a dear child, woe, woe! And Yentl cried; why shouldn't she cry when she had no children, a misfortune! No matter how many times she had consulted the rabbi, it did no good! And Breine cried because everyone was getting married and her daughters were still at home looking for bridegrooms—five grown daughters, God help me! Young wives gazed at the bride and cried for her as well as for themselves. They knew very well that this "veiling the bride" really meant: A Jewish girl is bound over by marriage—she is transferred from one authority to another, from her father's to her husband's. Those who knew the groom and remembered his first wife, poor Feigel, wept for Esther now. They knew that Esther wouldn't be having it easy with him. And others wept because they remembered that their own fathers or mothers had died or that a child was lying deathly ill at home and there was no hope for it. And others cried for the sake of crying, because the klezmorim, the musicians, were playing a sad song, and the tears came of themselves.

And so all were crying and especially Esther—she had not wept as much in her whole life as she did now. She hid her bright, lovely face in her white handkerchief so her tears wouldn't be seen. The fast, the sorrowful music, the weeping all around her, and the many wretched thoughts merged together in her mind. She felt as if her strength were ebbing and she was going to fall senseless. Suddenly everything turned dark: black, yellow, red, and green pin-wheels, large and small, spun in front of her eyes, and then, far, far away, everything appeared brighter, and then finally she felt light, easy, and good, very good! She imagined Mother Rachel's tomb, saw it opening up, and a corpse in white shrouds emerged and motioned to her with its hand, beckoning toward itself, toward itself . . . Esther wanted to cry out *"Sh'ma Yisroel—Hear, O Israel!"* but couldn't. It seemed she had died; she was lying on the earth, covered with a black sheet. Her mother was standing over her body, wringing her hands and hitting her head against the wall, wailing over her poor only daughter. Then she felt them lifting her up and carrying her around the town past the shops as they shouted and shook an alms box in which to collect money for the burial of the dead. And thus she was borne to her burial place. There they placed over her body a black canopy, as is the Jewish custom when a bride dies, and they lowered her into the earth, into the grave, and then she heard a very familiar voice. She listened to the voice and it seemed to her it was Yosele singing. It was Yosele chanting the Kaddish for her, the prayer for the dead, and the whole congregation responded with an "Amen." Esther listened to every word that Yosele intoned for her Kaddish and to the congregation's answering "Amen." . . . Suddenly she heard someone falling on her grave, and several people began to scream, "Take him away! Take the father away! Take away the father from there!" Esther revived and realized she was sitting on the same stool they had placed her on for the veiling ceremony, sur-rounded by women and men who were shouting, clamor-ing, splashing water in her face, and rubbing her ears and nose; they were unbuttoning her dress, loosening her un-dergarments, and Zlate was crying, "Esther! My daughter!

God be with you! The bride's fainted! Let them take her to the canopy! Never mind the veiling, in God's name!"

"Hush, Zlate, don't shout!" spoke up one of the women. "Don't shout. Here comes the bridegroom's family—stop shouting, sha!" Alter Pessi's entered. He was elegantly dressed, looking well scrubbed, festive, and healthy, with a freshly shaven neck and a considerable paunch, his cheeks quite florid, his lips pursed. Behind him came the two escorts, the Uncles Beinish and Moshe-Abraham Zaliaznik, wearing beautiful silk prayer shawls and carrying braided Havdalah candles in their hands. In his hand the bridegroom held a *pruchas*, a ceremonial curtain from the Ark. He went over to Esther and threw the cloth over her head, and all the women showered them with hops and oats, crying out, "Mazel tov! Mazel tov!" After this ceremony the klezmorim began playing a *freylachs*, a rollicking tune, and all the women clapped their hands as Zlate began to dance. At last she was happy: God had had pity on her—she had lived to see Esther married. Zlate danced the *freylachs*, hopping and spinning, her arms akimbo, her face glowing, as a mother's face should when she marries off her first daughter. When they saw Zlate dancing, Yentl and Breine linked arms (till then the two sisters hadn't spoken for three years, had been mortal enemies, at sword's point), and both of them danced together toward Zlate, bouncing and shaking as Yentl sang,

Hop, skip, sister mine,
I'll complain any time.
You're not me and I'm not you
Still we're sisters through and through.

The klezmorim were playing furiously. Zlate, Yentl, and Breine were dancing, embracing, and kissing each other resoundingly. All the women were clapping along, hopping from side to side in place, and shouting, "Faster! Faster!" In their midst suddenly appeared Reb Kalman the matchmaker, his sleeves rolled up to the elbows, he tucked up his caftan and began dancing a Russian kazatzka, squatting low and then leaping to the ceiling. When Beinish saw this he grabbed his brother-in-law Moshe-Abraham Zaliaznik, and both of them began to do a Jewish dance, placing their arms on each other's shoulders, heads thrown back, eyes shut, stamping their feet, turning in place. Menashe and Ephraim, Zlate's young, lively boys, also couldn't contain themselves and jumped into the circle, prancing about like little calves—hetz-hetz-hetz! With every minute the circle of dancers grew larger and larger as they all joined in a chain and circled the room, shouting to the klezmorim, "Livelier! Faster!" They all hopped, danced, bounced, and clapped, and it turned into a jumble, a tumult, a racket, a din, as you would expect at a Jewish wedding.

XXVIII

A Yampeler Coachman Delivers a Very Strange Passenger to Lazer

As long as Lazer the coachman had been driving passengers from Mazepevka to Kashperev and from Kashperev to Mazepevka, never had he landed such a profitable passenger as the one God sent him once in the middle of the month of Elul through the good offices of a Yampeler coachman, bless him. While greasing his coach Lazer promised to bring the passenger to Mazepevka in record time, even before sunset; he could depend on his horses, he wasn't going to pamper them. The horses had to get them there in a hurry, and there would be no excuses.

"May it be God's will that this be true," the Yampeler coachman said in Polish to the passenger and then in Yiddish to Lazer, "Why should I lie to you, Reb Lazer—I really got you a rich fare, a big spender! I bet you'll get a lot out of him. To these people a ruble is nothing. Where can I find such a fare for the way back, Reb Lazer?"

"Don't speak in Yiddish! Why talk Yiddish?" Lazer responded in Hebrew.

"Why, what is it, Reb Lazer?"

"What is it? Don't you see how the gentleman is grinning like an unwashed corpse. What if he understands everything we say? Let's stop talking about him."

"He understands no more than a dead man. When you pass the black mill, Reb Lazer, it won't hurt to ask him for a little extra. It's springtime and the road is muddy. I'm afraid you're both going to have to get out and walk, and I have a feeling that passenger in your cab looks a little weak to me. So don't get lost, Reb Lazer, and go in good health because God is God and brandy is brandy—you understand me. Go in good health!" the Yampeler coachman said to the passenger, doffing his cap.

While driving out of Kashperev and taking the dirt road to Mazepevka, Lazer the coachman asked his passenger if he was from the seminary, because a year ago at this time he had taken two passengers, Polish gentlemen from the semi-

201

nary, very fine people. But someone from the cab was speaking to him in Yiddish.

"You didn't recognize me, Reb Lazer?"

Lazer the coachman almost fell off his perch. He looked around on all sides, under the coach, above him, and could not figure out where the voice was coming from.

"Reb Lazer! Ha-ha-ha! You didn't recognize me at all? Take a good look!" the passenger said again and laughed loudly. Lazer the coachman was beside himself. He halted the horses and stared at his passenger intently.

"You can go and skin me alive, kill me on the spot," said Lazer. "I don't recognize you! Something about you is familiar to me and something not. Are you maybe Menashe the clockmaker's brother-in-law?"

"What clockmaker? What brother-in-law? I'm Shmulik the cantor's son—I'm Yosele, Yosele Solovey."

"What!? . . . How are you? Greetings to you! And I, dumb ox, sit here like a calf, looking and looking—what a head! So how are you? Giddyap, giddyap, my eagles! Lift your feet, my carcasses! We have a guest, a guest! After all, a guest! So you're Shmulik's son? If you were to skin me alive I couldn't have told that you were Jewish. You're wearing your hair long, so I thought you were from the seminary. You're really Yosele Solovey? Nu-nu! The more you live the more you learn! I still remember your chanting in the Cold Shul. Ay, Yosele! And I, dumb ox that I am, I'm standing and looking so long, you could paint a picture of me! What do I know? He says a gentleman, let it be a gentleman. Go figure who it would turn out to be! Ay, Yosele! Giddyap, my delicate ones! Giddyap, giddyap, my carcasses!"

Lazer the coachman and Yosele Solovey were both delighted to be in each other's company. Yosele joined Lazer on the driver's seat and questioned him about everything that was going on at home, not omitting anyone. Lazer answered all his questions, as well as he could, without leaving anything out. He even told him about his old horses that he had just traded at the Kashperev fair and on which he had been cheated because the horse traders there are great scoundrels. . . .

"Such bastards, I tell you, you can't find their like even if you were to travel all over the world. They can confuse the shrewdest customer. They addle your brain so that you don't know which way you're going, left or right! Worse than gypsies. What am I saying—a thousand times worse than gypsies! Giddyap! Croak, my afflictions! Oats you want? My troubles I'll give you with my poverty as a dessert. May your hides burn!"

"So how is our neighbor, Zlate the shopkeeper?" Yosele asked, his heart pounding.

"How should she be?" answered Lazer. "She's making a wedding."

"What do you mean, making a wedding? For whom is she making a wedding?"

"For her daughter."

"Her daughter!" Yosele asked and lurched toward Lazer. "With whom? When?"

"She's marrying her daughter off," answered Lazer. "What's her name again? I forget her name. That Kashperev fair and those horse traders have so mixed me up that from there to here I've forgotten everything. May your bones burn, my carcasses, giddyap!"

"Her name is Esther. Nu? She's marrying? When? To whom?"

"To what's-his-name, that Haman, the moneylender, the devil knows who he is."

"Yenkl Meir Pinni's? Berl Moshe-Lippe's? Itzl Abraham's? Simcha-Dan? Getzl-Menasha?"

"No!" said Lazer, scratching his neck with the whip. "Ach, what's his name, devil take it? It's right at the tip of my tongue! He's rich, a black year to him, stuffed with money. He's sort of stout, has no children, his house is the third from the new synagogue—if you know where I mean."

"Maybe Alter Pessi's?"

"Alter, Alter! A violent death to you nags! Alter, Alter!"

"So she's marrying this Alter, Reb Lazer? How did that happen?"

"Do I know how? Or why? Or when? I just heard he was taking her. How come I heard you'd gotten married yourself and were very happy? Is that true, Yosele, my boy? Giddyap, carcasses, may you have eighty black years! Do you think we'll have a clear night tonight? Even in the middle of Elul, eh? God willing, maybe we'll even be able to reach the walled inn by morning."

"What do you mean by morning, Reb Lazer? You promised to get me there tonight. What does this mean, Reb Lazer?"

"I promised? You can see for yourself we're not standing still. We're keeping on going."

"Urge the horses on, then, Reb Lazer. Let them go a little faster, I beg you."

"A little faster? I suppose you keep 'fast' company, young man. It's easy to tell someone else to run a little faster! I'd like you to be a horse and see how you would go flying uphill."

"What kind of uphill? You don't even see any hills! I'll give you another three rubles, Reb Lazer, another five, just go faster, I have to get there faster, you understand me."

"Maybe you want to get there faster? You've convinced

me. . . . Giddyap, my eagles! Another fiver, may you both sink into the earth! Giddyap! Giddyap! It'll be all right!"

Lazer lashed the horses, beat and whipped their hides, jabbed them mercilessly, all the while cursing the Kashperev fair with its horse traders. Yosele returned to the cab from the driver's seat and soon was deep in thought, his hands behind his head, no longer hearing Lazer's goading and cursing or his singing in a deep voice a song without beginning and without end.

Fantasies, images, dreams—these Yosele had experienced from childhood on. He always welcomed his soaring imagination, its fantasies, its images of golden mountains.

Yosele had succeeded only with difficulty in tearing himself away from Bardichev for a few days and was now going home. In the coach from Bardichev to Kashperev, Yosele had imagined how he would ride into his hometown and no one would recognize him. He would ask to be taken to Shmulik the cantor's synagogue. Shmulik would look at him astonished. "Whom do you wish to see?" he would ask. "You don't recognize me, Father? It's me!" he would answer, falling on his father's neck. An uproar would follow. "Yosele is here!" His stepmother, the cantor's wife, would certainly wish to be the first to run and tell Zlate and Esther the news: "You know whom we have as a guest? Our Yosele has come home!" But Yosele wouldn't let her do it; he would rather go himself and pretend to be a stranger, using some pretext. He would begin talking to them about Yosele Solovey, all the while looking at Esther to see what she would say. Then he would suddenly reveal himself to them, as Joseph did to his brothers in Egypt, and would announce, "It's me, Yosele!" Esther would redden and tears would come to her eyes. Then, when he was alone with her, he would tell her everything, face-to-face, everything that was in his heart, everything that had happened to him. He would hold nothing back from her. He would reveal all, and Esther would forgive him. He would tell her how he had longed to come home but that Gedalye Bass, may his name be erased, hadn't let him; instead he had dragged him from one town to the next, always putting his request off for later, later! Then, when he was about to come home, another calamity, Perele the Lady, had befallen him, and he had been snared in her net, sinking into the depths of degradation, realizing his mistake too late. . . .

He knew what a foolish thing he had done, how badly he had treated everyone. How could he not have asked the advice of his elders! To commit such a blunder, to enter into a marriage without asking a father—it made no sense at all! He knew it full well, but what good is wisdom if it comes only with age? He would not deny to Esther that partly Perele's charms and partly her money had turned his head. He still could not fathom how he could have forgotten his loved ones. How could he have exchanged Esther for Perele? And for what reason? Was it really for money? What did he need her money for? Yosele would tell Esther how he had suffered, what an ordeal he had gone through in that month with Perele, how difficult it had been for him to manage to get home, how Perele had insisted on going everywhere with him—nothing else would do—how he had finally succeeded, pleading with her, lying to her so that she would let him go alone, how loathesome his life had become, how restricted, barren, and dark his world was, how his heart drew him home to her, to Esther, and for her sake he was prepared to do anything, even to die! Let her know everything at last, and whatever she would require of him he would do. He would obey her every word, do whatever she asked. For her sake he would risk his life, even run to the ends of the earth with her!

And Yosele began to fantasize how he would run to the ends of the earth with Esther, and in the midst of this fantasy he fell asleep in the cab of the Yampeler coachman, awakening only when they drove into Kashperev, where he was transferred to Lazer's coach. From Lazer he had heard the awful, bitter news of Esther's marriage, and now his fantasies began to work in another direction.

XXIX

Lazer Drives the Horses Hard
and Brings Yosele Home Late at Night

Other thoughts, other fantasies mingled in Yosele's head after hearing from Lazer the news that Esther was marrying someone else—Alter! All his earlier dreams suddenly disappeared, vanished. He became furious at Alter, at Zlate, and even at Esther; they had become in his eyes totally mad, thoroughly guilty. Only he escaped blame. It never occurred to him to ask himself whether it was he who had been at fault. He was growing impatient for the moment he would arrive home at last. Every minute seemed a year.

"Is it still far?" he asked, prodding Lazer, poking his head out of the cab for a minute and touching his arm.

Lazer snorted and spat. Apparently he wasn't pleased to have been interrupted in the middle of a sound sleep. The horses had also been dozing, running out of sheer habit. The air already had a springtime aroma; the sun was beginning to set. One part of the sky was painted with a broad red stripe like blood washing over the entire western heaven. A cool breeze stole into Yosele's cab, touching his long, curly hair, caressing him, stroking his face. He leaned back in the cab and dozed off. The breeze was blowing, the coach was rocking, the little harness bells were tinkling, the horses were switching their tails, and Lazer was yawning, droning on with the same sad song that had no beginning and no end—and all that made Yosele feel even more melancholy. He fell asleep.

He dreamed he was still a child. He was in Mazepevka on the steep mountain that, when he was a child, seemed so frighteningly high to him, reaching almost to the clouds. There on the mountaintop, as they would tell in *cheder*, grew all kinds of rare and fragrant spices. Concealed in a cave was a treasure that Mazeppa had stowed away, not telling anyone where he had hidden it. There was also a crystal palace, so he had heard in *cheder*, and in that palace lived a wicked queen all alone. Every night, when the moon rose, they heard her wailing and calling out in the sorrowful voice of an owl. At those times it was perilous to go there by yourself. . . . He imagined he was climbing the mountain, scrambling up, making his way higher and higher, but the top of the mountain was still far off. He began to crawl quickly on all fours, like a gnome, going higher and higher, but the top of the mountain was still far off. He looked down and began to tremble with fear when he saw what a great distance he had climbed, but the top of the mountain was still far off. He broke out in a cold sweat; he was lost. He could not see a living soul, not a dwelling or even the ground below, only mountain and sky, sky and mountain. He felt his strength ebbing, felt sick to his stomach, faint . . .

He woke up but immediately fell asleep again and

dreamed he was in a thick forest. He was lying stretched out on the grass, one hand holding a platter of Purim treats and the other hand stroking Esther's head. Esther was singing a song quietly, a song called "The Young Soul," by Goldfaden, that they used to sing as children:

> Past midnight the time, the world was at peace,
> All creatures were mutely reclining,
> Only the moon full and round did not cease
> As it strolled among stars brightly shining.

Suddenly he spied in the distance a large white cat stealing toward him. With feline grace she silently edged closer and closer. She was right upon him, digging her claws into his neck, beginning to suffocate him, strangling him. He felt his throat being torn, he wanted to cry out but could not. He looked into the cat's eyes and it seemed to him she was smiling. He took a closer look and recognized her as Perele. He wanted to scream but could not. . . . A ferocious black, shaggy dog stood over him, gnawing and biting him. He took a closer look and recognized him as Gedalye Bass. . . . With all his might he tore himself free and in a voice not his own cried out, "Oy, Father!"

"Oy! Father!" Yosele cried out loud and awoke from sleep, bewildered. "Tphoo-tphoo-tphoo!" He spat three times to ward off the devil. "Where are we, Reb Lazer?"

"Where are we, you ask?" Lazer answered him in an angry voice, now walking alongside the horses, berating them continuously. "Oh, it's still quite a way off. May your bones rot, carcasses! We've gone more than halfway up this hill. May a vile end befall these creatures! How I've pushed myself to the limit! Forgive me for asking, but it wouldn't be such a bad idea to take the trouble and walk alongside for a while. It might be easier for my horses, may their hides burn!"

"But aren't we almost to the town, Reb Lazer?" Yosele asked in a whining voice.

"Soon, soon, you understand me, soon. Right after this hill there's still a sandy stretch, then a forest, then again sand, and then it's straight on the dirt road into town."

What could he do? Yosele took heart and followed behind the coach. His head felt heavy, his legs ached, and he felt a tightness in his throat. The poor horses drew the coach up the hill reluctantly. They would certainly have stopped on the spot, ignoring the curses Lazer showered on them, but he gave them to understand full well with his whip that they had to keep on moving. The moon, which had sliced its way through a corner of the sky, floated higher and higher. The breeze turned cooler, and Yosele trudged behind the vehicle like a person sentenced to exile. "You can climb back into the coach now, if you please," Lazer said to him, stopping for a moment. "In less time than it takes to swallow a drink we'll be home."

These few words of Lazer's revived Yosele's spirit. If he hadn't been ashamed he would have embraced and kissed the coachman. Even though it took much longer than it takes to swallow a drink, they eventually arrived in Mazepevka.

Never had Yosele so appreciated the town of Mazepevka with its foul-smelling mud, its small, dark, sleepy little houses. Like a potentate entering his domain, he derived pleasure from every sight. He could barely sit still. When he stuck his nose out of the cab he had to cover it immediately with his hand because of the stench. Like a child, he bounced up and down excitedly, talking to himself: "There's Zalman-Eli the slaughterer's house! There's Zemach the rich

210

man's house! There's Arke the shoemaker's house, and there are the shops. . . . Sha! There's the old synagogue, and there's Zlate's house, where my father lives. . . . What are all those lights there, eh? Reb Lazer, take a look, please, how lit up it is at our place! Oy, *vey iz mir!* Is it raining?"

"What rain?" Lazer wondered, driving the horses like a madman. "It's not even beginning to rain. What else will you think of?"

"Why, then, is it so shiny? Sha, I think I hear musicians playing. I hear a drum and cymbals! What is that—a wedding, or what? Reb Lazer, do you hear a wedding?"

But Lazer wasn't saying a word. He was thrashing and whipping the poor horses, who were happy to be home so they could rest up at last—they had run enough! They jerked their tails up, let loose with their last ounce of strength, twitching their heads with every lash of the whip, as if to say, "Old fool! Why are you whipping us? We know when to run and when not to." And with a whoop and a crack Lazer's carriage came to a halt near Shmulik the cantor's window, almost sending an axle through it. Yosele jumped out and ran over to the house. In the half of the house where Shmulik lived it was dark and a key was hung on the door to show that no one was at home. But in the other half, where Zlate the shopkeeper lived, it was brightly lit up and lively. The musicians were playing, and he could hear people dancing, stamping, and shouting, "Faster! Faster!" At the door a knot of peasants had gathered, eating sunflower seeds and laughing. He approached and asked one of them what was going on.

"Zeh zhidevske visilye!—A Jewish wedding!" they answered in Russian, laughing and pointing toward the house. Yosele elbowed his way through, stepped into the room, and was devastated by the scene he now saw before him.

XXX

The Guests Force Themselves
to Have a Good Time as Yosele Arrives
at the Height of the Celebration

"With effort," our Jewish sages said, "the Jew endures!" With effort the Jew survives his short time on earth, with effort he marries off his children, with effort he enjoys himself. A Jew, when he wants to be merry or celebrate a happy occasion, has to force himself to do so. "Jews!" he then shouts, "Jews, we have to be merry!" And they gather together and force themselves to drink, because it isn't the way of Jews to drink, and whoever will not drink will have the wine forced down his throat. He has to be merry even though he may not feel like it. He must dance even though he may not feel like dancing. It is a joy to behold Jews getting together at a celebration; for not long after the first two "forcings" they begin to clap and sing without urging:

> Let's drink, dear friends, all through the night
> Glass after glass of wine so bright,
> Down the gullet clear out of sight,
> The only way to make things right.

And soon enough one's caftan begins to feel so heavy that one has to throw it off and stand in bare undergarments, forgive me, with the small tasseled ritual undergarment on top; then it is easier to dance. All form a circle and hold hands. Men stomp their feet and jump in the air, tossing their heads from side to side, and turn glazed eyes to the ceiling as if in the middle of prayer. And whoever is stubborn and refuses to dance is pulled by force into the circle and made to spin and move his feet in rhythm. That was the way Shmulik the cantor was made to dance at Esther's wedding. If you had not seen him then, you have never seen a more sorrowful person in your life. Oy, was that a bitter dance! Shmulik felt more like crying from the drop of brandy someone had forced down his throat, and he had become even more despondent than before. But it made Zlate happy to see that Shmulik was also dancing in the circle along with everyone else. When she saw his feet moving in the dance, she went over to observe how the men were dancing in their, pardon me, ritual undergarments. But no one cared: at a celebration it didn't matter, it was no tragedy. Zlate began clapping and singing in a voice quite hoarse by now, as you would expect of a mother of the bride:

> You're called a kugel
> No matter where,
> Standing here or standing there,
> In the oven or in the mouth
> To the north or to the south,
> You're called a kugel
> No matter where.

It was hard to tell whether it was the few drinks he had been made to drink or that it simply happened of itself, but suddenly Shmulik the cantor felt the festive spirit rise in him. He joined the relatives, Reb Kalman the matchmaker in their midst, to drink whisky with abandon while munching sour pickles—a well-known antidote for drunkenness. They downed so much liquor and ate so many sour pickles that when Shmulik looked at Reb Kalman he saw two Reb Kalmans, and Reb Kalman himself saw two of everything as well. Somehow this vision of two Reb Kalmans emboldened Shmulik all the more and he had the urge to laugh out loud. Suddenly everything became comical to him. He looked over at Zlate as she sang the "Kugel Song" and laughed so uproariously that Zlate stopped singing and dancing on the spot. She sniffed and stepped to the side while Shmulik held his stomach with both hands and writhed with laughter. The sight of him inspired Reb Kalman and all the relatives, who also began laughing, and they felt so merry they exchanged hats and yarmulkes. Zalman-Ber the ritual slaughterer found a cap somewhere, tucked his caftan up, securing it with a belt at the waist, tied his beard (Zalman-Ber had the longest beard in Mazepevka) with a kerchief, and performed a German dance while singing

> Let's all be German
> Stuffed and drunken.

And Shmulik together with Kalman and the relatives dissolved in laughter, and then Alchenon the *shamesh* also had the urge to show off. He fixed his earlocks behind his ears, puffed up his cheeks, and, eyes flashing, he danced a Russian dance to the tune of *Hayom t'amtzeynu*. Also Shimshon-Yenkl the tobacconist turned his eyes upward, sat on the ground, and, twirling a tassel from his *tallis-kotn*, sang a beggar's song, "*Oy, biv sobi sviatei lazar. . . .*"

Now Reb Kalman the matchmaker could no longer contain himself and had to exhibit his comedic talent; he donned a dress and pretended to be a pregnant woman and put on an entire show. . . . Well, they all had a great time at Zlate's daughter's wedding. Shmulik didn't stop laughing, downing one drink after another. All at once Zalman-Ber the slaughterer switched from playing a German to being a cantor, Shmulik and the rest of the crowd serving as his choir. Zalman-Ber put on a white shawl as a *tallis*, faced toward the wall, and began to sing the doleful melody from the *ne'ilah*, the last prayer said on Yom Kippur:

> You're old
> You're cold
> Don't know it
> Can't do it
> So why do you try it at all?

And Shmulik, Shimshon-Yenkl, Reb Kalman, and Alchanon the *shamesh* sang along with him like members of the choir, gesticulating with their hands and screeching in frightful voices the *ne'ilah* melody:

> Oy, oy, oy, oy, oy!
> Ay—ay!

And the guests couldn't get enough of it, were falling over one another with laughter.

Yosele Solovey stood and observed this scene, searching the crowd for someone, but the one Yosele wanted to see was no longer there. The crowd was so drunk that no one noticed Yosele standing in a corner, leaning against a wall, taking note of each and every guest. Yosele felt a pounding in his temples, his face burned, the whole room was spinning around like a wheel, he saw shimmering lights in front of his eyes, like a shower of gold, and he felt sharp cat's claws digging deep into his throat, suffocating him, strangling him. Yosele grabbed at his throat and ran outside.

The night had grown darker. Small black clouds were starting to move across the sky, swallowing the moon and then spitting it out. A cool Elul breeze was blowing. The sad sound of an owl hooting was heard, as if it were submerged in the ocean. It became quite chilly, but Yosele was warm, so warm that he mopped the sweat from his face with the hem of his caftan and felt that his body was on fire. He had fled the wedding so as not to hear the playing of the klezmer, the dancing and singing that poured venom into his heart and made him burn and sear as with a hellish fire. Yosele ran, and following after him was the mournful tune of the *ne'ilah* with its merry words. Yosele covered his ears so as not to hear the singing and fled like a madman, not knowing where he was running.

XXXI

Shmulik Chants the Seven Benedictions in a Mournful Voice

Wearing a veil, as is expected of the mother of the bride, Zlate attended the veiling breakfast the following morning. Around her were gathered her sisters, Breine and Yentl, and some of the relatives, all wearing veils and quite dressed up. None of the men had arrived as yet. The male relatives had gone off to shul, and most of the out-of-town guests weren't too eager to attend the veiling breakfast. Instead they went

216

to the market bargain hunting, perhaps an odd job, God willing, might also come their way. The *shamesh*, the rabbi's personal assistant, and his wife might do Zlate the honor of dropping by again. But it was the local wives who came to help prepare the table, slice honey cake, and share the bride's happiness. Since only close friends were there, it was fitting to have some honey cake and drink a toast to the mother of the bride. The helpers did so and wished her well with all their hearts.

"May God grant, Zlatenyu, that you have a lot of *naches* from your daughter. She should never know grief. May she grow old with him in honor and respect and, God willing, next year at the *bris*, don't forget us, Zlatenyu. We are, after all, bearers of good luck. Whenever we go to a wedding, in a year there's always a *bris*—that's the kind of luck we bring. It's a blessing."

"Amen, let's hope so!" Zlate answered with a pious expression. Breine glanced at Yentl, Yentl glanced at Breine, and Zlate at both of them. The three sisters communicated among themselves much more with those glances than others did with words. They understood each other quite well.

Later the men began to filter in and seated themselves at the table, imbibed small amounts of brandy, and toasted the bridegroom, Zlate, and the family. Alter's face glowed under his new velvet hat. He looked much younger than his years, quite boyish, in fact. This, however, was not true of the bride, who was veiled and clad like a pretty gentlewoman but did not appear happy at all. Her face was ashen, almost yellowish, without a drop of color. Her black eyes beneath her long eyelashes were altogether quenched, without luster, and looked larger. Her cheeks were slightly sunken. Her new veil was adorned with pearls and diamonds like a crown. In her expensive silk dress, trimmed with velvet and gems, ornamented from top to bottom with jewels, Esther looked at that moment like a princess. The lively, happy Esther had now assumed a dignified, sedate, quiet, serious manner. Just like a bride, the wives thought, admiring her lovely clear face.

"What an elegant lady she is, may no evil eye harm her!" the wives said among themselves, nodding toward the bride. "She is as pure as the driven snow. Such a jewel to have in one's house, don't you agree, Frume-Sara'nyu?"

Frume-Sara'nyu certainly agreed it was a privilege to have such a jewel in one's house. Why deny it? In the meantime the crowd had begun to wash up, passing around the copper large-handled pitcher and the damp, black towel. Shmulik entered the room.

"Welcome to you, Reb Shmulik!" said Zlate in a friendly voice. "Why so late? Please wash up and sit down at the table. Did you forget we needed you to say the *shiva broches?* Where is your wife, Reb Shmulik? Seems to me you're upset today. What's the matter?"

"I have a guest," Shmulik said in a grim voice. "A guest. My son has come back."

"Yosele?" they all cried out at once. "Yosele is here? God love you and your guest! Where is he, then?"

"What's the difference where he is? He's at home," Shmulik answered, not moving from the spot. "He doesn't seem to have any strength. He came back late last night— in fact he arrived just as day was breaking. Apparently he caught a cold, although he keeps complaining that his head hurts him. He's running a very high fever and is more dead than alive. We've already applied cold compresses and rubbed his temples. Nothing helps."

"He has to sweat!" a few cried out at once. "The best remedy is to have him sweat it out. Sit down, Reb Shmulik, why are you so upset? Sometimes it happens a person catches a little cold. God willing, he'll get better."

Shmulik stopped to say a word to Zlate. Zlate looked at Esther and shook her head. And Esther had to muster all her strength so as not to fall in a faint when she heard that Yosele was back. She had to be stronger than iron to keep herself from running from the table shouting, "Why, Yosele?" But she simply asked Shmulik one question as her eyes blazed with their old intensity: "Did he come alone?"

"Alone," Shmulik answered, standing absolutely still, in a state of shock next to Zlate, not knowing what to do.

As if struck by lightning, Esther leaped from her chair but quickly sat down again. For a split second it was as if she were lifted up and then dropped back down, so that she remained seated at the head of the table, stunned, all her senses numbed. In that one moment Esther lived through more than most people live through in a year. An awful thought flitted through her mind for a brief second, she was ready to spring up, leave all the guests, the wedding and everything connected with it, and run over to the cantor's house to see Yosele. She felt pulled in that direction— pulled and torn by the desire to be there! But that thought lasted only an instant. She quickly reconsidered: she was, after all, a bride, an *eyshes-ish*, a married woman. The battle that Esther waged in that instant was formidable. Two op- posing feelings were struggling within her: on one side stood the Tempter himself, who urged her, "Foolish Esther! Why are you listening to them? Yosele's come back. He is lying sick in bed. He's surely waiting for you, and here you sit—for whose sake? Listen to me, Esther! You're young, you're pretty, you need to enjoy life. Live, live!" And on the other side she heard other words, "A Jewish daughter? Reb Abrahaml Slaviter's grandchild? Love? A bride? *Harey at m'kodeshes*—'Here you are consecrated, united, bound, an *eyshes-ish*, a married woman'!" And the other, the Tempter, had his say again, "Whose fault is it? They've bound you, tied you up, fettered you. Nonsense! You're a human being. You need to live. Listen to me, Esther! . . ."

And Esther continued to sit in dignity at the table, as a bride should at her veiling ceremony, but she was frighteningly pale, benumbed, her face shining despite the veil, her jewels sparkling and shimmering, adding all the more to her beauty. The wives admired her, enjoying and delighting in gazing at the beauty of this radiant, charming bride.

Sorrowful and plaintive was Shmulik the cantor's voice as he chanted the *shiva broches*, the Seven Benedictions, and Esther imagined his voice was coming from the bowels of the earth, from the Other World. Those were bitter *shiva broches*. Holding the wine cup in one hand and clutching his throat with the other, in the style of the old-fashioned cantors, and throwing his head back, eyes shut, Shmulik attempted the coloratura runs in his old, cracked voice, and with a sob ended the *M'samayach chosn im hakaleh*— "Gladsome be the bridegroom and bride"—so sorrowfully that the guests were deeply moved. Everyone at the celebration felt troubled, bereft, and downcast, not knowing the reason why, in the manner of Jews who grow sad in the midst of joy even while fêting the bride and groom, God Almighty! What is it in Jewish singing and Jewish music that evokes only sorrowful thoughts? . . . And the wives, standing along the sides of the room, responding to the prayer with "Blessed be He, blessed be His name, Amen," let a tear fall when they looked at Zlate and saw how she wept and lamented. No one was surprised that Zlate was crying; they all knew how it felt to marry off a child.

"In spite of that," the wives confessed, "may God grant that children marry and that we live to see each other on happy occasions!"

"Amen—may it be so! May it be so!"

The wives bade goodbye to the mother of the bride, kissed the bride, wishing her that she live to see celebrations of her own children, and Esther looked at them in bewilderment. Her head and her heart were elsewhere; all she wanted was for the guests to leave so she could be alone and cry her heart out. And here the women were crowding around her, kissing her and wishing her the best of everything.

God helped; the crowd began to thin out, and Esther could steal off to her little room to recover from the ordeal she had endured that day. Only a few close relatives remained in Zlate's house, the in-laws and Reb Kalman. As usual after a wedding, the house was still in turmoil: on the long table were strewn empty bottles, overturned glasses, pieces of bread, chewed-over bones, and nearby several chairs lay overturned. Two or three poor folk who had come too late for the veiling ceremony were licking off the plates, stuffing leftover chunks of challah into their bosoms. The wedding officials, while downing a last glass of wine, were adding up the gratuities dropped into their wretched collection plates by the wedding guests. They paid no attention to Zlate, Breine, and Yentl, who were shooing them out. "Go in good health. It's time to clean up, make some order."

Zlate was frantic, as you would expect of a mother of the bride; the corners of her silk kerchief were tied at the nape of her neck, her face was flushed, and her voice had become so hoarse one could barely hear her speak. Nevertheless she refused to rest, flitting about embracing everyone, bidding goodbye to each one with her eyes, not with her voice, as her words couldn't be heard. Zlate acted like someone who had moved heaven and earth to accomplish a much-sought-after happy outcome. God knows if Zlate herself realized what she had achieved for her daughter, for her one beloved and devoted daughter, whom she had given away, placed in bondage, sold forever! When did Zlate have the time to reflect? One minute they were talking about a match and the next there was a betrothal party and the next minute a wedding. It was no small matter to put on a wedding! Zlate, Basya the wholesaler's daughter, would not countenance any ordinary wedding; she wasn't, thank God, from a family of tailors or shoemakers. Even if God had punished her with widowhood, and made her a poor widow at that, she was nevertheless Abrahaml Slaviter's daughter-in-law. How would it look for her only daughter to go to the canopy without a silk dress and that for Esther's wedding there wouldn't be a crowd of guests around the table, so that the whole town afterward would be talking about it? Lord in heaven, Zlate thought, may I live to see no worse wedding for my younger children!

In a corner, among the relatives, a loud argument had broken out, a dispute over the marriage broker's fee. Reb Kalman was shouting at the top of his lungs, clutching Moshe-Abraham Zaliaznik's beard with one hand and with the other covering Alter's mouth so that he couldn't speak. Alter was perspiring freely and wanted desperately to say something, but Reb Kalman wouldn't permit it. "Listen to me. Listen!" he shouted. "Let me finish talking. Let me, and then you can speak!" Moshe-Abraham and Beinish, the two brothers-in-law, as well as a few of the other kinsmen from the groom's side became involved, hoping to find a way to satisfy both parties, but it was a waste of time. Alter was hard as steel, would not bend an inch even if you cut him in half! "Nu, what do you say, Reb Shmulik, is this fair, is it, they should cheat a matchmaker this way, a matchmaker, ha?" Shmulik the cantor was sitting off to the side, glum and preoccupied, wishing to help out his old friend Reb Kalman in any way possible, but Reb Kalman would let him utter no more than his usual "What is there to say?" and then cut him off. "That's exactly the whole problem here," poor Reb Kalman complained. "Do you know what's going on here, do you? We're talking exactly about . . . in the first place, how do they say—it should be as agreed, but here it turns out to be a heartache. We should have to talk about the fee all over again, we should, and especially—eh, Reb Alter, listen to me, Reb Alter!"

"It's time for the evening service!" announced Moshe-Abraham, clearing the windowpane with his hand and peering outside, where the sun was beginning to set. The men stood up, belted their caftans with kerchiefs, and took a count to see if there were the required ten men present to start the prayers. The bridegroom, Shmulik the cantor, both brothers-in-law, Moshe-Abraham and Beinish, the three relatives from Alter's side, Reb Kalman, and both shameshim—exactly a minyan! They washed their hands, said kitores, the incense blessing, and ashrei—"happy is he"—following which Shmulik faced the wall and began to chant the Eighteen Benedictions in his dulled, broken voice. The wives—Zlate, Breine, and Yentl—felt privileged to be hearing a Kedushah in the house. . . .

When Esther, still in her room, heard Shmulik's tearful voice, she went to the door, peered out, and saw the men and women rising three times on their toes for the Kedushah: "Kadosh! Kadosh! Kadosh!—Holy! Holy! Holy!" She stood by quietly, not knowing what to do. She was now a

223

married woman like the rest of them; the rules applied to her too. Breine winked at her from across the room, pointing to her forehead. Esther didn't understand what she meant and blushed. After the Kedushah her Tante Breine went up to her and pointed out that a strand of hair was showing immodestly from under her head scarf. Esther had thrown off the bejeweled veil and had put on a silk head scarf and another dress. Esther the young girl had turned into the young wife. She seemed to have diminished in size and had entirely changed in appearance. A cloud had suddenly settled on her bright, pretty face and she looked several years older; only her radiant eyes shone in the dim light like two bright stars in the sky. At that moment she was even more beautiful than before.

"If you wish," Zlate said to her in a hoarse voice, "if you have time, come with me to the cantor's wife to pay a sick call on Yosele."

Were a cannon to have gone off near her ear Esther would not have started as she did upon hearing those words. Only a minute earlier she had been wondering how to invent a pretext to visit the cantor's wife to see Yosele, and her mother had suddenly solved her problem. But Esther's face didn't betray that her heart was pounding in her breast as if it would leap out. She answered her mother quite calmly and quietly, "All right, I'll come if you wish." She really wanted to throw her arms around her mother's neck and cover her with kisses. Mama'nyu, dear heart. Dear, dear Mama! thought Esther, and with the other women quietly passed through the dining room where the men were all standing facing the wall, fervently praying the Shmoneh Esreh. Mama'nyu, lyubenyu! Esther thought in her heart and walked slowly, feeling as if she were walking on air.

Shmulik the cantor's house was pitch dark although it was

still twilight. No light had as yet been turned on. In a corner, on a bed heaped high with blankets, lay Yosele Solovey, surrounded by pillows, and near him, on a stool, sat the cantor's wife. "Shhaa, he's sleeping!" she said as the women entered the room chatting among themselves.

"No. I'm not sleeping," said Yosele and sat up in the bed as if his heart had told him that not far from him stood Esther.

"How are you feeling?" the three women asked in the same intonation, regarding him from a distance.

"It wasn't meant for me, it seems, to be at your daughter's veiling breakfast," the cantor's wife exclaimed to Zlate. "Go figure on such a turnabout. As if we didn't have enough troubles! A guest arrives and suddenly he gets sick. Sit, Zlatenyu! Breine dear, Yentl, my darling—sit, sit down, sit! Sit, Estherl, why are you standing?"

The women looked at Yosele from across the room, shaking their heads, each suggesting a favorite cure, a sure remedy for headaches, for nausea, for sticking pains, for any ailment. They seated themselves near the window and were soon engaged in lively discussion about the wedding, the dinner, the veiling breakfast, and the wedding presents each side had given. Though Zlate was very hoarse, she spoke with animation, complementing her words with gestures, demonstrating how furious she was at Frume-Sara. "Imagine that Frume-Sara! You all know that Frume-Sara? Did Frume-Sara have the right to say that at her younger daughter's wedding there were twice as many guests and a hundred times as many wedding presents? Nu, I ask you, how do you put up with that?"

"Why should Frume-Sara's words bother you, Zlatenyu? Let me better tell you what Tzippeh-Reizl said about her

225

youngest daughter. God in heaven, if ever I had an enemy anywhere, I'd wish it on them, my God!"

The conversation among the four women became so engrossing that they almost forgot about the patient. Yosele sat on his bed, a towel wrapped around his head. From under the towel his long, curly hair hung loose, his face was deathly pale, yellowish, but his eyes burned with their customary fire. When he saw Esther enter he wanted to leap out of bed, but some force riveted him to the spot, frozen, unable to utter a sound. Esther remained standing, gazing at him for a long time from a distance, and only after the wives had become deeply engrossed in their conversation did she approach the bed and ask him, "How are you feeling?"

Those few words were uttered with such softness, with such true devotion, with so much love as only a sister can convey to a brother. There was no response from Yosele, but his expression, his wry little smile, said it all. She moved closer to him, and as if it had been planned beforehand, sat down on the stool next to him where the cantor's wife had just been sitting.

Esther imagined that Yosele's eyes had grown larger. He looked at her strangely, not with the same friendliness as before.

"How are you feeling?" she asked again.

"Oy, Esther!" he answered, placing his hand on her head.

In those two words one heard the cry of a person crushed by tragedy, the kind of tragedy for which there are no words. Esther sensed he was very ill, but what kind of illness it was she had no idea. She did not remember how it had happened, but her hand was now in his hand. His touch seared her as with a flame and she imagined her entire body was on fire. She was drawn to him, pulled as if by a magnet, and again that terrible thought flew through her head.

Again the two powers were battling inside her: on one side the Tempter whispered in her ear that there was still time, she could still be happy, she was young and healthy and fresh. She mustn't bury herself alive. She must live, live, live! And on the other side she heard another voice, "A wife, a bride, just from the canopy, Zlate's daughter, an *eyshes-ish*, flee!" And her hand remained in his, burning, burning, as if it were on fire. . . . Suddenly Yosele's tongue loosed and he began talking; he talked incessantly, confusedly, mixing things up, his words disconnected, as he clutched her hand in his. Suddenly his face seemed to ignite, his eyes burned, he threw off the towel wrapping his head, and moved closer to Esther, saying to her passionately under his breath, so no one else could hear, "It makes no difference, Esther, that you're married or I'm married! They say I'm sick. Who's sick? Say the word and I'll get right up as healthy as ever and go away with you from this Godforsaken Mazepevka! Listen to me, let's go while there's still time. They'll run after us? Who cares! Oy, let's get out of here, be free, and then everything will be all right! I'll take you far, far away from here and you'll be mine forever, mine, mine! Esther! Oy, Esther, Esther!"

Esther didn't have time to comprehend exactly what she was hearing. She was drawn to him with a frightening force. She was prepared at that moment to throw herself into his arms and run off with him to the ends of the earth. That fine fellow, the Tempter, again appeared, this time in the guise of a good angel, an intercessor, and again began whispering in her ear, "Foolish, foolish Esther! Here is your happiness right in front of your eyes. Your fate is now in your own hands! Choose—a life in Paradise, a sweet life, a life of bliss, in happiness with a beloved companion, with him, with Yosele, forever, for all time, or a bleak, miserable existence right here, in the mud, with that coarse lout, with that scoundrel, that Alter. Foolish Esther!" . . . That fine soul, the Tempter, with his sugared words, and Yosele with his fiery eyes, with his passionate words, almost persuaded Esther. They almost prevailed. Never before had she so longed to live happily as she did in those few minutes. Never before had the world seemed so wondrous as it did then. Esther trembled in every limb. She was ready to run off with him, to soar up to the heavens, to plunge into the depths of the netherworld, relinquishing, forgetting everyone and everything as long as she could be with him, with Yosele! . . .

And Yosele kept on talking to her with increasing ardor. His eyes burned with a penetrating fire. "Oy, Esther, Esther!" he cried, but so quietly, almost whispering, "Oy, Esther! Esther!" He leaned toward her, opening his arms wide, trying to embrace her. Esther felt him so close to her that she jerked back, sprang up from the stool, and involuntarily clasped her head, which was modestly covered by her wifely kerchief. Like a dream, like a bolt of lightning, the terrible thoughts vanished, and Esther the young wife, Esther the Jewish daughter again emerged, and she saw her mother near her.

"Are we leaving?" Zlate said to her. "We got to talking a bit! They have good reason to say women can talk your ear off."

Before leaving, Zlate suggested to the cantor's wife a few more remedies for the patient, and Breine, on her part, added that if they could manage to have Shachneh the *shochet* come today and exorcise the evil eye, it would surely help.

Esther stood just inside the door and turned her head once more toward Yosele sitting on the bed. From across the room she imagined she saw the spark in his eyes, which were looking at her piteously. Her heart was deeply stirred, and there awakened in her a new feeling, the feeling of a person who has seen someone struck down and to whom she did not wish to extend a helping hand. She could see him sitting in exactly the same position as before, arms outstretched to her, and his sorrowful words were still ringing in her ears—"Oy, Esther, Esther!" . . . She remained standing for a moment more at the door. That terrible thought was again flitting through her head, that good fellow again appeared before her eyes with his sweet words: "Go back, Esther, go back—your whole life depends on this minute! One word, my child, one word only—go over and say that one word and you'll both have happiness!" "Go back to hell, you Ashmodai, you king of demons!" answered an inner voice. "Go away—you haven't come to the right place! A Jewish daughter doesn't do the things you ask of her! A Jewish daughter would rather be sacrificed for another's sins before committing such a deed—and a married woman too! Run, Esther, run away!" Esther gathered all her strength and tore herself from the demon's grasp and followed her mother home.

Passing through the dining room, she found the same group of people seated around the table, complaining to Alter. "Just look," one of the groom's kinsmen exclaimed, indicating Esther with his eyes, "Just look, Alter, over what kind of stuff you were bargaining a measly fifty for!"

As if over hot coals, Esther fled the dining room for her little bedroom. On her bed, her face buried deep in pillows, on a pure white pillowcase cleansed by an outpouring of hottest tears, there emerged the pure heart of a chaste, virtuous, though unfortunate, very unfortunate, Jewish daughter.

XXXII

Yosele Finds Himself in a Bad Way, and Lazer the Coachman Talks Like a Philosopher

Yosele Solovey survived three difficult, frightening weeks. They had almost given up hope that he would live. Shmulik couldn't understand how a person could have the strength to endure as much pain, as much agony as Yosele had endured. "Take her away from me, that cat!" he had screamed. "Don't you see her? She's creeping toward me. She wants to grab me by the throat and suffocate me, choke me!" Another time he would shout, "Give me back my Esther, she's mine!" To that Shmulik would answer, "What are you shouting for, silly? Here is Esther. She's standing right here with us, silly!" Again he would howl, "Esther! Give me back my Esther! How can you let her go out into the woods alone? There's a dog there!" And another time he would sing out loud like a cantor, throwing his head far back and gazing at the ceiling, then exclaim, "Do you hear, do you hear how they're playing in the church? In the church they play beautifully, it's a delight to hear it, ay-ay-ay!" and at the same time he would throw himself about and shake violently.

Only a father could endure the heartache brought upon Shmulik by his son in those three weeks. He didn't sleep nights, always sat up with Yosele, putting ice to his head. Yudel Doctor, a respected physician in Mazepevka, said it was a kind of fire in his head—*vospalyenya mozga* was the medical term for it, and it was, he said, a dangerous illness. What didn't Shmulik do to try to help Yosele? He fasted, visited Zelda's grave in the Holy Place several times, asked a *minyan* in the shul to say prayers on his behalf, until finally God helped. The illness subsided and Yudel Doctor announced that the crisis had passed. The patient had now come to himself and would live. Shmulik burst into tears of joy like a child. The rest of the household wept with him. Wailing broke out as if it were a tragedy, God forbid. When Esther, who had visited several times a day for news of the patient, saw Yosele sitting up in his bed, she was unable to control the sudden outpouring of tears, although her face was smiling.

Esther would pay frequent visits to her mother, pretending she wanted to look in on her brothers, and then she would slip out to Shmulik the cantor's house and sit for a few minutes till Alter would send for her to come home. Only God really knew with what a heavy heart Esther returned home. "Estherl, why aren't you drinking anything?" Alter would say with a smile. "Why aren't you eating, Estherl?" Every morning she could barely wait to run over to Shmulik's, come home, and again go back. "Seems that you visit your mother very often, my dear!" Alter would say with a loving little smile that cut her like a knife. "A frequent guest, my soul, becomes tiresome, heh-heh! A little wife should stay home, take care of things, take care of things!" But these words didn't move Esther. Her mind was totally taken up with but one thought—Yosele; Esther desired only one thing from God—that Yosele get well!

Sitting in shul on Shabbos, reading her prayer book, Esther prayed fervently to God that He grant Yosele more years. At night, lying in her bed, Esther often cried, praying to God on Yosele's behalf, "God in heaven, give him strength! Give him more years!" And God heard Esther's prayers. Yosele got well, the crisis passed, and, God willing, he would fully recover. Esther had no words to thank the Almighty One for the grace He had shown. When she arrived home Alter saw her face glowing, shining, and was thrilled. "That's the way I like to see you," Alter said to her, gazing at her face with a loving smile. "That's the way a young bride of three weeks ought to look. Fine—that's the way, that's the way!"

Esther ate her supper hurriedly, sitting restlessly, almost choking on every bite, and could hardly wait for the moment she would be able to leave the house. Since Yosele had rallied and was sitting up in bed, he was not left alone for a moment. Good friends gathered around his bedside asking him how he was feeling and whether his strength had returned. What had he been ranting about all that time he was ill? What had he been imagining when he kept talking about birds, about churches, about carriages, dogs, cats, and other things? What was it all about? But Yosele answered not at all, he was profoundly melancholy and his eyes stared out strangely dead.

"Leave him alone!" Yudel Doctor said angrily, chasing the visitors out. "Leave him alone! He needs rest, and you're bothering him with foolish questions."

"What are we doing that's so bad? We're asking him a few questions. Is that such a sin?"

"Did you ever see such a thing? Am I asking for something so unusual?" Yudel Doctor said, getting angrier. "Did you ever hear of such behavior? I'm telling you he needs to convalesce, like a woman who's just had a baby. You can talk to him later. Better give him some nourishment, a glass of tea, a little broth, some milk, anything."

"The patient wants to eat!" This was such welcome news that they all suddenly flew into action. "What can we give him to eat?" The cantor's wife went off to the neighbor's to try to borrow a quarter of a chicken. Shmulik began running about the house looking for anything he might give the patient to eat. Esther ran into Zlate's, made a fire, and put up some broth. Standing at the hearth, her hands clasped to her heart, and gazing at the flames as she listened to the pot sizzle, Esther sank deep into thought, remembering how almost two and a half years ago she had stood at this very hearth next to Yosele. How different it all was now! How much had changed, how much water had flowed under the bridge, how much heartache, trouble, and pain she had suffered in those two and a half years! Could she have known then, when Yosele spoke to her, that she would now be a married woman, Alter's wife? She vividly recalled how Yosele had taken her by the hand, had held it such a long, long time, squeezing it, how his eyes had shone, sparkled through tears, how he had vowed he would always, always be the same Yosele as ever! . . . The same as ever? she now thought. God knows, God knows!

For the first time since Yosele had returned and had fallen ill Esther reviewed Yosele's changeable behavior. She had not had the time to think of anything other than Yosele's illness. Her mind was filled only with thoughts of how Yosele was faring. What was the course of the illness? What did Yudel Doctor say? What was his temperature? How many days till he would begin to sweat? It could be said that during that time Esther was totally consumed with one thought—Yosele is sick—and that was enough to drive all other thoughts from her head. When her mother, her Tante Breine, her Tante Yentl, and other experienced people said he was in grave danger and if, God forbid, his fever didn't break and he wouldn't begin to sweat, he would be a goner, Esther grew cold all over. She felt a tightness and heaviness in her chest and lived in dread of what might happen. How happy she was when she heard that the patient was sweating at last, thank God!

"And what sweating!" said Yudel Doctor. "What sweating! Just look and you'll see what real sweating is! If a patient of mine doesn't sweat three bucketsful, it's not sweating, you understand me!" God only knows if Yudel Doctor ever had such a grateful friend as he had in Esther when she heard these welcome words! And imagine how she felt when Yosele sat up and asked for something to eat! "Thank you, thank you, dear God! Thank you, beloved Father!"

The door to Zlate's house suddenly opened and a woman's head appeared, in an oddly elegant hat draped with a lady's veil.

"Does Shmulik the cantor live here?" she asked.

"Yes, in the other half of the house. Come, I'm going there myself," Esther answered as she took a pot of broth in both hands and walked with the woman to Shmulik's.

"How is he feeling, Shmulik?" the other one asked, walking with Esther.

"How should he be feeling?" Esther answered. "He's well, thank God. One survives, and you don't ask why."

"He's well?" the other one said, surprised, looking at Esther and thinking what a pretty young woman she was. "But Yosele told me before he left that Shmulik was very ill, gravely ill."

"Hah?" said Esther, looking at her curiously, thinking, Who can this woman be? She said, "No, you're mistaken. It's Yosele who was so sick, not Shmulik."

"Yosele?!!" the woman cried out in alarm.

Esther asked her to lower her voice as they were now at the door and there was the patient himself.

Esther entered, carrying the pot in her hands. The woman ran in ahead of her, opening her arms wide. But they both remained standing stock-still in the middle of the room like blocks of wood, not knowing what was going on. His head turned to the wall, Yosele was sitting on the bed and was singing, making gestures like a cantor, placing his thumb under his Adam's apple in the old cantor's style. Everyone present was standing dumbfounded, staring, stunned and confused, not knowing what it meant. Yosele's singing was strangely wild, frighteningly sweet, and profoundly sad, like a sob from the depths of his being, its sound pierced the soul, moved the heart, penetrated to the very marrow of one's bones. The singing had no form, no sequence; it was simply liquid, exquisite, extraordinary sounds, almost inhuman yet superbly sweet, fluid, and gentle, yet wild and bizarre. Suddenly he let out a horrid crowing sound, "Ku-ka-ri-ku!" and burst into a crazed, loud "Ha-ha-ha!" so that everyone's hair stood on end and all were thunderstruck, staring at one another.

"Oh? She's here, the cat! The cat!" Yosele screamed out, pointing to the woman. This was Perele, his wife. "Do you see her? She's here again! She's here again! Grab her! Drive her away! Chase her out! She wants to choke me, suffocate me! Why don't you say anything? Hov-hov-hov!"

And Yosele sprang half-naked from the bed and lunged at Perele, who was cowering behind Esther, holding onto her back as both of them trembled like two lambs. Yudel Doctor ran over to him, grabbed him with both hands, and tried to force him back to bed. But Yosele resisted. He wrestled with him and tore himself from his grasp. He ran up to Esther, grabbed the pot of hot broth, and poured it over Yudel Doctor.

"He's deranged!" shouted Yudel Doctor. "Why are you all standing there like statues! Tie him down, restrain him! Don't you see he's gone out of his mind!"

* * *

A few days later poor Shmulik had to tie his son down
himself, restrain him as Yudel Doctor had ordered, and take
him to the Makarevka rabbi. Whoever did not witness
Shmulik in his cotton short coat, a green scarf wrapped
around his neck, holding onto Yosele with both hands so he
wouldn't throw himself from the carriage—whoever did not
witness this sad scene could add ten years to his life. "A
person really has to appreciate his own good luck!" said
those who accompanied these unfortunate passengers.

Lazer the coachman had not anticipated that in the same
coach in which he had only a month before brought Yosele
home, ruddy and healthy, he would now be bringing him
back in this condition. He let out his bitter heart on the
poor horses, and, walking on foot with Shmulik alongside
the carriage, Lazer held forth in a long commentary: "Do
you hear, Reb Shmulik? It's crazy. You must know what a
coachman's life is like. You meet all kinds of people in this
world. You go, you run, this one here, that one there. It's a
circus! I swear to you, you can believe me, I'm a man with
grandchildren, may they be well, I'm a grandfather. If you
think about it, you come to realize it's a rotten world. Feh,
really!"

Epilogue

"I don't know what's wrong with my daughter, Esther!" said
Zlate, sitting at the market surrounded by a group of shopkeepers, her sister Yentl among them. "Since her wedding I

never see her looking happy. She seems to be going down-hill. I don't understand it. She has a good life with her husband, *keyn eyn horeh*! Do I know what the matter is?"

"So what's new about that?" remarked one of the group, "All wives are like that. While they're still single, marriage seems like the best thing, but once they're married it loses its appeal and excitement pretty quickly. It becomes no better than a rag. I'll give you a groschen for the whole thing!"

"And I'm telling you," said another, "that she's pregnant and nothing more! My youngest daughter-in-law—do you remember her cheeks? As soon as she became pregnant she turned as pale as death! It's pregnancy, I tell you!"

"Let it be so!" cried Yentl. "From your mouth into God's ears—a healthy pregnancy! If I see it I'll believe it!"

"Why shouldn't you believe it?" an older woman broke in. "We've seen things like that happen before. A wife doesn't have children for years, and with God's help, she starts hatching them one after the other like a brood hen. With God's help, Zlate, maybe there'll be a *bris* next year."

"Amen!" answered Yentl. "A cat washes itself and a good friend says a blessing. . . ."

No one knew what was wrong with Esther. They could see only that with every day she was growing thinner and more drained, flickering out like a candle. Alter didn't spare any expense; he sent for Yudel Doctor, who examined her and said, "She is simply not well; she has a pain near the heart and there's pressure under her stomach." He pre-scribed cod-liver oil, Sholvi, Lipova Tzvit, and other po-tions and told her not to catch a cold or get a cough. "If you catch cold," said Yudel, "it can be very bad!" He told her to drink a lot of milk, eat a lot of butter, and always have on hand a good berry brandy—in other words, to take good care of herself. But Esther continued to shrivel up, flickering out like a candle, and no one knew what the matter was.

Shmulik has long since been put to rest in the New Cemetery. There are now in Mazepevka a few more hungry souls, a wretched widow with several tiny children. As usual, they are helped out. Zlate's older sister, Breine, took a large kerchief in hand and, together with another woman, went about the town collecting donations for the cantor's wife and her small children.

Perele the Lady lives, for all intents and purposes, like a widow, but they say she isn't too badly off, she has plenty of money and goes every year to Franzensbad. Her father, Meir Zeitchik, has to work hard to squeeze a hundred-ruble note out of her—"Like pulling teeth," says Malkeh, his wife.

Leah'tzi the maid also didn't fare too well with her lover. Her fiancé, Levi-Mottel, he of the suit, the boots, and galoshes, vilely cheated her out of her last few groschen and got himself a new bride, one not as pockmarked as she. Poor Leah'tzi worked as a servant for another three years and married a shoemaker. Those "highly interesting romances" have long been forgotten. She now lives the life of an ordinary housewife. All she lacks is a cow. She once tried writing a long letter to her "madam" asking help of her, but she hasn't received a reply to this day.

"Try again. Go over to Henzel Scribe," says her husband, Henech. "Let him write another letter for you. Maybe you didn't write enough."

Reb Kalman the matchmaker is still living. He is quite old and stone deaf but is still arranging all kinds of matches in his head. He is still pairing up young bachelors and grown girls with widows and divorced men.

Gedalye Bass continues to travel about somewhere with

the Shedlitzer cantors. He keeps hoping God will send him another rare find like Yosele Solovey. But his luck has run out, and a rare talent like Yosele Solovey's cannot be found these days.

The town of Strishtch is still there, and Berl-Isaac is now the owner of his own house and a fine shop. Winters he wears a handsome fur coat with fox trim, and he has a seat by the eastern wall in shul. He's a respected citizen—after all, Reb Berl-Isaac!

In the Jewish town of Makarevka, some years back, one could come across in shul or on the street a tall, slender young man with long, sparse hair, a large, yellowed *talliskotn* covering his shattered heart, wearing a strange cap on his head. His throat was always wrapped in a warm scarf, his eyes were hidden behind a pair of blue spectacles, and on his feet he wore one shoe and one boot. His habit was to come into a house without speaking a word, quietly wash up while mouthing the prayer, seat himself at the table, and wait to be served something to eat. After grace he would rise and leave wordlessly. He rarely spoke a word to anyone. Even more rarely, he would stand facing a wall and suddenly begin singing, but so sweetly, with so much feeling that those passing by would delay their errands, stop and listen to how the madman was carrying on like a cantor, chanting the *V'al ha'mdinos bo yomer* so beautifully and also the other prayer from the High Holidays, *Yalos*, in the most pleasurable way. But it seldom happened that he would sing anything through to the end; right in the middle of producing coloratura trills and ornamentations he would suddenly burst out laughing, meow like a cat, bark like a dog, or flap his arms like a rooster, crying out in a strange, crazed voice, "Kukuriku!" frightening the onlookers. Women would look

239

at him, shake their heads, wipe their tears away, and groan piously, "What a pity. This too is a poor creature of God, a sinful human being, merciful Father! Learn a lesson, Jewish children! Such a beautiful voice—and in it a dybbuk, heaven protect us. May it not happen to anyone. God pity his mother or father. Let me die, dear God, rather than suffer such a punishment!"

People took great pity on him, would always give him some food and drink, occasionally an old shirt, a used garment, or a groschen. Only from the young boys, the pranksters, did the poor madman suffer torments and indignities. The rascals would run after him, pointing their fingers at him, taunting him, jabbing and pinching him, tugging at him, flicking his nose, and shouting, "Nightingale! What are you—a nightingale or a rooster or maybe even a crow? Sing something for us, crow!" But he tolerated all this stoically, without so much as flinching, answering no one, always walking with his head held high, looking at everyone through his blue spectacles arrogantly, as if the whole world were his. . . .

Do I need to tell you that this was Yosele Solovey?